THESE VENGEFUL WISHES

THESE VENGEFUL WISHES

Vanessa Montalban

zando
YOUNG
readers
NEW YORK

zando young readers

The characters and events in this book are fictitious. Any similarity to real persons, living or dead, is coincidental and not intended by the author.

Copyright © 2025 by Vanessa Valdes

Zando supports the right to free expression and the value of copyright. The purpose of copyright is to encourage writers and artists to produce the creative works that enrich our culture. Thank you for buying an authorized edition of this book and for complying with copyright laws by not reproducing, scanning, uploading, or distributing this book or any part of it without permission. If you would like permission to use material from the book (other than for brief quotations embodied in reviews), please contact connect@zandoprojects.com.

Zando Young Readers is an imprint of Zando.
zandoprojects.com

First Edition: February 2025

Design by Neuwirth & Associates, Inc.
Cover design by Jenna Stempel-Lobell

The publisher does not have control over and is not responsible for author or other third-party websites (or their content).

Library of Congress Control Number: 2024943593

978-1-63893-028-0 (Hardcover)
978-1-63893-029-7 (ebook)

10 9 8 7 6 5 4 3 2 1
Manufactured in the United States of America

To my loving husband, Leonardo—
Had I only one wish, it would always be you.

For all the women in the shadows
and all the shadowy women

Three rules encouraged for Santa Aguas Residents

1. Do not roam the woods at night.

2. Mustard seeds are to be collected and stored by thresholds for the family's well-being.

3. When traveling on roads, never stop for a woman in white.

PROLOGUE

THE BOY HAS NOT RETURNED *to see me, and I am hungry. Night always draws them near. They think the dark can hide their wickedness. But I see into their rotten hearts.*

This one follows me deep into the woods, his hands snatching hungrily for my dress. His mind is too gone with drink to realize that his fingers graze nothing but air.

I can see what he thinks will happen tonight. What his imagination has led him to believe—no cry or claw could keep him from what he wants. But he has yet to feel my bite.

The moon bears the only witness to his death. She is the only one who pulls away the shadows from my visage so that he may take me in full. A monstrous face. He dies thinking it.

When I taste his blood, it is sweet and warm, and when I bring up my hand, I can see myself once more. The night becomes richer, its smells and sounds once again clear, no longer as if coming from underground. It's how I hear the boy . . .

In an instant, I am there. The Sevillas' pull as much my curse as it is my yearning. The highway road between us glitters black like obsidian.

It's the boy and his friends, drinking and laughing by Dead Man's Street, as they like to call it. The Sevilla boy talks to the one he claims to love, but I have yet to see proof of it.

In the distance, a truck's headlights come barreling down the street toward them.

The Sevilla notices this, too, and pulls the girl with him, though she shrinks back.

He runs a hand down her face. "Hey, I promise you, it's fine. We're invincible." He nearly drags the girl toward the road.

The greedy one with fiery-red hair cups her mouth. "Don't be scared! We've all done it. And we're alive!"

In the middle of the road, the Sevilla boy spreads out his arms. The truck is speeding closer, going down the hill that'll climb back up on a blind turn, right toward them.

The girl shakes off his hand, and the Sevilla laughs. "Fine, I'll show you." He sits down, takes a cigarette from his pocket and lights it.

"Stop it! Get up, you idiot," the girl yells. All their friends stand at attention. The headlights climb over the hill, illuminate the boy's dark eyes, making him appear feral. The girl screams.

Seconds before he's hit, the truck swerves to the right, crunches over grass and gravel. It rights itself back on the road with barely enough time, releasing a stream of honks before disappearing into the night.

The Sevilla boy seems almost disappointed. He knows that's not his fate. He knows I wait, he thinks he is clever.

He crushes his cigarette and lets out a howl. His friends all laugh. But the girl, the girl is afraid, as she should be. The Sevillas are never to be trusted.

1

MY HEEL PIERCES ONE of my mother's prizewinning hybrid roses, pinning it to the damp earth. It's one of her rare black Baccaras that look like mulberry velvet. An untouchable rose meant for photo ops and awards, and here I am trampling them like they're nothing.

I almost laugh. Almost.

The alcohol rushes to my head, tilting the world under my feet. But I manage to dislodge the rose off my heel and stumble back onto the garden path of mosaic sea glass and imported stone. But this trek is quickly becoming an obstacle course, because the sprinklers hiss to life, chopping sewer water in my direction. Tugging down my dress, I make a clean break past the jets.

Anthony isn't so lucky. Water blasts the front of his pants, and he throws his head back in a cackle. "Yo! It looks like I peed myself."

I roll my eyes. It's my own fault. It's what I get for drunk texting him when I'm lonely.

"What if your mom catches us?" he tries and fails to whisper.

I catch him by the collar before he stumbles back into the caged poisonous gloriosas, and he lets out a choked sound. Like a hyper puppy straining on its leash, though he's built like a bull, making all the dainty flowers appear more vulnerable with him among them.

"As long as you don't break anything, she won't care," I say, tired, annoyed. It's been a long night, and the massive grounds of our estate only make it that much harder to sneak back in. I'd hate to admit how beautiful the gardens actually are. They were featured in *Veranda*'s list of "Charming Home Garden Designs." A feature Mom's spent the last year obsessing over, along with whatever fad diet the Miami housewives of Coral Gables are fixated on, leaving her extra catty and malnourished.

I wonder what she'll fixate on next. Because I guarantee it won't be me.

When the article said, "Marina Navarrete has a magic touch," they weren't exaggerating. The endless sea of flowers and exotic plants my mother selected is spellbinding, the smells intoxicating. The perfect place to get lost in and never emerge. Sink into the tilled dirt until you're just one withered weed in a field of meticulously arranged roses.

Anthony grabs me around the waist, squeezing me to him like a boa. The ring I wear on its long chain presses into my sternum, but tonight has made me numb. He starts kissing my neck as we trudge forward, huffing away the strands of my short curly hair from sticking to his mouth. "God, you smell good."

I extend my neck, mouth tilting. "That would be the flowers." We approach the side of the house, moving toward the French doors of my room.

"I've missed you so much, C." He stumbles again, leaning more of his weight on me.

Wish I could say the same.

"Promise—" He hiccups, or burps; it's hard to tell. "I'll be so much better this time. Treat you like a *QUEEN*."

I shake him off, not planning on holding my breath. "Who said we're getting back together?" It's not like we were anything before. I'm not harboring any romantic notions about what we mean to each other. Just two empty hearts, one goal: distraction.

He grabs my arm, turns me to him. His face contorts into what I imagine he considers a sincere expression, though his eyes kind of cross. "I'm serious!" he shouts, wincing at his own pitch. "I think I might love you."

Somehow he makes the words sound more absurd than they are. I shove him toward my bedroom. "Go inside and sleep it off."

His shoulders slump, bloodshot eyes shuttering. I point again and he goes. Just as I'm about to follow, the light above my bedroom flickers on, and I wait.

My mother's face looms, peering into the dark fog of her precious gardens. Her eye mask is pulled up, her bronzed skin glossy against the moonlight. Finally her gaze trickles down to me and hardens.

We stare at each other for a few moments, and I can't remember the last time we took stock of each other like this, pausing to acknowledge that we exist in the same sphere. Taking a second to recall how someone related could be so outrageously different.

Finally she shakes her head and steps away, taking the lights out with her.

"Told you she wouldn't care," I whisper to the dark.

ANTHONY IS ALREADY SPLAYED OUT across my bed, his massive form taking over the entire queen-size mattress. Doesn't matter. I don't plan on sleeping anytime soon.

I take a long shower, plucking the silky robe from the towel warmer once I'm finished. Even through the bathroom wall, Anthony's snores rattle through with enough force that I'm surprised he hasn't woken up the entire house. I can just imagine David barging in, red-faced and snarling until he realizes I have one of Miami's future prominent football players under his roof. The next generation to lead us into the playoffs. Oh, he'd bitch at my mom for sure. David hasn't liked me since the first moment I refused to call him *Dad* in front of his friends, adding that it wouldn't make sense until he passed the infamous one-year mark of my mother's divorces. But still, his dislike wouldn't stop him from gushing at Anthony's feet. It'd be almost funny to watch.

I bypass my bedroom, going into the adjoining sunroom where I'd left one of my half-painted canvases set up. It's one of my charcoal pieces from my Nightmare series—the chaotic purge of colors I dispel once in a while after a haunting dream. The paintings I don't show anyone.

I give the piece a lopsided look. The frothy silvers of a watery surface and algae-green streaks are kind of growing on me. It's a lake with no sky, a watery grave with no escape. But there's something else there, too, in the center of the water's depth—an almost sinister leeching of color, bone-white, a blank space in the canvas that won't absorb the paint right no matter how many times I go over it. If I close my eyes, I can practically see that shade of void-white peering at me from a dark place. Like the blank eyes of someone waiting, and it stirs something in me.

Something I can't pinpoint but since I've been numb for so long, feeling anything at all feels . . . good.

I shut off my electric kettle, sit on the stool, and place the steaming cup of tea beside my palette. A wet ring forms over the Dorset Academy's student pamphlet beneath. A summer art intensive program in England, just a few miles south of

Stonehenge. They have the highest success rate in placing graduates in high-level curating positions and top universities. The faces on the pamphlet's glossy cover all have toothy grins, and everyone stands with linked arms in front of the academy's impressive building. When my friend Cristina first told me about the program, I thought it sounded a little cultish, thanks to the school's spiel about "creating the atmosphere of a home and the bonds of a family." But I did my research, and it's not bullshit. Their alumni are well-respected artists I've been following for years, university directors for art programs all over the country. They post photos together on holidays, in galleries, gathered around dining tables and fireplaces as if they really were family. They claim to recognize brilliance, and have a track record to prove it. I flip the pamphlet over and read the back. "Students will have the assurance of a lifelong mentorship, the confidence that they will be guided and nurtured. Our program is highly selective . . ." I sigh.

Originally, I'd propped the pamphlet here for motivation, but I feel like it's had the opposite effect. Like the pressure of getting accepted makes all my work seem underwhelming, basic, and overdone. Weak.

What's worse is that now my backup is the only sure thing I have.

Earlier this evening, right before taking a stroll into the wine cellar and uncorking a two-hundred-dollar cabernet, I'd gotten a ping on my email. An acceptance to University of Miami's School of Law, where I'd applied only to please my mother. Where the only scholarships available are strictly for those pursuing a degree in anything that doesn't involve the arts. At UM I can stay close and get a "useful" degree and have the curated life of an elite socialite—like her. Every inch of me recoils at the thought, and I have to stop myself from taking it out on the painting.

It's not like I don't enjoy the perks of having money. Mom's only been married to David for nearly a year. Before that it was Robby or Bobby with his unhealthy obsession with Britto sculptures and fish tanks. An interchangeable array of wealthy men to keep our life cushy. But it meant being stuck in shitty situations with shitty people for money. It always came down to money with her, and from the brief conversations I've overhead between David and his gross golf buddies, it doesn't matter if the money is legit or not or who they screw over in the process.

As for Mom, part of me understands her. During the periods between her husbands and boyfriends when it was only us, being broke sucked. I was six when she graduated from community college while pulling shifts at a Mexican restaurant and juggling full-time courses. I remember staying in aftercare until closing time. I remember how she'd fall asleep on the couch in her uniform under a fort of textbooks while I stuffed my face on stale chips from her shift. I know if she wanted to, Mom could run a business of her own with the gumption of an army general, but something in her always pulls back. Something always comes up to make her plans flop—I've seen her struggle; I know how bad things can go in the blink of an eye.

She truly believes University of Miami would mean a surer future for me. A future where I wouldn't have to rely on other people to keep me stable, where I wouldn't have to live paycheck to paycheck, or find myself stuck. And to her, me being an artist would mean I've failed to live up to those expectations. It would mean I've squandered the sacrifices I never asked her to make.

We have not come this far only so you could choose to be a starving artist, Cecilia.

I crack the charcoal pencil, grab another one, and shade the void of white with the brightest reds, killing the effect of calming waters, making it instead look generic and abstract like a reprinted shower curtain.

It takes me hours to fix it into something decent, until the morning light filters in and highlights the sequestered shades I'd tried so hard to keep buried. Reveals all the imperfections.

I'm so close to grabbing the damn thing and chucking it out a window, when a police siren blares from outside and the entire room fills with flashes of red and blue lights.

And I think, it's about time they showed up.

2

I PERCH ON THE HOOD of my mother's Mercedes as her husband is escorted out of the house in his robe. An FBI agent cradles David's head as he tucks him into the back of a nondescript car. My mother wails from the porch, in such a state that she's actually out in broad daylight without makeup and primped hair.

Our entire driveway is ringed with cops. Some of the neighbors have even stridden right past the gates to see what's going on. It's an absolute circus. Part of me knows I should feel guilty. My anonymous tip is what brought this on, but then I remember what a terrible person he is. How he would flirt with my friends, the things he'd whisper about me under his breath, the way he'd treat my mom at parties, as if she were some lapdog. Even she deserves better than that.

I overhear his lawyer explain that David's been under investigation for months, after they received some pretty incriminating evidence.

"Oh no," I whisper. "Who would do such a thing?"

And why would someone with so much to hide keep his home office unlocked? I mean, the man employs a full staff; anyone could've done it, really.

A smile twitches at my perpetually downturned mouth until I catch Anthony waving me over from behind a column. I raise a brow but walk over to him, realizing I'm also still in my robe.

What a portrait my family must make.

"What?" I ask, gesturing to the driveway. "Kinda busy here."

Anthony bares his teeth in a wince. "Yeah . . . it's wild. What'd he do?"

I sigh, watching my mom nod tearfully as their lawyer speaks low into her ear. She's been perfecting those doe eyes for moments like this.

"Apparently, we've been living off stolen money. He got caught running some Ponzi scheme with his investors."

"Dammn—" He elongates the word with a wince. Anthony still hasn't come away from his hiding spot. "That sucks, babe. But, yo, I gotta head out. Mind if I take the route back through the gardens?"

I give him an assessing look. "I don't care. Are you embarrassed?"

He does that obnoxious *what-do-you-mean* face. "Nah, Ceci. I support you, babe, no matter what. It's just"—he shrugs—"my scholarship depends on a squeaky-clean persona. You know how it is."

"Right," I say.

He gives my chin a playful tug. "Call me later, 'kay?"

I pull away. "We'll see."

"Ah—" He laughs, backing away with a wagging finger. "There's my Ceci. Keep a stiff upper lip. It'll all work out."

He disappears through the maze of shrubs, and I turn around to the now mostly empty driveway. My mother hugs the lawyer and sobs into his shoulder.

Suddenly this pressure forms in the back of my throat, like a roiling cloud right before it thunders. Not because I know this is the last I'll see of Anthony, or even because of the arrest that I know will change everything; it's because I get this rogue glimpse of the suffocating numbness inside me that nothing can penetrate, and the full extent of it leaves me hollow.

I don't care. I really don't—and it's that emptiness that terrifies me.

IT'S BEEN WEEKS of lawyers and courts. Honestly I had no idea it would turn into such a big case. I'm just relieved our part in this Ponzi fiasco is over, even if it does mean moving to some backwater town.

My mother taps her black nails over the steering wheel as we make our way up the winding highway. She's taken to wearing black these days like a widow; I even caught her wearing a veil as the IRS foreclosed on David's property and stripped it down to its bones. The potted yellow plant that comes with us to every house is wedged between us. Everything else we were allowed to take is in the hitched trailer behind our newly purchased *used* car. Until her lawyers can poke enough holes into her prenup to make it look like Swiss cheese.

Despite the tint of her oversized sunglasses, I can tell Mom's eyes constantly flicker to me. I continue to scroll through my friend Cristina's Instagram account, finding photo after photo of my other so-called friends and Anthony at the beach. There's one of Cristina in some outrageous yoga pose in her bikini while Anthony holds her legs. I read the time stamp again—Saturday morning. The day after the hearing. The day they took everything and my mom finally stopped crying long enough to sit me down and proclaim we were moving to the town she grew up in after she migrated from Nicaragua with her tía. It was the day I'd almost texted Cristina with *I need you*, words I don't say to anyone, ever, but she'd texted me first. Not to check in, but with a paragraph of emojis to announce that she'd been accepted to Dorset. She was already shopping for Europe.

Even now, the hot jealousy comes up like stomach acid. My uglier thoughts assume her alumni mother had something to do with it, because Cristina's *collage* art can't merit the supposed "brilliance" that Dorset seeks. But I try really hard for those thoughts not to take root. Instead, my brain spirals with questions, the main one being why I haven't gotten my letter yet.

As soon as I get accepted, I can move to the other side of the world and start over on my own. Mom can have free rein and find whatever husband she wants—the rich ones always seem to show up out of thin air. But I can finally be done moving my life around for her.

Once the tension in the car mounts to an unbearable peak, my mother whips back her glasses and glares in my direction. "Mirá, Cecilia. En serio? Do you honestly have nothing to say to me?"

I put down my phone. "What do you want me to say?"

"Um, how about 'I'm sorry for everything you're going through, Mom. Can I help you in some way?' Don't you even have questions about where we're going? 'Cause I can tell you right now, you're in for a rude awakening. This isn't some impromptu vacation to the Alps. There's no luxury in this god"—she slams a palm to the steering wheel—"forsaken"—again and again—"place."

I take in a settling breath. "I don't care about that stuff."

Her laughter is cruel, a little demented. "Oh, of course not. Try not to flash that Cartier band when you say it next time. Or let's see how that curly fringe holds up after a week of Garnier shampoo!" Her nostrils flare, her chest rapidly rising and falling.

An angry wave of blood rushes to my head.

I pull back my sleeve, unclasp the damn bracelet, and fling it out the window.

My mom's eyes bulge, glazed with disbelief. "What in the hell is wrong with you?"

"I told you—I. Don't. Care!"

She slams on the brakes, pulling over to the side of the road and reversing. I sit back with my arms crossed as she gets out of the car, slams the door, and searches the ditch, nearly slipping in her heels on the little hill that separates the wilderness from the highway. Let's see if she doesn't get attacked by some cougar for being desperate.

Oh, the irony.

Finally, after twenty minutes she comes back into the car, sweat pasting her pixie-cut hair across her forehead, but the rose-gold band is in her grasp. She throws it into a cup holder. I can't believe she actually found it.

"We'll be stopping at a pawnshop before getting into town."

Even though I know she won't ask for it, I clasp my cheap silver necklace and the old brass ring that dangles there. It's the only thing I own that belonged to my mother before everything changed, before the money, and it's not worth much more than the sentimental value.

"A pawnshop?" I can't understand why she's acting like this. "Don't you have a ton of cash saved up? I mean you've been divorced three times. Didn't you get settlements?"

Her arms are rigid. This time she doesn't glance in my direction. "I was one of his investors," she whispers with unbearable quiet. "I was . . . he took everything except the house in Santa Aguas. El hijueputa nos pelo."

A sickening feeling settles in my stomach. My throat is so dry it takes me a few tries to ask. "What about . . . my college fund?"

She settles her stiff back onto the seat, dropping the glasses back onto her face, but it doesn't hide the escaping tear of frustration. "Gone."

3

I FEEL SICK. I try conjuring up that bubble of wrath that came over me when my mom said she lost my college money, but mostly I just feel exhausted. What was I expecting anyway? That I could make plans and they'd work out? That I could fall back on any kind of reassurance from her?

She'd been played, but she was also careless. And I've come to expect that when it comes to me, but never when it comes to her money. Plus a part of me can't help but take the blame. I did this. David could've gone many years without getting caught, but something tells me Mom wouldn't have seen that money again anyway.

"They sell sodas out back. Grab me a Coke, will you?" Mom doesn't glance away from the mustached man behind the counter. She's been locked in conversation with the pawnshop owner for the past half hour, and these are the first words she's directed at me since our conversation in the car.

Another weight seems to settle onto my back. "Diet or regular?"

"Regular," she says, and it's the first good news I've heard in days considering all the lectures she's ignored from me about diet soda.

I push away from the glass display case with every type of handgun imaginable, as if it weren't clear enough we're in the Deep South. There's an ache in my lower back from how long I'd been leaning on the glass, staring at the woman sweeping the store.

I didn't mean to stare, but her Roomba-like movements nearly lulled me to sleep. What kept my interest, however, was how the woman purposefully avoided the two ceramic bowls filled with little seeds by the door. She was more preoccupied with my mom and the mustached man as if making sure there wasn't any flirting going on.

I head to the store's side door. If you could even call this a store. It feels more like an indoor recycling dump. I have to keep scrunching my nose before the layers of dust on dozens of VCRs can infiltrate and trigger my allergies.

Once I'm outside, I inhale the blast of humid air and follow the electric drone of the vending machine that must be in the back. There's a palpable static of electricity as I get closer to the building's rear, and I almost expect to see a mound of radioactive waste.

There's a mural on this side of the building that you can't see from the parking lot. Some quintessential Florida things like alligators and swamps with turtles, cypress trees, and . . .

I round the corner and my throat goes dry.

There's no vending machine here, but there is something dead. I swallow back the scream as I come face-to-face with a veiled horse skeleton. Some kind of taxidermy gone wrong. The horse head is on the body of a woman made of wood. The entire thing is erected on a pedestal with half-melted votive candles and more of those yellow and red seeds I saw inside. A scatter of men's shoes are piled at the base.

It's some kind of altar. The mural behind her spells out LAST CHANCE against a backdrop of dark woods. There's an uncomfortable wrongness in my stomach.

The head is what most throws me off. I'd think it was a saint statue, like the millions I've seen in Miami, but I've never seen a saint with a taxidermic horse head.

The thing is grotesque. The cheeks carved to appear skinless, revealing its sinewy muscle beneath. Glass eyes painted way too realistically. And the most absurd thing of all is that it's wearing a bridal veil.

What the hell is this place?

A click from the back door makes me jump. Someone's hauling out a garbage bag, and before they can turn around, I bolt back to the front of the pawnshop, feeling ridiculous the moment I'm back inside. It's a statue, not a monster.

I find my mom and the mustached man now counting out cash, so I'm assuming things are going well.

I move close to her side. "I . . . didn't see a vending machine. I'll just wait for you in the car."

"Fine," she says, not looking up from the stack of money piling higher. She looks practically naked without her jewelry. "Straight to the car and lock the doors."

You don't have to tell me twice. No matter how much I rub my arms, I can't get the prickly sensation off my skin or the horse face out of my memory.

THERE'S STILL STATIC lingering on my skin as I wait in the car, a residue from whatever vibes that dead horse saint was giving off. I can feel it on the back of my neck and down my spine. Can practically taste it across my lips like an impending storm.

I twist up the volume on some crackling station playing a Mexican ballad, hoping I can repress the image of the dead thing's face. But the glove box flops open and I jump. Suddenly I'm five again, hitting it with my feet, barely tall enough to see over the dashboard. A memory of waiting for what felt like forever in the dark, hours in the car in some back alley of an Italian restaurant. My babysitter had bailed, and my mom's date didn't know she had a kid. I had to be a good little girl and stay put until she was finished.

My stomach turns with an old ache.

As Mom finally exits the pawnshop, she almost knocks over a stack of audio equipment in her haste to get out. An open-mouthed old man sitting on a crate and smoking a cigarette eyes her in her Dior jumpsuit like something that magically crawled out of a magazine and materialized on the sidewalk. She stops in front of him, says something with that side-hip charm, and in two seconds the man is handing her one of his cigarettes. And lights it for her.

Sliding into the car, she hands me a wad of cash. "Here." I notice she's not wearing her wedding band. "This is just a start, save it. You don't have to worry about us going broke, milagrito." She squeezes my thigh before peeling out of the parking lot, dangling the cigarette between her lips. I'm still holding the money, a bit dazed, feeling like anything but her little miracle.

"Opportunities are never far. If there's one thing we can count on, it's that," she says, but her tone has a bitter edge.

"Good thing one of us is optimistic." I tuck the cash deep into her purse.

THE ROADS IN THIS TOWN are so dark, guarded by an endless tower of thick trees, that it's hard to believe anyone lives here at all. It's like this place exists inside a bubble, one that causes a slight ringing in my ears and an unsettling tightness in my stomach. Maybe there's a power plant nearby, or I'm slowly dying from the radioactive poison they dump into these small farmland lakes from the many slaughterhouses and their animals pumped with antibiotics.

Maybe I watch too many food documentaries, and there's a completely different reason for the unease worming its way under my skin.

We pass a large tattered sign that reads, WELCOME TO SANTA AGUAS. ESTABLISHED 1887. Someone graffitied the entire bottom of the billboard with BEWARE LA CEGUA in what looks to be blood but is really drippy red paint. After unsuccessfully trying to coax the one bar of service to illuminate me on what la Cegua is, I ask my mom, though I've been determined not to talk to her again for the rest of the trip.

"What's a Cegua?" I ask, my tone gruff.

She blows out a breath, hands tightening on the wheel. "You saw that, huh?" I stay quiet so she continues. "It's some weird town superstition. La Cegua is an old Nicaraguan folktale about a beautiful woman who lures men into the woods." A glance at my expression. "I know. Then she petrifies them by showing her true face—which some claim is a horse skeleton."

I sit up from my slouch. That must've been what the sculpture was all about.

"And do people here worship her or something?"

"Some do. Some believe she'll grant you wishes if you're good. Honestly, I think it's all a cautionary tale to keep men from being cheating assholes. But people here swear they've seen a Cegua stuck, roaming Santa Aguas. Poor girl." Mom shifts in her seat, gaze darting toward the woods.

"Maybe it's true, though," I say.

"Sure, whatever." She rolls her eyes. "There's a horse-faced ghost here kidnapping drunks for kicks. And she chose this town because of its *charm*."

Something in my stomach twists. "Kidnapped drunks?"

At this my mom's face finally sobers, takes on a pale tinge. "You know I'd actually forgotten all about it. But yeah, there were . . . cases of men disappearing near the woods for a few days. Some would come back"—she holds up a hand— "scratched, bruised, and scared stiff, but none of them could remember where they'd been taken. Again though, they were *skunk drunk*. Could've been some teenagers just being jerks and messing with them."

"That'd be seriously messed up." We're talking kidnapping people for *days*, and only some of them would come back. What kind of place is this?

Mom shrugs a thin shoulder. "Yeah, well, people can be messed up. Especially in these small towns where they have nothing better to do. There's some dumb annual festival to keep her at bay—horse masks, the guys showing their affections through competitive lance throwing and eating contests."

I scoff. "Because nothing says *love* like impaling something followed by indigestion."

We share a smile and immediately both look away.

"They also get a little weird with their prayers and offerings," she says, recovering. "But basically I think it's made up to draw in tourists. It doesn't mean this place is safe though."

"If it's fake, why wouldn't it be safe?"

"Hello? Because bored people can be dangerous, and anyone can easily go missing in these backwoods." Another shifty glance at the surrounding dark forest. "Anyway, change of subject."

And by that she means no more talking. My brows lift as she turns up the music.

"Fine," I say, but it's not really. I don't understand why she's being so skittish. We apparently owned a house here for years, and she lived in this town most of her life. Don't know if these so-called kidnappings and fake Cegua sightings had anything to do with her avoiding this place for so long. Or if she forgot about this town for another reason entirely.

After a while, Mom announces we're almost to the house. The headlights illuminate the haze of fog sticking close to the ground and the little smattering of rain. Her chin nearly touches the steering wheel as she looks for the turn. My eyes blur with sleep, and I think for the briefest of moments I see a silhouette in white appear within the dark wall of trees, but I blink and the figure is gone. The weird taxidermy and stories have obviously gotten to me.

"There it is," she says, voice a little reverent. We pull onto the barely visible gravel road, going past the open giant metal gates that creak with the wind.

Then the house comes into view.

My eyes nearly fall out of my head as I lean forward to peer up at the monstrous mansion just as a streak of lightning cuts across the dark.

The mansion is peaked and angled, growing like a giant thorny bush in the middle of the forest. An honest to god Victorian castle left here to rot.

"Whoa." My mouth goes dry. It's not at all what I expected. The steep, high-pitched roof seems to pierce the night sky.

"I know," my mom says with a sigh, parking in front of the massive entry portico and double-wide doors. The burgundy brick walls are heavily clad in ivy, making the mansion appear almost impenetrable, half-swallowed by the ground. It's difficult to gauge what the building really looks like in the dark, but I can make out the arched beveled-glass windows and the prominent chimneys protruding from two turrets that also seem to spear into the dark clouds.

"You used to live here?" I ask, more than a little awed.

Another heavy breath, and the light seems to ebb from her eyes. "I wished—I mean," she's quick to amend, "I *really* wanted to live here. I used to think this place was the peak of elegance." And it is elegant. A gothic, almost haunting elegance. "I spent a lot of time here," she continues, but there's a bitterness to her words. "Mostly cleaning it with my aunt. I bought it years after I left town and haven't been back since. Anyway, it's probably a wreck in there so watch what you touch. The electrician is stopping by tomorrow." My mom exits the car with her overnight bag, making it clear that's all she'll share on the subject though none of this makes sense. I know the method well. I recognize the moment her walls slam down, and it still takes an effort not to flinch.

The wind stills. The house's wrapped English ivy stops rustling as if the building itself has paused to watch us.

I hurry my steps and meet her by the door, a disquieting snake knocker staring back while Mom fumbles for the key in her purse.

She has to rattle the door a bit to get it open, and the wooden thing squeals in a cry of protest. The noise echoes around the dark space. The ancient quiet seeping out with every hallowed step I take inside.

The air feels hot, so much so that I thought Mom came in beside me, but she's still waiting outside the door, her eyes shining.

"Are you . . . coming in?"

I see her swallow. But still, nothing.

"Mom. What are you waiting for? Come inside."

That seems to break whatever daze she's in, because she steps into the house, and I swear the air seems to ripple. Then again, I'm running on very little sleep and the humidity of the deserted house is as thick as meat fat.

I look for the light switch, and I find one with two little buttons but neither of them work.

"That's old," Mom says from the other side of the room, clicking on the more modern-looking light switch and illuminating the foyer and grand staircase. "Like the furnaces and most of the fireplaces, the old switchboards were disconnected."

With the lights on, I can really take stock. I stop in the center of the room—the foyer, because it's a house that calls for those kinds of words. The ginormous antique chandelier in the center with missing crystals looms above my head as I take in the braided wood floors and coffered ceilings. The walls are paneled in dark oak and every massive painting is displayed high in a flaking gold frame. It's an array of romantic marshy and forest landscapes, probably Florida in precolonial times. When my gaze lands back toward the door, I notice the cylindrical jars on either side. Both of them are filled with thousands of those same red and yellow seeds from the pawnshop.

"They're mustard seeds," Mom says before I can ask.

Mustard seeds. "More town superstitions?"

Her eye roll says it all.

"Mom," I finally manage, "what is this place?" And I mean more than just the weird mansion.

She glances around, too, holding her arms together. I've never seen her look so meek. "Home. For now." She shuffles her way toward the stairs. "Tomorrow we'll get the rest of our stuff. I'll probably drown myself in the tub or maybe jump from the tower balcony—still haven't decided."

I ignore this. It's her usual melodrama. "What about me? Where do I sleep?"

She spreads out her arms, stopping for a moment before making a right at the stairs. A bottle of wine she must've had in her bag materializes in her hands. "The possibilities are endless. Take your pick."

And she disappears, leaving me alone in this house that may or may not be haunted. In this unfamiliar town in the middle of nowhere. Maybe I should find a tub to drown in too. I decide to make a left at the stairs, finding the farthest room I can from hers.

4

STARING UP AT THE CRACKED vaulted ceiling of my bedroom in the daylight, I get the impression I'm living someone else's life. Like an out-of-body experience where my soul has been temporarily dropped into some gothic painting or a Guillermo del Toro film.

I check to see if my phone has messages but there's nothing, not even a single bar of service, which has been the case since we crossed the manor's gates last night. I slide my feet off the bed, meeting the plush rug beneath, and take my necklace from the beside table, slipping it on. The room is surprisingly clean with only a hint of dust, as if it were recently aired out. But there's a distinct scent of lavender and wood rot. I wonder if eventually I'll start smelling like the room, too, or if my scent will leave an imprint. It's what tends to happen with every house, we leave and take a piece of each other.

Like many of the rooms, it has a modest bed with frilly lace sheets. The walls are a faded teal, like the Caribbean Sea, topped with gold leaf stenciling, and there's a little library nook in the corner, and a vanity with a cloudy mirror. But it's the bay windows with their beveled glass that sold me on this particular room. I knew my choice would pay off in the morning and it does not disappoint.

The view from my room faces the back of the manor and its expansive grounds. A huge clearing with a disheveled garden. There's a stone pathway that snakes and curves within the wall of concrete girdling the towering pines. The morning light filters in soft amber patterns and evergreen shades—the concave glass paints the room in rainbow.

I can imagine myself painting here for hours, getting lost in all the offered colors of the woods and sun. But that reminds me everything is still in the U-Haul and this might not be home for long. No matter how magical this place seems, it's not powerful enough to keep Marina Navarette in one place for too long.

I take extra pains with my makeup, conquering a flawless wing tip and the shimmering glow of highlighted cheeks. Because, like my mother says, *Just 'cause you're sad doesn't mean you can't paint on a pretty face*. And if there's one thing I can do well, it's putting on a mask.

Flouncing my curls, I step out into the hall, enjoying the creak the old wood floors release like a greeting. In the daylight, I can really take in how amazing this place is. We've never lived in anything like it. Always new construction homes with pale walls and floors, plastered shelf nooks, and fake lilies in cream vases. Everything here is lived-in, worn down, and moody. Like my soul—not to be dramatic. I can almost make out the marks on the walls where many people must've passed, trailing their fingers.

Along the wall, the frames containing different genera of labeled flowers slowly shift toward striking portrayals of Indo-Christian art. Interesting, because it's more common in Central America than middle-of-nowhere Florida, and I wonder again what's the story with this house. Painted in cubist techniques with bold red and brown tones, there are women in beautiful, off-the-shoulder gowns and rebozos. Children with frowning mouths and big dark eyes that seem to follow me as I walk. They're all striking—dark-skinned and elegant. Not my mom's style of art at all so I know these must've been here long before she bought the house.

I keep exploring, not yet ready to step back into the reality that waits for me downstairs. I wind through the corridors, finding different rooms and a small alcove at the very end of a hall where it grows dark and chilled. A hallway that seems to lead nowhere. It's no longer art, but a gallery of family portraits. The alcove ends on a tall, floor-to-ceiling oil portrait of a brooding man with a serious mustache. The plaque on the bottom says, GERARDO ALFONSO SEVILLA-BECKMANN. Judging by the painting's placement, I'm guessing he was an important dude. Maybe even the man whom the house was built for.

Around his portrait, there's a set of more modern photographs illuminated by a flickering sconce light. I cross my arms, peering closer, finding myself far from where I started or any natural light.

These photographs are of different young men throughout the ages, posing with a gruff countenance that seems to be inherited. I find no women in the frames. The spouses, sisters, and mothers weren't highlighted at all in this family.

The Sevilla-Beckmanns definitely don't look like a happy bunch.

My attention eventually snags on a series of the same boy. First as a toddler on an old swing in the woods. A hawkish kid with very high cheekbones and a tin lunch box. There's something familiar about him—maybe in the way that he's alone in every picture or that he seems preoccupied with something in the distance. There's something lonely in his expression. Always looking away from the camera.

Except in the last photo of him, where he's staring directly back as if assessing me too.

In this one, he's a little older, about my age. His hair is dark and curly. Eyes a bit protruding over hollowed cheeks. Striking, in a disarming way.

He's standing by the house in a forced pose. Behind him there's a clear pathway into the forest, arched with large magnolia trees—before the concrete wall must've been built.

I can almost picture something reaching for him from the dark woods at his back, and a chill runs down my spine.

Find me.

I stumble back. I swear I hear a voice whisper in my ear, but when I look around I'm still alone.

Come find me.

My eyes lock with the boy, and I squint to make sure I'm seeing this right, because I know his expression changed. It changed.

There's a crack, and the ceiling above me opens like a mouth. I scream with everything I've got as a face materializes from the dark.

"GAVE THIS ONE A FRIGHT." The cable guy tells my mom in the kitchen with a chuckle. She's looking sparkling new, as if the hellish few weeks didn't just happen.

"What about the Wi-Fi?" she asks, ignoring his comment and the story he's undoubtedly about to spill about how he was coming out of the attic only to find me waiting beneath like a mouse caught in a trap. I know because he just finished telling me the story, as if I didn't experience it with him. As if my heart weren't still beating in my ears.

The house is already getting to me.

He puffs his chest in lament, adjusting his tool belt. "Well, there's a bit of an issue. Looks like there's something wonky with the ethernet line, and really the estate isn't exactly wired for access points."

My mom pinches the bridge of her nose. "Just tell me how much it'll cost."

"And how long it's going to take," I say. No internet, no mobile service, no TV. My mom and I will strangle each other before the day's out.

He sucks his teeth. "I'll get a crew out here and give you an estimate. Let me talk to Carl and see what he thinks, and I'll get back to you."

My mom places her mug down. "Who's Carl?"

He looks confused, pointing his thumb toward the dining room where a man is currently poised on a ladder, fiddling with a loose wire from the ceiling. "Ugh . . . your electrician, ma'am. Says he's been working with Gabriel—"

She waves this away, as if he's the one off topic. "Get whoever you need, but get it done quickly. Please," she adds, already turning around, trying to figure out the giant cast-iron range.

"You got it." The cable guy leans toward me. "And don't worry about those ghost stories they be telling about this house. I checked the whole attic and didn't find any bones." He winks.

Great. Fantastic. That completely puts me at ease.

I lean against the counter. "What ghost stories?"

Mom shoots the cable guy a glare, but he raises his arm innocently. "Figured you knew seeing as you own the place."

"You mean, la Cegua?" I ask, and the guy's face lights up.

"Ah, so you do know a little something. But nope, I meant the Sevilla boy and his family curse—"

Mom slams down one of the stovetop's metal burners, as if disassembling it will get it to cooperate. "Don't listen to this nonsense. It's an old house in a small town—people have nothing better to do than make up stories."

The guy fixes his tool belt. "Now, I don't know about no Cegua, but the curse is as true as toast and as old as this town. My great,

great-granddaddy worked with Gerardo himself when the Sevilla sickness took hold."

I think back to the portraits upstairs. The mustached man with eyes of molten metal.

"He was the owner of this house?" I ask.

"He was the town founder."

"He was a drunk," my mother snaps, annoyed. She turns to me, abandoning the stove. "Look, the only thing the Sevillas were cursed with were bad choices that led to untimely deaths."

"Untimely deaths before their thirties," cable guy says with a huff. "Six generations of young men died tragically, and one of them went missing. A little more than bad luck, I would say."

Missing? Someone went *missing*?

My face must ask the unvoiced question.

"Yup. The Sevilla boy. Last one of them."

Oh my god. So many questions rattle in my chest. Like did they die in this house? When did the boy go missing? Is it the unsmiling one whose expression seemed to change? The one who I swore spoke to me?

But that's impossible.

Mom looks just as disturbed but not surprised. Not surprised at all. Of course she'd know. She'd lived here most her life.

"Why the hell would you buy this house, Mom?"

"Well, I imagine she got a pretty good deal on it," Cable Guy interjects.

I feel her walls come down again like a guillotine, but she doesn't deny it. Of course. Of course she wouldn't care about the horrific backstory of some building that has nothing to do with her. It'd come down to money.

Mom pinches the bridge of her nose. "This is giving me a headache. How about instead we worry about the Wi-Fi before we have another tragic death on our hands."

That wipes the jovial expression from the man's face, and he stalks off grumbling about rich city folk.

Mom couldn't care less. She smooths her hair in a soothing gesture and takes my spot on the stool.

"Cecilia, help me out," she says, gesturing to the stove.

She's already got the thing on, but she's basically asking me to cook the eggs for her. Since she's previously burned *water*, I gladly take over. I need something to do besides spiral on thoughts of generational curses and ghosts.

I voice my next-pressing concern instead. "What are we going to do here without internet? I really need to check my email today."

Mom shakes her phone as if that'll get her messages to go through. "I need to stop by the post office to reroute the mail. There's a little internet café next door you can check out."

I don't know what an internet café is, but I can tell mom's mind is already ten topics away. She leans across the counter, wiggling her shoulders. "I got some wonderful news this morning." She pauses, waiting for my reaction.

"Oh yeah?" I crack an egg into the pan. "Another haunted house go on the market?"

"Very funny. *No*, Liam—the lawyer—called to tell us they're fighting to get some of my gifted assets returned to us. That means the sale on those assets can at least cover your tuition for the first two years at UM. Plenty of time for me to figure out our next step. Oh, and the divorce is finalized."

I turn off the stove. "Wait. What?"

She fixes a rogue strand of hair. "Well, I wasn't going to stay married to someone who robbed us."

"No." I shake my head. "I mean—I haven't decided to go to UM yet. I haven't heard from Dorset. It's still a possibility."

She raises a brow. "The summer program all the way in Europe? They're not even affiliated with a real university, Cecilia. Didn't you already try the whole starving artist thing?" She tries hiding the smug edge to her smile by taking a sip of coffee.

Bitterness consumes my insides like a parasite. She's referring to the time I couldn't take living with her anymore and ran away. I was sixteen and a group of older friends, an ex-boyfriend to be exact, let me crash on his couch for a week. No one would give me a job. Their water and electricity was always being shut off, and the place had a continuous stench of weed and takeout. I felt like I was living in a nonfunctioning commune. To top off the humiliation, he'd started seeing someone else while I was still living there. So I left, then came crawling back home. Just sneaked back in one night, and Mom and I pretended like I'd never even left.

Like she'd known I'd come back eventually. I never knew whether to be grateful to her for letting me preserve my dignity or whether I should continue hating her for not trying to get me back sooner.

The plate of eggs clatter as I set it down with too much force.

"We'll talk about it later. Now, sit down and eat," Mom says, as if *she'd* been the one to prepare us breakfast. "Maybe you can talk to the guidance counselor in school on Monday."

The fork hangs halfway between my mouth and the plate. "School? You can't be serious."

She scoffs a laugh. "You didn't think you were going to drop out in your senior year, did you?"

"No, of course not. I thought—*Mom*, there's only a few weeks left. It already sucks that I had to leave before graduation with my friends, but to start a new school *now*? It doesn't make sense. I can finish the semester online."

"With what internet?" She throws her hands up. "You heard Carl—"

"That wasn't Carl."

She ignores this. "He said this place is a dead zone. And you really want to graduate with one of those obscure online high schools? Imagine how terrible that'll look on your transcripts. Even if you got accepted already, it still doesn't look good."

"Who cares if it doesn't look good?"

"I care!"

We're both leaning forward now, plates forgotten.

"Why are you making this so difficult?"

Her hands slam onto the counter. "Because I don't want you to end up like me!"

We stare at each other, chests heaving. I put the napkin over my plate and toss it into the massive sink, which rattles on its antique legs like a loose tooth.

"Well, that's the last thing you should worry about, because I'll never be like you."

My mom's staring at me like I've slapped her, but the words are already hanging between us, heavy as lead, and there's no taking them back.

It's then my phone decides to pick up a single bar of service and ping with a message. We stare at each other for a single beat longer before she turns away.

I pick up my phone and nearly jump when I see the Dorset email sitting in my inbox. But it's not at all the answer I was waiting for. The letters burn into my heart, searing deep.

We regret to inform you . . .

5

THERE'S A HEAVY PRESSURE on my chest. A pit widening in my stomach, threatening to eat away at every organ. Because my work is not enough. *I'm not enough.*

They don't want me.

The last bit of the letter repeats in my head, the simple note and deviation from the standard form rejection—*Ms. Navarette, your work shows a lot of promise.*

A promise that doesn't quite deliver. And I see it. There's something missing in my portraits, in the colors, in the shape and form or wherever the emotion seeps out from. It's not there. Maybe I should've submitted something from my Nightmare series—the charcoal drawings I usually keep tucked away under my bed or buried deep in the closet. The paintings that crawl their way to the surface after one of my lingering dreams. But they're way too messy and unrefined. Too personal. The oozing poison of darkness spilling from a dark, hidden place.

Driving to town, my mom and I don't say a word. Both of us maintain a stoicism that seems hereditary. There's been a wad of pain lodged in my throat since I opened the email. I wouldn't be able to talk about it even if she asks. And she hasn't.

We're silent as we pass a yellow caution sign that reads, HIKE AT YOUR OWN RISK, and in the downtown area, my jaw clatters on some of the cobblestone roads in desperate need of maintenance. At least in the town center of Santa Aguas, there's some semblance of civilization. People mill about lazily. Cars drive below the speed limit. Even the thick gray clouds seem to move slower here.

It looks stuck in time—not a Starbucks or McDonald's in sight.

It's not the prettiest town. Mostly neglected historical buildings turned into banks and pharmacies and some colonial-style homes. The power lines are everywhere, crisscrossing over roads and buildings like a messy chess board.

But at least the people are diverse. My fear had been that we'd be the only non-Caucasian family for miles, which is the risk you run in Floridian small towns. Already I'd been missing the food: the bakeries on every street corner, the bodegas and obscure botanica shops that contribute to Miami's flavor. But I catch sight of Mexican taquerias and a Nicaraguan fritanga, and count about five psychic shops.

Why would a population of like a hundred people need that many psychics?

Mom parallel parks in front of one of them, leaving me face-to-face with the mannequin outside wearing a threadbare wedding dress and tattered veil. There are more men's shoes at her base like I'd seen with the horse statue from yesterday.

"I'll wait in the car," I say, tearing my gaze from it.

Mom takes the key out of the ignition, heaving a breath. She places the huge Dolce glasses over her head to peer outside. "God, I hate being back here." When she looks at me like she wants to say something else, I think she might bring up our earlier conversation. I think maybe I should apologize, or maybe she's changed her mind about sending me back to school when our whole world has just been upended because of her bad decisions.

But instead, she flips the visor, checks her lipstick, and shakes herself up. "We just got to make the most of it. Like not stay in the car and sulk." She hops out before I can respond, and it's as close as she'll come to saying, *Don't make me do this alone*. As close as we'll get to an actual conversation. So I get out, too, because I'm *not* sulking.

I only have a second to grab Mom's arm and pull her back before a camouflage-painted pickup truck comes roaring down the road, nearly taking her out.

"Hey!" she yells.

This leathery-skinned man sticks his middle finger out the driver's side window.

"At least the locals are friendly," I huff, but then several people stop to ask if we're all right, and Mom quickly assures them we're fine.

"I can't believe that man still has a license," she says to me.

"You know him?"

"Just your local resident asshole."

After checking both sides of the street, we cross another road and make it to the post office, where there's a parked car riddled with bumper stickers. Like it's a miracle they can see out their back window. I read some of the stickers, noticing a theme. It's a bunch of rock puns.

A mossy rock says, I'M REALLY LICHEN YOU! Another one is of two pickaxes that reads: I'VE GOT MY SCHIST TOGETHER.

I snort, getting a blast of cool air as Mom opens the post office door. There are a few people busily checking their PO boxes and only one person ahead of us.

Off to the side, behind a register, there's a guy my age, biting his tongue as he seals a package. His dark hair is artfully messy and naturally highlighted with lighter brown strands in that unfair way boys inherit beautiful nail beds and long eyelashes. He's wearing a fitted T-shirt that says, HAVE YOU BEEN HELPED TODAY? But it doesn't look like a uniform. At least none of the other tellers are wearing it.

Finishing his task, he looks up, meeting my gaze. He's totally caught me checking him out, but he smiles wide anyway—an unabashed swoop of his mouth taking up most of his face. I turn around quickly, studying the display of greeting cards as my mom is helped next.

I'm only going to be here for a short time. It would be pointless to get distracted by a townie, even one who looks like that.

There's an older man at the teller talking too loudly for the small space. He's got a hat tucked under his arm and pants smeared in dirt. It'd be impossible not to eavesdrop, but when I hear *sinkhole*, I don't even try to pretend.

"Swallowed up the Myers' new crop last night. Haven't seen one that size in years!"

He goes on to tell the teller that it's been at least twenty years since the last sinkhole, which prompts both of them to go quiet.

Great. A town known to swallow you whole at any given moment. This move has just gotten better and better.

I pick up a Santa Aguas postcard and roll my eyes, reminded of the stack I have under my bed from all over the world, unsigned and undated. I've been getting them on my birthday every year from the sperm donor—which is what I call the absent man in my life who couldn't be bothered to meet his kid. I skip past another card—one that says: THOSE WE LOVE ARE NEVER LOST, THEY ARE ALWAYS WITH US. And I wonder if that counts for those who were never found to begin with. Like my father. If he really is always with me. I clear away the intrusive, sentimental thought. *Always* is the same as *promise*: bullshit.

"Hi!" A voice crops up beside me and I jump. It's checkout guy. "Sorry, didn't mean to scare you."

Oh god, why is he talking to me? I randomly select another card, slanting a quick glance at him. "Hey."

"I'm Jamie." He leans against a column, but it doesn't diminish his height. "Are you . . . new in town?"

Now I face him. "I am. Are you the welcoming committee, Jamie?"

He laughs. "Afraid I can't claim that title yet. I'm pretty new here too. Well, it's been two years, but I haven't seen you around or in school. Will you be going to Beckmann?"

I give him a blank stare. "How do you know I'm not a freakishly young-looking forty-year-old?"

His eyes widen. "I—"

Easily flustered. How adorable. "Relax," I say. "I'm kidding. If Beckmann is the high school here then, yeah, that's where I'll be going. Unfortunately."

He rubs the back of his neck, and I'm not sure if it's to flex his bicep or a nervous gesture, but it's cute. "It's not that terrible, I promise. I've moved around a lot and as far as schools go it's . . . well, they're mostly the same, aren't they?"

"Crummy food, overworked teachers, a demoralizing social hierarchy of hormone-fueled teenagers?" I give the card display a whirl. "Yeah. I've moved around a lot too."

I catch his smile from the corner of my eye.

"Cecilia?" my mom calls, raising an inquisitive brow at Jamie from the door. "I'm ready."

"Yeah, I'll meet you outside." I turn back to the boy. "I'll see you around, Jamie. In the halls of Beckmann."

"Or anywhere really," he replies. "It's a small town, and a forty-year-old teenager would be hard to miss."

I snort before walking away.

Outside my mom nudges my shoulder with hers. "Not even two seconds in town and already picking up strays."

"I so was not," I say, but just then, the post office door blasts open and Jamie is running outside.

"You forgot this," he says, handing me a card, slightly out of breath.

"I didn't—" I start to say, but he's already turned and walked back in. When I look down, it's a simple greeting card that says "See you later," with a picture of an alligator underneath. A reluctant smile tugs at my lips.

"Hmm, cute," my mom says reading over my shoulder, but her amusement is short-lived as a motorcycle comes rumbling down the road loud enough to rattle the storefront windows.

"Oh my god." She looks mildly panicked.

"What's wrong?" I ask but this is ignored as her attention follows the motorcycle's path toward a parking space, and as if an internal string is plucked, my mom basically levitates toward the man who's releasing the motorcycle's kickstand and pats her thighs while she waits.

"Gabriel Delgado," she says in a slightly nervous singsong.

He takes off his helmet, revealing aquamarine eyes and a soft smile reserved for my mother. "Marina."

My god. What kind of men do they breed here? Must be whatever the local slaughterhouses dump in the lakes.

The guy is tall, dark-skinned, and muscular. And he's tucking my mom's small frame into his in an embrace that seems almost *intimate*. He's young, but then again it's moments like these that I remember Mom's still young too. Having a kid at eighteen means she's barely in her midthirties.

He pulls her back to get a good look at her. "How do you still look exactly the same?"

Her breathing is shaky. "No." She laughs. "Not exactly."

The response makes him flinch, though I can't imagine why. "You look good, is what I meant."

My mother flushes. She backs away, gesturing to me. "Gabe, this is my daughter—Cecilia. Cecilia, this is Gabe, an old friend."

"Hey," I say, crossing my arms. "It's Ceci."

Now it's my mom's turn to roll her eyes. She hates that I shorten my name, considering she agonized over what to call me when she was pregnant and was determined it wouldn't be anything tacky.

Gabe takes me in, studying my face, a little struck with whatever he finds there. "Wow. You look just like—" He aims another strange glance at my mother but finishes the thought with a little laugh. "Just like your mother."

I stare at him. Almost willing him to say what he means. I know I don't look just like her. Despite our nearly black hair and bronzy complexion, my eyes are too narrow and dark. My brows too thick. My lips too puffy. Whereas her features would be considered delicate, mine are clearly intense. I wonder if he ever met my father—before he decided traveling the world would be preferable to sticking around. Mom says my dad was a quick fling after she left this town, but who knows if that's the truth.

I slide my ring on my chain in thought. I notice Gabe tracks the movement.

"I want to thank you," Mom says, brushing his arm. "I know I don't say it enough. Or call like I should. But the way you've kept up the house all these years, and with everything else . . . it means a lot."

He studies her for a moment. Every glance between them feels measured and heavy, as if they're wading through an ocean of shared history. "No biggie. I didn't want to leave the house unprotected."

"Right," Mom agrees. "Squatters."

Gabe hesitates. "Yeah, that." He checks his watch and gets back on his bike. "Anyway, it's great to see you again. Ceci . . . I'm glad I got to meet you. I'll come by tomorrow when I meet up with Carl."

"Leaving so soon?" Mom asks, and it's not her usual tone of voice. It's sincere.

He smiles at her. "I'm meeting my mom for lunch, but I'll give you a call. I just passed through town hoping I'd see you."

Mom's face goes pink. "Tell Irma hi for me."

He nods once at this and he's off, my mom staring after him with a tender expression.

I peer at her, and she notices.

"What?"

"Is he an ex?"

She snorts. "*No*. Gabe was my best friend."

I chase after her as we head to the car. "Nothing more?"

She shakes her head. A scatter of leaves sweep past.

"No, nothing more." We climb in the car and she's quiet for a moment longer, tapping her nails on the steering wheel before continuing. "I . . . I was always too caught up wanting something different."

I take advantage that she's actually talking. "Different how?"

"I don't know. I wanted something that could shake up the boredom of this town. Something dangerous and thrilling. So I overlooked him again and again." She glances at the rearview mirror with a *tsk* of her tongue. There's a world-weary regret in the sound.

"And was my dad . . . dangerous and thrilling?"

Her eyes seem to go darker as they meet my own, as if she sees him there in my face's hidden features. "Yeah. That he was."

6

THE COLD SEEPS UP MY FEET. My fingers trail the wallpaper, the banister, and finally find the glass knob that leads outside.

Wind seizes the sea of leaves across the back garden, funneling them into the sky. A tidal wave of movement brought on by my steps.

I'm being led. There's a static under my skin that's building and building. Tugging at my chest toward the woods.

I can smell it through the fog of sleep. The damp, sweet smell of decay and morning grass. The overgrown weeds and ivy cutting into the soft skin of my ankles. My legs move for me. Behind me, the manor stands quiet and watchful in sentry-like warning as I approach the forest. Everything glitters with a sheen of dew, including the dozens of spiderwebs in varying degrees of spun silver.

Tell me your desire.

My gaze stays trained ahead. To the glimpses of shadows weaving just beyond the trees. To the beckoning flash of white—another tug forward.

What's in your heart?

It's a feeling that digs under my skin at least six-feet deep.

Come find me, and make your wish.

"Yes," I think I say. I make it to the mossy concrete band of wall. So flimsy, like the last line of defense to keep us tucked away from the forest.

Or to keep something out.

I step closer. Compelled to see what's on the other side. There could be a place where the concrete barrier has crumbled. Or a door. One you could walk into and never look back. Something's there—beyond the vines. If I could just . . .

"Cecilia?" Hands clamp on my shoulders, spinning me away. I gasp in breath as if I'd nearly drowned. The haze of sleep disintegrates, but my thoughts are stringy as cobwebs. My mother is still in her nightgown, wide-eyed and panicked. She shakes me again. "What are you doing out here?"

Sensations return all at once. The cuts on my skin. The imprints on my feet from walking barefoot over stone. The hazy recollection of a voice calling out to me from the dark.

I blink, taking entirely too long to figure out where I am. The backyard, too close to the woods, and the sun is barely out.

"I . . ." I swallow. "I think I was sleepwalking."

The panic in her expression morphs to concern. "But it's been ages since you've walked in your sleep."

I know. Not since I was little. When I used to dream of my dad. I rub away the deep chill across my skin, and when she realizes I won't keep walking toward the forest, she lets me go.

Mom eyes the woods warily. "I'm having Carl install an alarm system once he figures out the wiring. You can't step foot in there."

"I wasn't planning on it," I say defensively. At least I don't think so. "It wasn't my fault."

"I know." Mom pinches the bridge of her nose. "But in general, since we might be here for a bit, there are rules that everyone follows." A deep sigh. "God, I can't believe I'm going to be one of those people."

"Rules?"

She nods with a wince, as if she can hardly lower herself to say them. "Santa Aguas rules. If you hear someone call for you from the forest, you don't answer. You don't stare too hard through the trees, and you never walk into the woods at night alone."

"But it's daytime."

"And this is Sevilla grounds. The rules here are different. Remember that, milagrito."

ON THE WAY TO SCHOOL, I try really hard to suppress what happened this morning. My mom's strange list of rules for surviving this town and the fact that I almost walked into the forest alone has my stomach in knots. I hate feeling so out of control. The idea of sleepwalking again is beyond terrifying. Especially since I'm apparently living in some hot zone for ghosts and horse-faced men eaters.

Tonight I'm wedging a chair in front of my door.

In town, Mom bypasses the café after she warns me that it has the worst coffee in all the South. Instead, she heads down the street to the only grocery store for miles, which is across from the high school that's built in that same Spanish colonial style as the other municipal buildings. Major's Depot Grocery is next to the only dry cleaner in town, the only movie theater, and so far, the only gas station I've seen since we first drove into Santa Aguas. Kids are already loitering around the school and in front of the Orion gas station sign looking as thrilled to be starting the day as I am.

I wasted an entire weekend in a haze, unpacking my room and pretending like I'm actually in a tower I never have to climb down from. Except now it's Monday and I haven't mentally prepared for my first day at this backwoods school, only to graduate in a few weeks with a bunch of strangers.

The Dorset family invites you to reapply next year.

I've gone through my portfolio pieces over and over again. I stare at the visor mirror for a long time, unable to find what's missing. Unable to make it right so it can come alive.

It doesn't matter anymore anyway. I know there are plenty of other art programs but getting accepted into Dorset would've been the proof I needed, the validation that art is what I was meant to do. But it wasn't, and now I don't know what I should want.

We wait for a group of friends to cross the street so we can get into the parking lot. It makes me think of my friends back home. How none of them have called to check in on me. Maybe they saw something missing in me too. Maybe they've all moved on.

Cristina has her acceptance letter. People like her are always wanted in places like that. Even when they don't deserve it.

My mom barely avoids clipping one of the kids, parking and talking loudly on her phone. A tinkling giggle that can only mean there's an unsuspecting man on the other end of the line.

"Oh, Liam, you are a lifesaver. Seriously, what would I do without you?"

I unwrap my breakfast. Her giggles intensify and I pretend to gag.

She shoots me a glare. "All right. Well, take care! Thanks again for the update."

She hangs up, her shoulders sagging. Must be tough juggling multiple personalities.

"Good news?" I ask, taking a bite of the stale cereal bar.

"Maybe." She sighs, switching to her normal voice with a creeping accent. "Liam thinks we may be able to jump aboard the lawsuit train and get a settlement for emotional stress." She takes a sip from her thermos with a look of disgust. "Esperemos."

"Suing the ex. Classy."

She makes a face at me then not so casually looks down at my outfit. A midnight-black Bergdorf sheath dress, jacket, and Doc Martens. My silver chain jewelry glints against the fabric like a star. If leaving Miami was Marina's funeral, starting school here is mine. "Just taking a page out of your book," I say.

Mom steps out from the car and I follow. "Wear what you want. You know, it'd really help if you tried to *learn* how to drive. Save us both a lot of time. You're not going to find an Uber in this hellhole."

"You don't even need a car here," I mutter. "Unless you're an out-of-town weirdo who moved to a haunted mansion in the middle of the forest. *Oh, wait.*"

Mom ignores the sarcasm.

We step into the grocery store of flickering lights and yellow linoleum. It has a subtle scent of old meat. She lowers her sunglasses. "God, this place hasn't changed." Customers stop to stare at us. "Go on, get the coffees." She points to the back. "Maybe by some miracle they stock Dunkin' now. I'll be in customer service buying a lotto ticket. What numbers?"

I think for a moment. "Twenty-three, six, and fourteen."

"You got it."

I make my way to the back of the store, getting stared down suspiciously by an old woman comparing two different cans of soup. I pretend I don't notice and search through what I think are the cold brews, but like everything else, the off-brand packaging looks local. I'm really hoping it's not sourced from the same supplier as the local café.

After paying for the two bottles and a bag of trail mix, I find Mom by the automatic doors chatting someone up. My chest gives a little flip as the guy's face takes shape. Jamie from the post office holds a grocery uniform vest in his arms and casually leans against a coin converter machine, smiling brightly.

"Cecilia!" Mom spots me. "Look who I ran into."

She grimaces at the bottle of iced coffee I hand her.

Jamie straightens off the wall as if jolted by an electric wire. "Oh, hey. I ran into your mom."

"I see that." I want to smile, which is odd for me, but I maintain a steady face. "Small towns, right?"

He laughs a little. "It's a hazard, yeah. So, Cecilia?"

"Ceci." I correct him quickly, taken aback. How can a person come off as nervous and confident at the same time? He doesn't back down or break eye contact at all.

"Right. Ceci," he says slowly as if trying it out, as if rolling it on his tongue to savor. That easy smile of his comes back in full force.

"So," Mom cuts in. "I just hired Jamie here as our part-time groundskeeper. We can finally get somewhere with his help. You said you had experience, right?"

My eyes widen. "Our *groundskeeper*? As in at our *house*?"

He glances between us. "Uh, yes, ma'am. I've worked in plenty of yards."

"This place is massive though," I say, cringing when I hear how elitist that sounds. "I mean, it's a mess."

Mom flaps a hand dismissively. "He's not afraid of a little challenge." A raised brow in my direction. "Obviously."

"*Mom*," I say.

"Not at all, ma'am. It's the old Sevilla house, right? I've wanted to see it for a while now." But his eyes stay on mine, and I don't know what he wants. Brownie points for good eye contact?

Mom's face pinches. "We can lay off the ma'am."

"Oh." He shifts. "Sorry, ma—I mean—"

"Marina's fine."

I turn away from them, studying the groups of kids eating gas station junk as they walk across the street toward school.

"I gotta go," I say, checking the time on my phone. "Wouldn't want to be late for my first day in hell."

Jamie grabs his backpack off the floor. "I was just about to walk over. We could go together if you want?"

Before I can say that I think I can find my own way when it's literally across the street, Mom ushers us toward the door. "How sweet of you! I think that's a great idea. Look at that, already making friends." She reaches over and gives me an uncharacteristic hug, squishing my crossed arms against my stomach. "Play nice," she whispers into my ear with a little snort of laughter.

I glare at her, and she beams back before practically skipping toward her car. She knows I don't make friends easily because I *choose* not to. Friends can be exhausting in my experience. They want you to make plans, be "on" and fun and social, share jokes, make commitments. Then when you ask them to be there for you, when you need them, when you actually want someone to listen, you're the boring one. The downer no one wants to be around.

Sometimes friends ask for too much, and I don't have enough in me to give.

"You and your mom seem close," Jamie says once she's gone, falling into step beside me.

"Seems that way," I respond, looking both ways before crossing, but I stop as I see my mother hesitate by her car. Jamie seems to realize something's wrong too.

She's staring across the street at something like she's seen a ghost. She's gone bone-white.

When I follow her line of sight, there's a girl my age with fire-red hair staring right back at her.

They're both paused in time, in varying degrees of disbelief. It reminds me of the time a coyote had stolen into our backyard, cornering my mom by the fence line while the rest of us stood frozen and useless on the deck. They'd stared at each other much like this, neither willing to budge, both of them afraid of the other—until

I couldn't take it anymore and gave a loud, solitary clap that sent the animal scurrying.

The girl's face takes on an unsettling grin as she mouths something—it looks like my mother's name.

Marina.

I almost use the same method and clap to startle them, but a large truck rolls past, beeping its horn and forcing Jamie and me back onto the sidewalk. Across the street, the girl is gone.

My mom glances back at me, hesitates. I can tell she curses, caught in between some inner decision. I lift my hand to wave, realizing how ridiculous I must look, but she nods back. And the decision to leave must win out because she gets into her car and reverses, pulling an illegal U-turn before she disappears down the main road.

"Was it me, or was that weirdly tense?" Jamie says.

"You saw that, right?" I ask, gesturing to where the girl had been.

"I did. You guys know her?"

I shake my head. "No. I mean, I don't know about my mom, but she hasn't been back here since high school. Since *her* high school years so I doubt they're old friends. You don't recognize her either?"

He shakes his head. "No, never seen her."

We cut across the small stretch of grass toward the front of the school. The girl hadn't been wearing a backpack so I'm not sure if she goes here, but I keep my eyes peeled anyway. The school building is shaped like a horseshoe, with classroom doors facing out toward the yard and arched hallway balconies cluttered with kids. Looks more like an oversized church than anything else.

Jamie waves at a few people before snapping his fingers. "Oh, I got it. Maybe your mom almost ran her over on the way here and she was waiting for her to like sue?"

Already, he seems to have my mom pegged. "Possibly."

He smiles. Objectively, he's got a nice, wide mouth.

Jamie opens the solid wood door for us, and the inside of the campus is just as cramped as the rest of the town. Long narrow halls with flickering bulbs stretch out down either side, ending on a stairway. But right smack in the entry is a large marble bust on a pedestal underneath the Beckmann High School banner. The kind of thing you'd expect to find in a funeral home. I recognize the sculpted man as Gerardo Sevilla-Beckmann. The same face that stares down at me with shrewd eyes from the manor walls.

"God, this guy's everywhere."

Jamie looks at it as if noticing it for the first time. "Him? Oh yeah. He's got a bit of infamy around here."

"So I've heard." I try my best to give the bust a wide berth, but the halls are just so tight, and the people come in like a flood. Jamie slaps hands with some of the people he knows and even side-hugs a few of the girls until he notices I haven't moved.

We move off to the side as I take a moment to collect myself.

"It's only like this for a few minutes," Jamie says, waiting patiently. "The senior class is like eighty kids. They clear the halls pretty quick." While he says this, the space seems to empty as kids slip into their classes. Neither of us seems to be in a hurry to follow.

"Hey, um, I hope it doesn't make you uncomfortable that your mom hired me."

"I don't care," I say, waiting until it's truly empty before attempting to find the administration office. "It's your free time, not mine."

"Oh. Right." He looks kind of taken aback as if I'd said something hurtful. And maybe I had. My friends would always tell me I have major resting bitch face and a droll voice to match. I think they were trying to be helpful? People think since I don't always react to the things they say that they don't bother me. I've just become an expert at brushing stuff off. At hiding my feelings. But I forget how it makes me come across.

I try to lighten my tone. "What's with all the jobs anyway? Don't you already work at the post office *and* the grocery store?" I lean a shoulder against a poster for prom—black-and-white theme. Internal eye roll. "When do you sleep, Jamie?"

He mimics my posture, seeming more relaxed. "I'm a terrible insomniac. I also volunteer at the nursing home on Wednesdays."

My eyes widen. "That's some . . . work ethic. What about after graduation? How are you going to juggle all that with college?"

He shrugs. "Not sure yet. I might not even do college. I guess I'm testing the waters. Seeing what's out there. See if I'm good at anything." A small laugh. This one forced. His jaw goes hard for only a millisecond but I catch it. "Anyway, it's not like we have to have it all figured out."

I shrug. "I mean, it is senior year. Don't we have to have like a set goal at least?"

The bell rings, but we both ignore it.

He leans in closer, arms crossed. The picture of ease. "I mean sure, but it doesn't have to be our lifelong career. You ever hear that people psychologically change every seven years? Or maybe it's ten. Anyway, we're constantly evolving. There's no age threshold where you have to decide what you want and do it for the rest of your life." As he talks, his hands become animated. Sounds like an argument he's had before. "You can choose to do different things that make you happy until they don't anymore."

"Oh, but give monogamy a chance," I say.

He snorts. "Maybe it doesn't apply to every aspect of our lives—"

"I mean divorce rates would agree."

"I guess they would," he says. "When it comes to passions, desires, those things change and shift with time. And it doesn't mean we're unfocused or wasting our lives." He takes on a surfer-boy accent. "I just feel like we're the machine that needs filling, not the other way around, ya know?" He rubs a hand down his face. "God, I sound like such an idiot. I swear I don't usually talk this much."

"You're just passionate about this. Which is a shame that drive will only last another ten years or so before your mind latches on to something else."

He smirks. "Yeah, exactly. Maybe if I was born with my dad's narrow-focused obsession, I'd have that lifelong career that could outlast the ennui."

"What's the obsession?"

"Geology."

Ah, explains the rock puns.

"We actually moved here so my dad could map out the limestone. Seems there's a lot of weakening spots around Santa Aguas . . ." He takes a look around at the empty hallway, panic crossing his features. "*Crap*, I totally made you late on your first day."

"Maybe I made *you* late."

His eyes soften in the corners. "Worth it."

"You might not think so once you get to know me," I say walking backward and adding space between us. I meant for it to sound like a joke, but he doesn't crack a smile. Before he can add anything, a teacher's crisp steps clip down the hall.

"What are you two still doing out here? Jamie, get to class. Are you the new student? I can show you to the office."

Jamie points two fingers to his forehead in salute. "Right away, Ms. Mariani." A dip of his head in my direction. "See you later."

"Alligator."

And the delighted expression on his face can really make a girl forget her way.

7

SCHOOL REALLY IS THE SAME anywhere you move. Despite Santa Aguas's abysmally low population count, the halls are overcrowded and the student-teacher ratio is grossly disproportionate. The school building, although campus shaped, feels like it would've served better as a historic museum, but with so much preserved land circling the town, I guess they had to work with what they had.

Everyone already has their cliques, possibly the same ones they've had since grade school, but I'm the new oddity and I can feel their eyes on me as I grab an unappetizing lunch. Living in the manor hasn't made blending in any easier. I've been getting weird looks all morning, and I've already had a few kids come up to ask me questions or fill me in on more town legends.

Have you heard of la Cegua yet? She lures men into the woods, men who drink too much, who cheat, who hurt. She leaves some of them alive, but changed. Ruined. Except for the Sevilla men—those she takes for good.

The manor is haunted and anyone who lives there is destined to go insane . . . or die.

It's taken all my willpower not to skip, to metaphorically retract the claws before I lose it. I'm curious about the Sevillas. I am. But I want something more than rumors.

At lunch, I find a decently clean table in the corner, empty and shaded. Again I search for a glimpse of the girl with red hair from this morning but maybe our schedules don't intersect. Maybe she doesn't go to school here anymore.

I'm about to take out my sketchbook when a tray plops in front of mine. Then another.

I look up. It's a girl I sat next to in my first period who had everything on her desk labeled and organized by color—Diana, I think the teacher had said. Beside her is Jamie. I haven't seen him since this morning either.

Someone else joins us, a girl with a septum piercing, thick eyeliner, and a giant bee brooch on her sweater. She kisses Diana on the lips and taps Jamie. "'Scuse me. You're in my spot." She has a pleasantly raspy voice.

"Right, sorry." He grabs his tray and slides cautiously beside me as if I might bite. His smile is apologetic, but I make room for him on the bench. I guess he's back to nervous mode.

"Good first day?" he asks quietly, shoving a paper with a bright red *F* into his bag.

I pretend I didn't see it. "So far."

"Hey, new girl," Diana says, twisting back her long braids and banding them with a velvet scrunchy. She has the prettiest eyebrows I've ever seen. "Ceci, like cesspool, right?

Her girlfriend's eyes boggle. "Di—what the fuck?"

Diana laughs and leans forward. "She's the one who said it! Ms. Cason introduced her this morning and called her *Cici*." She pitches her voice high and reedy—an uncanny impersonation of our first period teacher. "Like Cicis Pizza? Then this girl said . . ." She flourishes a perfectly manicured hand toward me, expecting me to finish. They all wait so I have no choice but to repeat what I'd said.

"It's Ceci. Like cesspool."

Diana claps, startling me. "Cason's expression was priceless."

"Damn," her girlfriend says with a laugh, spearing a mandarin orange with a sharp black nail, not noticing that her bell sleeve has gone into her food. "That lady swears like our names are that hard. My last name's Casador, and she's forever calling me Ms. Candor."

"Mine's Navarette," I offer. "She didn't even try saying it."

They laugh.

"I'm Myra, by the way." She reaches over to shake my hand. There's a pen-drawn tattoo of a rose vine along her arm, and I might spot the hint of a sketchbook spilling out from her tote bag. "This is Di, the love of my life—" This makes Di's cheeks darken. "And the goofy one beside you is Jamie."

Jamie takes a sip of his water. "I wouldn't say goofy. More like uniquely charming? Or persistently handsome."

"Sure," Di says, folding a napkin over her lap like we're at a dinner party. "Whatever you say."

He takes a fruit slice from her tray, and Di looks scandalized. "Besides, me and Ceci go way back."

"Really?" I say, slanting a brow in his direction. Overconfident-mode is back in full force apparently.

"That's right. I mean we have inside jokes. You know all about me and my strange affliction for work."

"Your sleeping habits?" I say.

"Exactly." He pops a grape into his mouth, smiling devilishly. "And I've already met your mother."

I huff a laugh. From this close-up, I can make out the subtle green shades of his hazel eyes. A color found in summer storms. When we glance up, I realize we have an audience. Di and Myra stare at us in fascination.

I take another bite of food.

Jamie opens a bag of chips. He chews quickly, inhaling the contents, and I get the feeling he's the type who's used to eating while standing up and moving around. "I also got a job working the Sevilla Manor grounds," he says. "Ceci's mom hired me."

"Another job?" Myra groans. "Jamie, they're not Boy Scout badges."

"But imagine if they were," Jamie adds.

Di ignores them, her expression lighting with interest. "So you *do* live there? The actual Sevilla mansion?"

I tear my bread into little pieces, readying myself for the outpouring of questions. "Only for now. I didn't realize the house came with a title."

Di chews, nodding thoughtfully, everything on her plate neatly separated. "Oh yeah, lots of places in town are named after the Sevilla-Beckmann family. Our school, streets, civil buildings, but your temp house, that's their legacy. It was the first thing they built back when Santa Aguas was all swamp and unexplored caverns."

"Before they were cursed?" I ask with a skeptical brow.

Myra sits back with a wicked smile. "Ah, so you're caught up on the lore."

"Kind of," I say. "I still don't get what makes it a curse."

This town really does love their ghost stories. The Sevillas could just be afflicted with some hereditary disease, but rumors of a curse suggest their deaths aren't as simple. Might as well be the one to ask the questions now.

"You want to take this?" Di points a thumb at Myra. "I know you want to."

"Oh, dare I?" Myra says, with the type of face that shows every crossing emotion, one of the hardest to paint, and the sparkle in her eyes proves she's interested in the topic. "This is like my mom's favorite subject. She has everything you can think of on la Cegua and the Sevillas."

A buzz suddenly fills my ears, as if I've stepped into a wasp nest. A shadow falls across the table. We all look up at the girl who seems to have come out of nowhere.

And it's her. The girl from this morning. She looks like a woodland sprite come to life. A cascade of fiery hair, a smattering of sun-touched freckles, and a startling vacancy in the dark green of her eyes. It makes me want to sketch her to life.

The empty gaze suddenly clears and she's sitting down beside me. A touch too close to shift comfortably.

"Hey," she says. "I think I saw you this morning. You're Marina's baby, right?"

Myra and Di give her the same looks I've been getting all morning, the oddity. Someone they've never seen before.

"I'm her . . . daughter. Yeah." The stillness around her is infectious, and again, I think of that coyote, that loud singular clap. "Have I met you before?"

Her attention lingers a moment on my necklace—the brass ring stark against my black dress.

"No, but our moms went to school together. A really long time ago."

"Are you new here too?" Myra asks and she had to have noticed that the redhead is dressed like a high-profile Realtor rather than a high school student.

"Sort of," she chirps. "I'm Adel. I hope you guys don't mind if I sit here. First days are the *worst*. Aren't they?" she asks me. I nod dutifully. I'm a little stunned; it's as if a switch has been turned on inside her. She grabs Myra's wrist, gushing over the pen tattoo. Talks about the tattoos she wants to get one day. Adel moves on to Di's outfit, mentioning a designer they both love. In a moment, she's charmed them. An extroverted full-frontal assault that I've never been able to replicate.

Jamie and I share a look and I'm secretly pleased he seems unaffected.

Adel swipes an unopened water bottle from someone's tray as they pass. She doesn't even spare the kid a glance, and he doesn't dare stand there longer than a few seconds before moving on.

She unscrews the top. "But I'm totally monopolizing the conversation. What were you guys talking about before? I heard curses and Sevillas." Her eyes glitter.

Myra's interest reignites. "Oh yeah. Ceci wanted to know what the deal was with the Sevilla curse. So, I was saying—"

But Adel interrupts. "Ah, the curse. I did hear you were staying at the manor. Funny since your mom used to clean it with her aunt and now she owns it." Her laugh is sharp, slightly mocking.

I clench my jaw, not appreciating the demeaning tone.

"Sounds like a full circle moment," Jamie says, and I note his perpetual smile is missing.

Adel either doesn't notice the tension or decides to barrel past it. "The curse, though," she continues as if picking up on a story she'd been in the middle of telling, "started with Gerardo Sevilla's first wife. She went mad before mysteriously disappearing. Gerardo took it hard. Remarried but then became like really paranoid. To the point where he cut Santa Aguas off from the rest of the world, vetted all the residents, and created secret passages in the manor so he would be harder to kill." She rests her chin casually on her fist. Dirt is packed under her fingernails, as if she'd climbed through mud. "But in the end, our dear town founder was discovered on the side of the road in a state of accelerated decay with trouser pockets filled with mustard seeds to ward off evil spirits. He was only twenty-nine and he drank himself to an early death as most drunks do."

Di makes a noise low in her throat. For some reason this prompts both her and Myra to check on Jamie who's gone very still and quiet.

"As most *cursed* drunks do," Myra amends, trying to put the story to rest. "Anyway, early deaths have been a theme for the Sevillas since, and la Cegua is to blame."

"Because some claim Gerardo's first wife was a witch," Adel adds, too seriously for what she's suggesting. "They say she's the

Cegua and she's been making the Sevillas pay for something. Though nobody knows what."

The Cegua. The beautiful ghost who haunts the woods and petrifies men. Allegedly. They blame la Cegua for an entire lineage of dead boys? People that lived in my house. I peer around the cafeteria and everyone pretends like they weren't just staring at me.

Does Mom believe this story too?

"Where did you say you were from?" Myra's brow crinkles in Adel's direction.

"From here," Adel says breezily. "I've just been away a while. Too many painful memories . . . for my parents." She watches me carefully. "You know, with Roman's disappearance and all."

Everyone at the table straightens at the name. I look around at them.

"Who's Roman?"

Adel takes a long sip of her water, hiding her expression. So Myra leans forward, her large, heavily lined eyes go soft with pity. "He was the last Sevilla. Only eighteen when he disappeared. People think"—she pauses, biting the side of her lip—"that his parents chopped him up and hid his body somewhere in the manor. That the Cegua made them do it, like she orchestrated all the Sevilla deaths before him. Everyone thinks she still roams those woods, punishing those who wander too close or remind her of her drunk husband."

I swallow hard.

"That's just a myth, though," Jamie says.

"I don't know," Adel adds musically. "Sometimes myths come from buried truths."

Jamie's already picking up his tray. "I think you guys are freaking her out for no reason."

The last thing I want to admit is that I'm more intrigued than frightened. "It's fine," I say, instead. "Even if I did believe all this, I'm not a Sevilla so it's not like I have skin in the game."

"But you're living in their house." Adel steeples her fingers. "Has your mom told you *why* you're living in that house?"

Before I can answer, the bells rings. The awkwardness of the morbid topic quickly dissipates as everyone gets up in a flurry of activity. But Adel and I keep our gazes locked. What is she getting at? We live in a mansion from the town Mom grew up in. She simply wanted it, and because she got to a position where she *could*, she bought it. Yet, when it comes with this tragedy attached, would a good deal really make it worth it? She has to have an emotional attachment to it besides having cleaned it once upon a time. An emotional connection that apparently wasn't strong enough to come back to her hometown and live in the manor but enough not to sell it all those times we needed the money.

Adel winks at me and heads toward the cafeteria doors, as if her work here is done. She leaves the water bottle on the table.

"She's a treat," Jamie says.

"Be nice," Myra warns.

Di's class is on the other side of the building so she and Myra step aside to say their goodbyes, as if they were about to leave on a monthlong trip.

Jamie remains close, creating a rift between me and the sea of incoming kids as we filter into the hall. He seems to settle quickly into caregiver role, no doubt something he does for everyone. "So," he starts, "kind of a lot for day one. Sorry if it got too intense."

"I told you it's fine. I don't care," I say harshly, my mind still on curses and ghosts—and the house that comes attached to them. But Jamie's dull flinch at my reply makes my heart squeeze. As if he's used to those kinds of responses. I don't have time to soften my words or apologize by the time Myra comes back throwing an enthusiastic arm around me and Jamie, which brings us all excessively close. She starts leading us toward the annexed science building.

"What do you say about hanging out after school?"

"With me?"

Myra laughs. "Yeah, of course. Di and I wanted to know if we could come over."

"Am I not invited?" Jamie asks.

Myra playfully pushes him away from my side. "Nope. Girls only. What do you say?"

I glance down at my phone's empty screen. I don't know what answer I expected to find there. There won't be any messages waiting. Nobody wondering how my first day went. I'd go home to an empty house and a silent room like I've done for most days of my life.

"Sure," I say finally, the words pulled out of me like teeth. "We can do that."

8

ON THE WAY TO THE MANOR, while Myra and Di bicker over which song to play, I do a quick internet search. After lunch, I couldn't concentrate on anything else besides the story. Besides Adel's question as to *why* we're living in this house. What's the real reason?

And a gut-wrenching thought struck.

When I search for Roman Sevilla, an old article comes up with a black-and-white photo of the manor. The headline reads, "Police Call Off Search for Sevilla Heir," dated March 12, 2000.

I stop to calculate.

My mom would've only been thirteen. This happened five years before I was born and before she skipped town, so it's possible Roman went to school with her, but impossible for him to have been . . . my dad. I think of the box of postcards in my room—never signed, just stamped from all over the world. The only contact my father's ever attempted. I'm not sure if it's relief that settles over me when I do the math and it can't be him.

Once we reach the driveway, both girls go a little pale. They look up at the manor, as if it'll open its ivy-lined mouth and swallow them whole. Inside, Myra's bag slides down her arm and drops to the floor. She takes in the entirety of the Sevilla manor's foyer with a slack jaw.

Di just stares at me. "Seriously?"

I nod. "Yup. This is it."

"So you're like *rich* rich."

"Apparently this place was a steal," I say. "Something about bones in the attic and haunted woods."

Myra squeals. "I hope we see something spooky."

I laugh. "You came for a tour, right?"

They glance at each other, then Di steps forward. "Nah, girl, we came for you. Girl talk. You know, shoot the shit. Show us to your room and get us snacks."

"Chocolate," Myra adds. "Because I am PMSing like crazy." She weaves her arm through mine. "And popcorn, too, 'cause we hungry. I want to see more of your sketchbook." She hoists her bag. "I can show you the stuff I have on Procreate."

A warmth spreads through my chest.

I start to lead them up to my room, but we make plenty of stops on the way as they point out different things they find fascinating, like the art, the bathroom with its claw-foot tub, the little closet with a laundry chute. I even show them Gerardo's portrait and Roman's photos.

The whole time they talk to me as if we've known each other forever, no awkward pauses or silent exchanges between them that I can't decipher. I'm oddly touched that they came here for me, but I wouldn't begrudge them their curiosity either. This place comes with its legacy of ghosts, and it'd be impossible not to feel lured by the salty air of magic.

In the hall of portraits, Di peers at Gerardo's severe face and shivers. "It's bad enough they're everywhere in town; sucks you got to live with them staring down at you like that. All judgy and shit."

"Um hello, my abuelita has a picture of Jesus and la Virgen María in every single room." A glance at me. "And I mean *every* single room. Bathroom and all." Myra points to another portrait on the right side of the hall. A clean-shaven man with not an eyebrow hair out of place. This Sevilla has light eyes and a splotchy complexion. A severity more skewed toward unhinged.

"Speaking of religion. Percival Eugenio Sevilla," Myra states, reading off the plaque. "This one was obsessed with spiritualism and saints. It was thanks to him my family came to Santa Aguas," she explains at my confused look. "He went on a campaign looking to bring in more 'like-minded' residents." She uses air quotes. "Even put out a nationwide ad for psychics, mediums, anyone with a penchant for the occult. There'd been lots of Cegua sightings at the time. So my great-grandma came at Percival's request and brought the entire family with her."

"She was a psychic?" I ask.

Myra nods. "It runs in our blood. My mom's more of a historian than a psychic, but I swear she knows whenever I'm hiding something."

"That's because you're a terrible liar." Di laughs, placing a kiss on Myra's cheek, which she pretends to accept against her will. With the hallway's low light, parts of Myra's makeup glow.

After studying some of the older portraits around Gerardo and Percival, we turn to the wall on the left. Roman Sevilla stares out from his frame, almost impatiently. I see the photos leading up to his. There's only one I assume is of his parents. He was still a little kid in the photograph, clutching his father's hand. His mother standing beside them with a solemn mouth and a bounty of curly hair down her back.

"What happened to his parents?" I ask.

Myra purses her lips. "I think his dad died earlier than most of the Sevillas. Didn't make it past his midtwenties." I stare at that viselike grip. A tether snapped. "I'm not sure what happened to his mom. I think she died of grief a few months after Roman disappeared, but she abandoned the Sevilla Manor and moved to Baltimore, so I don't really know."

The pale woman staring out of frame. Barely a footnote in the Sevilla history. Barely a place for her on this wall. I don't see any portraits of Percival's wife, nor Gerardo's. Not a single space reserved for the women who ran this household. For the first wife that could be la Cegua. It makes me wonder why the mustard seeds and horse-faced effigies. Why not honor the woman she was? It took the threat of death and monsters for her to be acknowledged at all.

"Can we go to your room now?" Di says quietly. "No offense, but this place gives me the creeps."

Myra touches another photo, leaving a smudge. "I low-key love it. Maybe not this hall of dead guys but definitely love the house."

And I have to admit that's my sentiment exactly. Because I do really like this house, despite its horrible history.

In my room, Myra and I show each other our art while Di delves into a romance novel she found in my library nook. When she compliments my work, I actually believe her. There's no undertone of competitiveness or any passive aggressive comments like there was between Cristina and me. When I casually mention the Dorset Academy, leaving out that I'd already been rejected, Myra seems unimpressed, lessening the sting a bit. There's only a brief moment of awkwardness when I ask where they want to study. Myra's going for the summer to an aunt's house in Mexico to study indigenous art. Di got a scholarship to a writing school near Boston. Both of them avoid each other's eyes after that, and I make a mental note that it's a sore subject.

They both get over it quickly though. Myra has little qualms about digging through the canvases that were poking out from under my bed, and though it makes my heart hurtle, I stand back and let her. Di comes over, too, once Myra pulls them out. My most volatile and despairing collection. My reserve, collecting all the darkest parts of me onto canvas. Self-portraits and landscapes.

The girls are quiet for too long, their silence weighing on my chest like a compressor.

"Ceci," Di starts, but can't say anything else.

"Agreed," Myra says, but doesn't elaborate. She turns to me instead, grabbing my shoulders and pulling me into her. "You have to submit these to art school. Or I don't know, put them up somewhere for more people to see."

"You . . . like them?"

Her eyes widen. "I *feel* them." She presses the center of her chest. "Right here."

It takes me a while to hear anything else but the pounding of my heart.

Once they're gone, I stack the canvases by my dresser instead of shoving them under the bed. One of the charcoal sketches I did ages ago stares back at me. I haven't seen this one in so long. I'd been practicing with different shading techniques and blending with oil pastels, and I'd drawn the first thing that came to mind.

But now that I look at it . . . at the overgrown wildflowers and spears of unfettered grass, the magnolia's distinct white petals and lichen-cobbled concrete of a gate, it looks unbearably familiar. A gate to keep out a forest.

I go closer to it. The creaks and echoes of a silent house pressing around me. I hadn't used colors other than black and white for this one. And yet, there's a mark of blue within the hatched sketches of foliage. A hint of something behind the trees, waiting.

I'd sketched the Sevilla grounds before ever seeing the place. Had I not been lured here this morning, I could excuse the drawing for any other forest. But it's not.

It's mine.

Come find me, and make your wish.

9

THIS TIME, I MANAGE TO SNAP myself awake before I can make it to the woods. A good thing considering I'd been about to walk off the ledge of my roof after having *climbed out of my window*.

My hands are still shaking. The chair is still wedged under my door. I can taste bile in the back of my throat. I could've died. I could've splattered onto the spindly rosebushes Mom's been trying so hard to revive.

I deliberate whether I should tell my mom, but I'm scared it'll give her more ammunition to leave. And despite everything, I'm not ready to go.

Without meaning to, I've fallen effortlessly into a group, and it's only been a week.

Myra and Di usually hang out with me after school before dropping me off at home. Jamie, even on the days he doesn't work, meets me at the grocery store every morning. He always happens to have an extra coffee in hand. I don't have it in me to tell him that it tastes like tar. I sip it and hope he doesn't notice when I dump most of it out before the first bell rings. I'm enjoying our tenuous routine too much to ruin it. Though I'd never admit it to him, I actually like hearing about his job adventures and listening to him ramble about the meddlesome old women from the nursing home. I notice he doesn't bring up his family or the fact that he stays after school to make up work for extra credit.

He's so electric, so outgoing—completely my opposite. He has to say hi to everyone, and I can tell he makes a great effort to walk at my slow pace, settling instead for tapping his long fingers across his pant pockets. And he smiles. He smiles as he talks, as he reads, his face flushing so easily I'm surprised he doesn't stay a permanent shade of red. He's also entirely too tall.

I realize what I like most about him though is that he's not a siphon. He's not one of those people who absorbs all the energy in the room until you're half-alive. That would suck from the marrow if you let them. In fact, he might be the opposite. Someone that overspills, that gives too much.

No. I'm not ready to leave just yet. I'll seal my bedroom door and window. I'll figure out what my subconscious wants me to see so it can stop leading me into danger while I sleep.

I head downstairs and find Mom heading for the front door with a carry-on case. She's got on a large-brimmed hat and what she calls her traveling heels. "Oh, good, you're up."

"Where are you going?" I ask, still wringing the shake from my fingers.

Mom props the case against the wall, riffling through her purse for something. "Meeting Liam outside of town at that little bed-and-breakfast we passed on the way here. You remember that sweet little place with the red roof and blue shutters?" I roll my eyes. It's like she practices these kinds of sentences in the mirror. "We just need to square up some of the details before the next court hearing." Her hand emerges from her bag with a twenty, and she places it on the entry table. "In case you get hungry. You'll have the car if you need it," she says knowing I won't drive it. "Liam sent someone to pick me up. Isn't that nice of him?"

I stare down at the money. "Why can't he just come here?"

She makes a face like I'm talking nonsense. "And see how we're living? No thanks." She seems to realize something. "Oh, by the way, how's school been?" Her cheeks go a little red, as if suddenly remembering her role as a parent.

I suppress the snort that'll have her hackles up. "Fine," I say. Classes have been reduced to refreshers and cram work, everyone preparing for prom and the ensuing traditional campout after-party that the locals seem more excited about. Apparently the campout is where all the *real* fun happens.

Mom goes back to fussing with her outfit, satisfied with the one-word answer. She takes off her hat, checking the mirror. "How's my hair look?"

"It's got an *Amélie* vibe," I say purposefully. It's what she'd told me after I'd cut off my own hair only for her to turn around and get a similar cut, except her hair is straight and shiny like a wet bar of soap while mine picks up static like a radio in a storm. My mother frowns, fluffing up her hair and shaking the bangs loose. I give her bag a pointed glance. "You staying long?"

She opens the door, tugging it behind her. "No," she says. "This is just por si acaso. You never know what can happen on the road, and there's no telling how long the meeting's going to take." She pauses by the threshold. "Will you be all right? Did you . . . did you want to come with me?"

I scrunch my fingers in the inside of my robe pocket. "No. I'm fine."

Her mouth is pulled down. "Sorry, I guess I should've asked you last night."

"I don't care." The words slip out, or if I'm being honest, they're produced deliberately.

"Right," she says with a deeper frown. "Well, I'll see you later." And the door closes behind her with a final thud.

The familiar pattern reemerges like a rebellious bout of black mold. There's no holding it back, and I'd rather not spend my Saturday dwelling on it. After breakfast, I go through the unfinished canvases stored in my large walk-in closet. They're stacked behind an old vintage sewing machine embedded into a worktable with wheels. I run my fingers over its cold metal pieces, feeling the charged residue of energy, and I wonder about the person who'd spend hours here creating something out of nothing.

I head to the back gardens with a canvas, escaping the eerie creak of the settling house and its forgotten rooms, and put in my earbuds.

Outside, the breeze hits me first, the scent of damp soil and wet leaves. It's early enough that some of the dew still clings to the grass, making me grateful I brought a blanket. I head toward the back, passing the abandoned greenhouse with cracked glass and spiderwebs, following what I'm sure was once a neat path of hedges and stone, now overrun with weeds. I make it to the manor's barrier, to the concrete rim my dreams are determined to bring me to. It's also the angle of the house from one of the pictures upstairs. Roman Sevilla standing in front of these woods.

Everything is overrun with bramble and palms now, vines and thick imposing trunks. Even with my music playing I can hear the birds, not the gentle chirping but the echoing squawk of a predator searching for food, and judging from the underlying smell of sweet rot, I think something died nearby.

I plant myself upwind, still close to the house so I don't feel as isolated. Something about its looming presence feels protective. Like I've got somewhere to run in case the wilds turn against me.

When I lay out the blanket and charcoals, I spend the next few minutes staring between the canvas and the tree line, trying hard to ignore the deprecating mantra of *shows a lot of promise* from circling over and over in my head.

"What is it you want to tell me?" I speak to the breeze.

A song croons in my ear. I sweep the compressed charcoal against the canvas, blow away the excess dust, and use my fingertips to smudge-draw what I imagine lies on the other side of those woods. The path, open and waiting.

Choose me, it says. *Look inside and walk deep, find the parts I keep hidden.*

The drawing slowly comes alive, so much so that I feel like I can step into it. If I hold it up, I can pretend I've created a shadowy portal through the woods.

The strokes become meditative, my thoughts curling inward like a dried peel. I feel my eyes closing, the world dipping under my feet.

The pen splatters ink on the page. I write yet another letter they won't reply to. Mama, perdóname. Forgive me. I tell my sisters how much I miss them. I recall the strength of their fingers weaving through my hair. Weaving through the baskets we plaited beside la laguna under a fading sun . . . I wish I could be there with you, I write.

I don't add the thought that I wish I never left. Letters can be stolen and read, and I will not make that mistake again.

A chill creeps across my feet. I tuck them under the large hem of my dress—an itchy fabric I'll never be used to wearing, but at least it's embroidered with my favorite flower, the sacuanjoche, to remind me of my land. Beatriz brings me a steaming cup of tea from inside, anticipating my needs before I can voice them. The smile I give her makes her wince, and I'd nearly forgotten why. The pulsing bruise on my cheek has dulled enough that the pain is no longer unbearable.

I watch my husband finish the circular garden door. He paints it the purest of blues, the color of skies and lakes. I'd dreamt of the door once and described it to him, and now he builds it for me as if this were a fairy tale. He rolls up his sleeves once more, his arms strong, strong, strong. Too strong. He wipes the sweat from his brow, turning to me with a grin full of teeth.

"Do you love it, my lucky bird? Is it everything you dreamt of?"

I nod dutifully, and he frowns, so I force my mouth to lift despite the pain. "It is everything I wished for."

And one day, I would go through that door, deep into the woods and never look back. Only then would I truly be a lucky bird.

The tinted charcoal falls from my grip, dashing a streak of bright blue onto my thigh. I can almost feel the ache on my cheek, still sense the repressed pit of fury and sadness swirling deep in my chest. What the hell was that? Was I daydreaming? I touch my fingers to the unbruised skin below my eye.

I look down at the canvas. It's the woods in front of me, except there's a door. A bright blue garden door, open and waiting like a mouth.

Come find me, and wish.

Make a wish, Cecilia.

I pull off my earbuds. There's a sharp whistling, the wind picking up speed. The sound forming voices. Someone hovers behind me. I'm almost sure of it, but when I whip around, there's no one there.

I get up, hit with an assault of wing flutters and the sharp crack of moving branches as a pair of long-beaked crows takes off toward the sky.

This is ridiculous. It's just me here, there's no reason to be afraid in broad daylight. I was dreaming, just dreaming.

She haunts the grounds.

A crash comes from the other side of the house, and I flinch. It's coming from the shed as if an animal is trapped inside. Based off the next thump, it's obvious that whatever it is, it's big.

I gnaw at the inside of my cheek. It could be hurt, but then again if I do help whatever's stuck, *I* could get hurt. The crashing sounds frantic now, and I swallow hard imagining something caught, eyes wide and fearful.

I inch my way toward the shed, wincing with each sound. My hand shakes as I reach for the handle, getting ready to open and run. Maybe I can make it to the greenhouse before whatever's in there comes out charging.

The shed door swings suddenly with a crash, nearly knocking me back before I get a chance to decide my next move. A bunch of rakes and shovels spew out with a clatter, and a very human person follows, stumbling to the ground with a loud painful *oomph*.

The fear tempers in my chest. Landing on his elbows, Jamie lies face down on the ground.

"Ow," he groans, rolling onto his back and staring up at the sky a little stunned. His eyes widen when they meet mine.

I crouch down, head tilted. "You okay?" I pluck the stuck-on leaf from his hair, watching as the color in his face deepens.

"Just fine," he says, coming to rest on his back forearms, striving for an unaffected pose. "Been here long?"

"I thought you were a defenseless, trapped animal. I was coming to rescue you."

He closes his eyes with a wince. "You weren't far off. I think maybe I overestimated my skills as an arborist."

I move the plow off his leg and reach out my hand to help him up. "I thought you started tomorrow."

He takes my offered hand, and with little effort from me he's back on his feet, dusting himself off. "I do. I mean, I was going to. Your mom said I could make my own hours and let her know by the end of the week. She gave me a key to the shed. Thought today was as good a day as any to start. At least come out here and"—he glances around the expansive grounds—"get a lay of the land." He starts picking up the array of scattered tools. "I texted the number you gave me," he says without looking up. "I was wondering if you'd be home."

A flush climbs up his neck.

I bite the edge of my lip, scooping up some of the tools. "There's no service here," I say. "We're supposed to switch carriers on Monday. I actually haven't gotten a call or text since we moved."

His gaze shoots up. "Really?" and it might be relief in his voice. "I mean, I'm not surprised. This is the middle of nowhere."

We set the last of the instruments against the shed wall. Again, the wind picks up speed, carrying with it a cool bite. My short hair lifts in a sweep of curls, my gaze drawn once more to the trees. There's that incessant tug again. The memory of the blue door still clinging to my skull. Still evident in my drawing.

"What do you think's in there?" I hold my middle.

He follows my line of sight, coming to stand beside me. "In the woods? I imagine it'd be more trees."

"Seriously," I say. "I feel like . . . I think there's something else. A path leading somewhere. Or something that got covered with time."

"A path?"

"Or a door." I don't know how to explain this. I point to the house. "There's a picture inside. Of Roman. He was standing right here, but everything looked different. The woods looked . . . accessible, almost inviting." Jamie's eyes narrow. Maybe I'm not making sense, but the daydream felt so real. "I think I'm going to explore a bit."

He laughs, then takes a closer look at my expression. "Oh, you're being serious. So let me get this straight, you want to check out an overgrown path leading to who-knows-where because a boy who went missing might've also gone down it?"

My brows lower in thought. I consider the trees, and think I know which way to go. "Yes." The scent of wet soil and rotting wood deepens. There's a slight prickle wavering under my skin the closer I walk toward the tree line. Like a static blanket draped over my shoulders. It's almost a physical pull to go inside.

My hands brush against the kudzu vines, parting them like a curtain, like I already know what to expect on the other side. Because I do. Because I was shown.

Blue the color of darkened lakes and rainy skies. The circular door is there. Darker than I imagined, weathered by age, perhaps. It is something out of a fairy tale. An archway moon gate of coral stone hemming it in.

And there's no handle. All I need to do is push through.

"It's real," I whisper.

Jamie shuffles forward, eyeing the entrance. "Your mom was pretty adamant about not going into the forest when she offered me the job."

"My mom's not here." I turn to him, already pushing the door open. It wails and gets stuck on something on the other side but leaves enough space for a body to squeeze through.

He still hasn't moved, and I'm a bit surprised. I'd taken him for the adventurous type. Usually I'm the one to stand back. Not caring enough to make the effort.

But the door is loud in the empty chamber of my chest. A spark I want to transform into a flame.

"You don't have to come," I say because I feel guilty. I've always been annoyed when I'm pushed to do something I don't want to do.

My stomach drops as he takes the offer and starts walking away without another word, back toward the shed.

The nerves finally kick in as I peer down what I can now make out is definitely an overgrown path through the forest. There's a trail of rotten wood planks over wet, marshy ground leading deep into the unknown.

Jamie is suddenly back at my side, and my gaze travels down to his hand, where he grips a machete, then back up to his resolute face. “You really want to see where this leads?”

A thrill works through me, fiery and bright. “More than anything.”

10

AFTER A WHILE, some of the tenseness slips away and we find ourselves slowing our stride along the path, barely stiffening when our shoulders brush. We walk over a decaying wood trail, jumping over the boggier parts of the marsh beneath. The daylight filters through the canopy of trees in soft angles, illuminating some of the wild mushrooms and flowers dappling the dirt. The trail is so deeply ensconced that it feels like nothing else exists outside of it.

Even the animals look different here. Their eyes glinting like glass in the shadows. Their furry bodies whisking up trees and disappearing into trunks like they were never there at all.

I've been so used to walking through orderly, precise gardens—magazine-worthy roses and elegant topiaries—that stepping into this is like unleashing some of the restraint in my own head. There's so much to look at; no two things alike. Each tree, vine, plant, or flower commands its own presence. Nothing feels tamed here, but endlessly growing and unhampered.

When the path grows narrower, denser, Jamie uses the machete to pull down some of the prickly vines blocking our way, his back muscles straining. “So are you usually home alone?”

I look back toward the house even though it’s no longer visible. “Yeah. My mom spends a lot of her days out. Tonight, she’s having a sleepover.” I pinch the sleeve of my shirt—finding it hard to keep the bitterness from my voice. “Meaning, I’ll probably have a new dad soon.”

“Ah,” he says, understanding my meaning. “I take it it’s a pattern?”

“It’s her non-failing recovery system after a separation. But like the saying goes . . . un clavo saca otro. One nail drives out another.” Once I’ve said this, I feel a wash of guilt. I don’t usually overshare the dynamic between my mother and me.

“What about you?” he asks.

“Oh, I don’t do relationships,” I say quickly, better to make that clear now before things get misconstrued. This is a for-now thing—a casual, mildly flirty friendship.

He gives me a strange look. “No, I meant more like how do you deal with that? Do you have somewhere else you can stay if you don’t get along with them?”

“Oh.” No one’s really asked my opinion on my mom’s dating habits. All my friends always thought she was the coolest mom, and that I was so lucky she let me do whatever I wanted as long as I wouldn’t judge her for doing the same. “I don’t really have a say. I’ve never met my father, and my mom’s distant relatives live in Nicaragua, so I doubt they know I exist. Besides, it’s her life. She can date whoever she wants.”

“Right,” he says after a moment. “But I mean, it’s also kind of your life too. You should have a say, and I’m sorry your options are limited.”

I hadn’t noticed we’d stopped. I swallow past an obtrusive ache in my throat to clear it, ducking beneath a palm branch and walking ahead. "What about you?" I ask. "Did you have a choice in moving around with your dad?"

He follows closely behind. "Oh, hell yeah. I don't know what I would've done without the option of moving in with him. My mom's house is a zoo. She used to be just like my dad—work was life, you know?" That explains his obsessive work ethic. Not that I bring it up. "Then suddenly she went from pantsuits to boho dresses and traded her flat in upstate New York for a barn house full of incense smoke and toddlers in the middle of nowhere South Carolina. She got remarried, and her husband's cool, don't get me wrong, I like him. And so does my mom, *a lot*, 'cause they've had like five kids together in the span of six years."

"Five!" I turn to look at him and he nods solemnly.

"Exactly. Two sisters—Jean and Taylor. Then there's the triplets—Cobain, Layne, and Corgan. And if you notice a theme it's 'cause they never moved past their grunge rock phase. They even take cross-country road trips in a Volkswagen van."

An image of a restless Jamie crammed in the back seat of a van with five little siblings draws out a smile. "They sound pretty interesting."

"They're cool. Happy, but I just—I always felt in the way, you know? The odd one out. At least with my dad, he needs me." He turns his face away, laughing. "I mean, checking out one of the most haunted cities in the world was also a selling point."

I study the tenseness of his back. I'm no one to psychoanalyze another, but Jamie is always so eager to help, to please. I can't help but wonder if it's because he really needs to feel necessary.

The path no longer has the wood planks but becomes a wide stretch of dirt dappled with little white flowers that tickle my ankles. We take a moment and stop, breathing in the forest's damp scent, and I break the silence. "You know, I get it," I say softly. "It's shit being someone's kid sometimes."

And though it makes little sense, he nods at this as if he knows exactly what I mean. Judging from the hollow loneliness in his voice earlier, I think he probably does. It sucks to want to be in control of your own life when you're at the mercy of adults too preoccupied with their own.

Jamie shoos away a dragonfly, seeming hesitant about what he wants to say next. "And that thing you said earlier, about not doing relationships—is that a rule?"

I press my lips together. "It is."

"Seems kinda lonely."

"It's not," I say. "You don't need to be in a relationship to be happy."

"No, of course not," he says quickly. "But I mean, what if you find someone you really like? Someone you're compatible with? Are you just going to avoid it because you're scared?"

I stop just as the path curves. "It's not fear. I'm being considerate. We don't stick around long, so why set myself up for a painful goodbye if I can help it?"

The odd look he gives me makes me stumble but Jamie's there, catching me before I can fall. He drops the machete, my hands grip his biceps, and his fingers press into my waist, just above my hip. There's a zap of electricity between us and I let go.

But the electric pull only grows stronger—stands my hairs on end. A buzz fills my ears, and weirdly enough I think I hear the distant sound of a horse.

"Tell me you hear that?" I say, holding my arms close.

Jamie takes a moment to recover. "I don't hear anything but I felt something. Like being too close to a power line. I thought . . ."

He trails off, but I know what he thought. That it came from us. Yet the pulse is too strong. The air thick with it.

"Come." I grab his hand, warm and buzzing, and pull him around the bend to a clearing that seems to appear out of nowhere.

We both let out a little sound of surprise: a huge watering well waits right in the center. It's about our height, the width of a miniature car. As if it continued to grow from the ground like a stalk while the earth slowly sank around it.

"Look at this thing!" I say walking toward it. "It looks ancient." The brick is collapsed in most places, with tiny bits of crushed seashells in the stonework. The well is so massive that the rim ends right by my shoulder, making it hard to look inside.

Jamie's expression is a little awestruck. "It probably is ancient. Doesn't look functional anymore. Look at these depressions in the ground." I see them. All around the clearing there are pockmarked holes. "Careful where you step. Looks like signs of a sinkhole."

We both circle the well carefully, meeting on the other side and my heart jolts in my chest. A portion of bricks has collapsed, the jagged edges rimmed with green algae.

But that's not what makes us hold our breath. It's the large stone steps that lead down into the deep, dark pit of the well.

11

"OKAY," JAMIE RELENTS. "But we'll go slow and if anything at all doesn't look right, we get the hell out and head back, deal?"

I pull out my phone, turning on the flashlight. "Deal."

The afternoon sun hangs heavy above us as we descend into the well's remains. The first steps are slippery, so we cling onto the rough stone walls. This isn't an unexplored place—there are hooks on the rock where I imagine lanterns used to hang. A few still swing eerily above us, their light long dead. The steps are man-made, carved and curling deep into the humid pit.

As we descend farther, I can still see my hands and feet and the outline of Jamie's back. It's a darkness that's bearable. The shadows of an almost familiar dark room.

Jamie warns me of a stumpy stalactite up ahead, and I duck around it.

A trickle of light suddenly flows up to greet us from the well's depths, making the flashlight hardly necessary. The air has a salty scent, and the dripping echoes of whatever's down here become louder and louder. It's like putting your ear to a hollow shell. Or the wailing of a ghost.

"How far do you think it goes?" I ask.

Jamie's fingers sweep against the bumpy surface of the glittering, milky-white rock. "We're about to find out."

And he's right. It doesn't take us long to reach the bottom of the descending pit.

My knees go weak once we enter a massive domed cave. Before the last jutting step, he holds me back, and a scatter of pebbles rain down into the pool of crystal blue water.

A lake with no sky. A hidden place, a—

"A cenote—" Jamie breathes. "An actual abandoned cenote."

"What does that mean?" I whisper. Because I feel like any sudden sound will shatter the illusion. The surrealness of this moment.

Jamie whips me toward him, gripping my shoulders. A giant grin strikes his face. "It's this. A sinkhole! A flooded sinkhole that's probably been here for centuries! I don't understand how. They're not common to Florida, but here it is."

I put my phone away. Sunbeams strike through the perforated ceiling letting in plenty of light, a cascade of roots and vines dangling like chandeliers above.

I clasp Jamie's hand, guiding us down farther until we reach the spring. The man-made steps stop abruptly, turning to a flattened muddy ramp hugging the cavern wall and sloping gradually down until it touches the water.

Right in the center of the large spring is a statue. Up close, there's no mistaking it's a woman cut from stone with a carved veiled face. The sculpting is so graceful, it looks like actual silk over skin. Her dress and veil molded to capture every movement, any hint of a ghost breeze. She's placed on a thick pedestal that serves as a tiny island at the lake's center. An achingly graceful hand forever reaching for a covered sky.

She's wearing a wedding dress, but carved without the accompanying horse face. Yet it's unmistakably her. The doom bringer of Sevilla men. The forgotten wife. The woman who haunts my dreams. This is what she wanted me to find.

"You think it's supposed to be the Cegua?" Now Jamie's the one to whisper as if reading my thoughts. Face so close, his words stir my hair and sweep my lips. I can almost taste the fear in them.

I can almost feel the weight of la Cegua's stone-eyed gaze beneath the veil.

"It's her." I feel the truth in my words. "I wonder who spent the time and money to build this. To bring her here."

I watch her for a few moments longer, but Jamie's moved on to study a patch of bubbly rock that reminds me of coral reef.

"This has to be prehistoric. Check out the speleothems—they're huge."

"The what?"

He glances back at me with another beaming smile. "The stalactites, the stalagmites, the columns, all of it! All these formations are mature. This has to have been here for a really long time." At my expression, he says, "Son of a geologist, remember?"

A nervous laugh bubbles out of me, my entire insides buzzing with a fiery thrill. We stare at each other for a few moments longer—it's clear what we're both thinking. This place is magical. We walk to the slippery edge of the lake. The water's surface is clear as glass, with some parts going no deeper than knee-level while other parts dip into dark and fathomless craters.

Jamie crouches down and dips a hand into the crystalline spring. "Man, my dad's mind would blow if he saw this. He used to take us to the cenotes in Mexico, but if he knew there was one right here . . ."

The feeling that's been pulling me here hasn't eased. If anything it's gotten louder, vibrating my cells like the first clang of a tuning fork. Something's telling me it won't abate until I go in.

Until I'm immersed and reach the statue on its pedestal that sticks out like a dais. This place feels familiar and strange all at once—sacred. I glance at the statue. Like the manor, it's as if I've finally reached something that's been waiting.

That's been calling.

I slip off my shoes, taking my socks off too and placing them inside.

"Jamie," I say, drawing his attention. His mouth, which has been slightly parted this entire time, only drops farther when he realizes what I'm doing. I shimmy out of my pants first. Then grab the edges of my shirt and slip that off too. My ring and the chain are cold against my chest.

I keep myself from looking down, from examining my exposed skin in front of a boy I'm only just getting to know. Keep the biting self-deprecating thoughts from entering my head and making me regret this. "Will you come in with me?"

Then without fear or second thoughts, I dive into the water. It licks at my skin like a frigid caress. I'm weightless, scattering a school of tiny silver fish, pushing off the sandy bottom that scrapes at my feet.

When I emerge, I toss my hair back and find Jamie watching me. A feverish color spreads along his skin.

"Well?" I ask, hoping to ease the tension with a baiting smirk. His eyes flare, and he peels off his shirt with more confidence than I expected. Then it becomes my turn to look away. My turn for heat to crawl across my neck.

When the water ripples at my back, I turn and swim toward him until we're under a ray of light. We avoid the areas where the color deepens to unfathomable blues and where the rock floor is littered with sharp rubble. In this part of the spring, the water comes up to my shoulders but it reaches Jamie's chest.

His bare skin is smooth, reflecting the wavering blue of the surface like a grid of electricity.

He wades closer. "It's kinda cold."

I nod, though I want to say that I'm burning up.

The quiet turns unbearably loud. Our breaths obvious in the tight space. In here, he seems different. I feel different. Like anything is possible. And when I sense us drawing closer, his eyes on mine flitting down to my lips, my body reacts before I know what I'm doing.

I splash him, right in the face.

There's a moment where we both float there stunned, but then he wipes a hand down his eyes. His mouth curves into a dangerous smile and I find myself swallowing. Hard.

"Oh, you're going down."

I yelp, but it's too late to move because he swoops down to pick me up and I cling onto his neck laughing like I'm someone else. Like I'm someone wild and free. He goes deeper into the water, and I know if I were to let go, my feet wouldn't reach the bottom.

But with my arms around his neck, my fingers in his hair, I'm not sure I'd want to.

He pretends like he's going to drop me.

"You wouldn't," I say, clinging harder. Our faces are so close. I see the droplets on his eyelashes, the freckles on the bridge of his nose. The enticing dip of his collarbone.

His gaze roams over me too. "No, I wouldn't."

I take the chance to study him up close. He's beautiful. But more than that, Jamie's a charge on a dead battery. But I worry about what it does to him and what it does to me. Because you can't expect to give and give without eventually running out. You can't expect that kind of kindness to last.

Something in my expression makes him move back, and the water recedes before he places me down and my feet touch rock again. I push back my soaked hair, the water cooling the heat of my neck.

My breath is deep and fortifying. "I'm going to propose something a little crazy."

"Crazier than this?"

"A smidge." I pinch my fingers to indicate the smallest of crazy. "How would you feel about keeping this place between us for a while? Our secret."

He studies me, and his flickering gaze is too penetrating. "I guess we could. We'd make it like our own hideout? Our metaphorical tree house?" My lips lift a tick, and he's quick to add, "But way cooler, obviously."

"Obviously."

He considers long enough that I begin to doubt he'll agree. "Okay," he says finally. "But I think we should promise to only come back here together."

"So we don't die where no one can find our bodies?" I ask innocently.

He blinks. "A terrifying way of putting it, but yeah, basically for that."

We both glance around the cavern with a new gravity. I suppose it could be dangerous. Especially if this really is related to la Cegua. The smart thing would be to never come alone, but when I agree to the deal, my fingers are crossed.

WE MAKE IT BACK to the manor the same way we'd come. The home springing out from the darkening woods like a lighthouse at sea.

Jamie and I stand by the fairy-blue door and stare back at the trail as if it would disappear on us. As if we imagined the whole thing.

"What are you doing tomorrow?" I break the spell of the moment, facing him.

By the look on his face, he already knows where I'm going with this.

"I'm coming back here, of course."

My smile is traitorous as it spreads across my face. "Good. I'll wear a proper bathing suit this time."

His brow lifts. "Don't do it on my account."

I smack his arm, which makes him laugh. "*Good night*, Jamie."

"Night, Cecilia."

And I don't have it in me to correct him as he walks off because the day has just been perfect, and I wait for the flash of annoyance to come on like an inevitable migraine, but it never does.

I don't linger outside with night approaching and my mom still gone. I go straight to shower after grabbing my canvas outside and a snack bar from the kitchen. The rest of the house is too empty of sound to explore on my own at this hour. But I'm too excited to sleep. I watch the mud swirl down the drain, wishing I had service so I could do research on the town and its lore. But then again, I'm also cut off from social media. There's no stumbling onto more beach photos of Cristina and Anthony. I can't see her feed where she's probably screaming about her triumph of getting into Dorset, reposting the same mediocre art—

I shut the water off. My skin nearly hot enough to turn the droplets to vapor. It's not like I can judge. I couldn't even get into the summer program to begin with.

In my room, I change and go for my sketchbook. My charcoal-tip pencil snaps on the page. I almost chuck it across the room, but that would mean having to get up from my bed again to retrieve it, so I sharpen it instead. The fine point scratches with a meditative hum, and I'm not sure what I'm drawing until I shade in the shadows of her veil.

A statue slowly materializes, starting at her crown to her pedestal-cemented feet.

I change little things here and there. Her arm pointing straight at me rather than at the sky. Her veiled face almost visible within the fabric-like stone.

Like this morning, the drawing lures me in. My head is swimming, before my eyes go blurry and everything doubles. The teal walls of my room fall away, leading me back toward the effervescent blues of the cavern.

Frigid stone meets the bare skin of her feet. Every step down the winding cavern stairs sends rocks clattering, their echoes like rainfall. And I know she's close.

I wait for her here, as I've waited for them all. And why should this one be any different?

Warring colors flicker across the cavern walls, forming images she's not ready to accept.

"Welcome, child," I say, my voice like grinding sand.

I come away from the pedestal, every step spindly and labored as I wake from the long sleep. The shadows flee around me, wary as they should be.

It is her turn to wait. The water is as cool as dead skin as I make my way to her. The smells of ancient depths and mud. The girl should be afraid, especially as she stares into the hallowed pits where my eyes should be. She tries to peer beneath my veil, but the bone-white surface of my face will reveal nothing but emptiness. And yet, she remains unafraid. As familiar with the void as I am.

It takes me time to decipher the feeling swarming to the surface of my empty chest.

Surprise.

I stop in front of her, head cocked to look into the dark eyes of the peculiar girl.

"What do you wish, child? What do you wish?"

She wishes for so many things. I can always sense it. She doesn't need to speak. I look deep within and hear her ugly truth. I nod once, and her hands reach for my veil. She can see that I am both humanlike and otherworldly, a contradiction of what I should be and what I am.

Achingly slow, she pushes up the fabric, her mouth opening in a scream that never sounds. Exposed to the air, my bones are jagged and sharp, a mask worn too long.

When I grab her hands, she jolts, looking down to find them stained red. Because in the end, they are all the same.

I wake with a start, a fallen branch pressed beneath my cheek. My nightshirt wet and muddy. I can smell the salty cavern air on my skin. I'm outside, by the garden door. The dream sifts through my mind like sand, but I can hear the voice as if it were still speaking.

What do you wish?

I scramble to my feet, rush into the manor and up the stairs to my bedroom. I'd forgotten to lock the windows and doors. I thought the sleepwalking would stop now that I'd found what I was meant to. But it's not over. Nowhere near over.

That night, I keep all the lights on, staring at my hands until sleep comes to claim me once more.

12

JAMIE AND I SPEND THE MORNING pulling down vines and picking out weeds, leaving parts of the earth tilled and ready for something new. We barely talk as we work, our minds already traveling through a door, down a trail, and into a well.

When we finally get to the garden door, and it's still there, I grab hold of his hand and squeeze, even if I drop it right after.

This time, on the path, we're cautious of the waning sun and incoming clouds, knowing our time here is limited before my mom gets home and it rains, but needing to see it one more time anyway.

Our descent into the well goes a lot faster, as we anticipate when to duck and weave around the jutting rocks. The roaring sound greets me first. The scent hits me next. Ancient—mud, stale air, and the iron smell of minerals.

The moment the veiled woman and I come face-to-face, I hear her words clear as glass in my mind.

What do you wish, child? What ugly truths do you keep hidden?

"Ready to go in?" Jamie bumps his shoulder with mine, startling me out of the trance, but he doesn't wait for my answer.

Like yesterday, we wade into the spring for as long as our skin can take it. Until our hands are properly crimped. At the foot of the statue, the pedestal is just wide enough for two people to sit back-to-back, skin to skin, and we do just that.

On closer inspection, the statue's veiled face tilts upward, her body positioned as if in midmotion, as if trapped before she could get away. She is eerie but completely entrancing. There's a deep-rooted sadness in the way she's carved, an anger even, the kind often depicted in fallen saints or solemn gods.

I wonder if a Sevilla ever came to this cavern. If this is where they'd come to pay their penance to the woman in white. To the thread-snipping fate of their futures.

Jamie tells me of other caves he's gone to with his dad for site surveys, the natural springs and canyons in different parts of South America. I melt as the hum of his voice vibrates along my spine.

"Could you see yourself doing what your dad does?" I ask.

"Studying rocks?" He shifts behind me. "I don't know."

"You seem to like it though."

"I do."

"Then what's the problem?"

He brings a leg out of the water, hugging it toward his chest. Casual, if not for the way every muscle on his back goes rigid. "There isn't one. I just—that's his thing. I kind of want to find my own. I do like the traveling. I like the science. I don't even mind the moving around that much. But I don't want—I don't want my life to be like his, you know?"

A prick stings the corner of my eyes, and I'm not even sure why but I nod.

"Out of all the caves I've visited, though, this place feels different," he says. "There's something special about it."

I accept the change of subject and glance around, mimicking his posture.

"I think so too." As if proving this, a sunbeam catches the shimmering cave wall, turning it into a drape of iridescent light, like the inside of an oyster, and the shadows of rocks transform into almost humanlike shapes.

"Maybe it's because it's ours," I say, a thrill dipping into my stomach. "At least for a little while."

"Ours," he repeats. A weighty significance in the word.

I tilt my head back, letting it tap against his. I don't need to look back to know he's smiling.

We spend the next few moments silent, save for the natural dripping sounds of the cavern. Every so often, I swear I hear a whisper. My name, over and over again. It's why it takes me so long to realize Jamie's been saying it out loud. "Ceci?"

"Hmm?" I reach up to hold my ring and slide it along my chain, a nervous gesture, purely on instinct, but my hands come away empty. No ring, no chain.

"Not to bring it back up, but, about our conversation on the trail yesterday—"

My hands roam around the pedestal, looking for any sign of it.

"Oh my god," I say, frantic now.

"What?" He turns around, realizing I've stopped listening. "What is it? What's wrong?"

I look up at him. "My necklace," I say, swallowing hard. "I think I lost my ring."

"Oh—" He glances around, peering down into the water. "Don't worry. I'm sure we'll find it."

As he says this, I see something glint in a shallow part of the spring. "I think I see it," I say, my heart settling. Without hesitating, I dive back in, keeping my eyes open as I swim down to what I'm now certain is my ring.

I reach for it, my fingers closing around the metal but it won't come loose when I tug. The chain seems to be snagged on something. Already I can feel the pull at my lungs to swim up but it has to come loose.

I bury my fingers in the soil, a sting ripping across my palm followed by a plume of blood, but I keep looking for the chain's end when something wraps around my wrist.

A hand materializes first. Long, gray fingers curl around my arm, pulling me close until dark eyes meet mine.

I scream, releasing nothing but bubbles.

His mouth moves so fast I can't make out the words. His dark hair floats suspended above him. His face is unmistakable.

Roman. The missing Sevilla.

Make the wish. Make the right wish!

I try kicking away but he won't let go until another hand wraps around my middle and pulls me up. As I'm being yanked away, the boy disappears as if he were never there at all.

We break the surface. I'm bucking wildly against Jamie.

"Hey, hey," he soothes. "You're okay. You're all right."

My head is shaking back and forth, back and forth, my wet hair slapping against my neck. My lips are trembling too hard to speak, and when I look down, my ring is clasped tightly in my fists, but the chain is gone.

I let him pull me to the water's edge where we left our clothes, my mind going through too many thoughts at once. Did I really see what I think I did? Could it really be the same boy who went missing all those years ago?

"Ceci, talk to me." Jamie pushes back my hair, cupping my face in his hands. "What happened?"

"I—I saw him." My chin gives a violent shake. The words spoken out loud makes it all the more real. "Jamie, *I saw him*."

He pulls back, giving me a worried look. "Who?"

Now I rub my own face furiously. "You wouldn't believe me," I say.

"Hey." He crouches down, forcing me to make eye contact. "Try me."

I hold up my arm, clutching it like the apparition did. "He grabbed me. I felt him. The same boy from the picture—the Sevilla kid. Just like how he looks in photographs but all gray and dead," I know I'm rambling but I can't stop. "Jamie, I swear it was him. He was—he was telling me to wish. To make a wish."

What do you wish for, child?

It's exactly what la Cegua has been trying to get me to do. Through the dreams or visions, she's also wanted me to make a wish.

And as outrageous as it sounds, I believe it. This place—this place deep in the forest has called to me since we moved here. Maybe even before that, I realize, thinking back to my canvases from the Nightmare series. The lake with no sky, the eyes waiting in the dark, forever waiting.

A wishing well in the middle of nowhere. They both want me to wish for something, but do they want the same thing?

Could Roman Sevilla have gotten lost here for good?

"He spoke to you?" Jamie asks, and I give him major credit that his tone sounds barely disbelieving.

"Sort of." I clench the ring tight in my fist, my hand still bleeding. "In my head. I heard his voice in my head, but his mouth was moving."

Jamie stands up, his shirt going on first while he hops around on one foot to put on his shoe, suddenly eager to get out of the cave.

"I think we should listen," I say.

This makes him pause. Almost fall. "Listen to what?"

I give him an inpatient look. "Wishing. That'll prove what I saw is real. If we make a wish and it comes true then—oh my god, I don't even know what then." My laugh sounds a little hysterical so I clear my throat. "Can't hurt, right?"

Jamie paces back and forth, still missing the other shoe. He keeps glancing at the water. When he stops again, he holds the bridge of his nose. "Okay. Okay," he repeats, crouching down in front of me. "Let's say you really did see Sevilla's ghost—"

"Which I did."

He holds up a hand. "And let's say this place really does grant . . . wishes." He groans. "Haven't you heard of the Midas touch or 'The Monkey's Paw'?"

My face scrunches. "The guy that turned things to gold?"

"Yes," he says, face deadly serious. "Because of his greed, he wished for the gold touch and literally starved to death because you can't eat gold."

Make the right wish.

"We can be careful," I say. "Wish for benign things. Even if it works, it won't be a big deal." But if it does . . . I can't imagine what having that kind of control would feel like. To know the outcome of things simply by wishing it so.

"That's literally the premise to 'The Monkey's Paw,'" Jamie says with a world-weary sigh, as if he's already given in.

Something about the sound doesn't sit well with me. I find myself doing the same thing whenever Mom or friends convince me to do things their way. But still, I mean, these are unique circumstances. It wouldn't make sense to not give it a try. Not when everything has been leading me here, to this moment—I look up at la Cegua—to her.

"Where the hell is my other shoe?" he says, frustrated. This is the most agitated I've ever seen him. "I mean, aren't you a little freaked out?"

"Of course I am," I say, standing now. "But, it feels kind of safe. I mean doesn't this place remind you of . . . home?"

"Home?" His brows pinch. "This place feels like home?"

I shake my head, eyes closed. I don't even know what I'm saying anymore. How to describe this sensation that I belong here. That

I feel deep down to the very root of my bones. A rope thrown my way finally within reach.

"Why don't we come back another day?" he says glancing up. The sun is no longer directly above us and the cave fills with more shadows, seeming to change the color of the veiled woman—the tilt of her head. "It's not like this place is going anywhere. We can think about it. Besides wishes are more coincidences than anything else. Stuff you bring on through your own state of mind. It's not like we can just say, 'I wish to be on some private island drinking piña coladas' and have it happen just like that."

He snaps his fingers, and at first nothing happens.

But then I find myself swaying. "Jamie . . ."

"I mean, it was kind of reckless of us to come here in the first place," he continues. "What if we got stuck down here? What if Roman *died* here and we're next."

"All valid points but . . . Jamie!" There is definitely something happening. The shimmering cave walls are turning a vibrant robin's-egg blue—like a vast sky and sea.

"*What?* Oh—" He's staring at me, and I look down. I'm now wearing a scarlet one-piece and a tie-on beach skirt. When I move my hand up, my fingers meet a floppy hat similar to the one my mom was wearing yesterday. I almost drop the fruity drink that materializes in my hand.

Jamie goes pale white, a stark contrast to the bright matching swimming trunks he's now wearing. When I toss the drink over my shoulder, it disappears entirely. The sound of the beach whooshes around us. In a second, we're by each other's side. My heart's racing a million beats a minute. Jamie's breaths come in quick, sudden puffs to the point I'm afraid he may hyperventilate.

I grab his face, forcing him to look at me and not . . . the island we're suddenly stranded on. "Jamie, listen," I say. "This isn't real. We are still in the cavern."

He glances around wildly. "H—how can you tell?"

I bite my lip and hug him tight. I press my ear to his chest, listening to his heart's furious beating. "Listen," I say. "The waves are an echo. I can still smell the damp rock. I can still feel the cool air. There's no sun in here, no warm sand beneath our feet. Just close your eyes with me and imagine us back where we were. Can you do that?"

His chin falls over my head, moving in a frantic nod. "Okay. Okay, I can do that."

And we cling to each other, eyes shut tight as the sound of the beach slowly recedes, and Jamie's taut chest settles to a survivable breathing pattern.

When we open our eyes again, the cave is back to normal except for the frantic cry of a seagull before it finds its way out of one of the cavern's perforated holes.

I pull away from Jamie, inspecting him for any signs of distress. Instead, his mouth slowly spreads into an expression of suspended disbelief and I find myself doing the same.

"Did that really just happen?" he asks.

I can't swallow past the dryness in my throat so I nod.

Jamie's trembling body comes to rest against a rock. He grips his mouth, face drawn and tight.

We both take a few moments to get a grip on ourselves. I feel lightheaded and electric.

"Are you okay?" I ask.

He's shaking his head yes, but it's definitely a lie. "This Sevilla guy, he—he was really here?" I nod again. "Ceci, hear me out, I think we should hold off on any more wishes for now."

What? My shoulders deflate because after what we just saw, the endless possibilities filter through my mind in alluring succession. So many opportunities, doors opening up with just a few words. My life finally going the way *I* want. "But look at what just happened—"

"I know," he says, running a hand through his hair. "That's exactly it. We don't know what we're dealing with here. Or how these wishes can affect everything outside the cave. Our *real* lives."

"But that's the entire point!" And I have to force myself to tone it down. Take a calming breath before I can convince him. "Jamie, just imagine what this could mean for our futures. The good we can do. I'll start with something small, something insignificant, and I'll be absolutely careful with how I word it. But it'd be crazy to leave here today and not at least try. We've been given this—" I look around. "This *gift*, and I'm not going to waste it."

Jamie's mouth is stern, but his eyes are generously soft like they were yesterday on the trail, when he said I should have a say on how my life is run. And he was right, my options were limited. Until now.

"I need this."

"A small one?" he asks.

I beam at him. "Tiny."

"How tiny?"

I pinch my fingers again. And with that, he doesn't say anything else, doesn't try to stop me from dipping my feet back into the water, closing my eyes, and making my wish.

13

ALREADY I WANT TO GO BACK to the cavern. But it'd be a risk.

A glance out my bedroom window shows it's slightly drizzling. A strong wind brushes the trees. My mom's also back from meeting her lawyer and Jamie's at work today. Meaning, I would need to go alone, and quickly.

I would need to break my promise to Jamie.

A sharp tug on my chest, but I'm already pulling on my boots.

Before creeping downstairs, I pass the hallway with the photographs, walking all the way down to the end, to the alcove with his photo. Roman. He looks as he did in the cave—one of those faces that seems angry even when smiling. I think it's the dark, heavy set of his eyebrows and the sharp angles of his face. I can imagine him settling that weighted dark stare on someone and making them squirm.

I know the feeling.

So far, I've looked through every room but none of them seem to have belonged to him. Most of the rooms have been cleared out and replaced with more modern furnishings, but others still look suspended in time, covered in dust-coated sheets. None hold his mark.

A quick glance outside tells me the coast is clear. From what I know, Mom hasn't ventured past the old greenhouse behind the manor. Nowhere near the slope of leaves and mold-covered pavers that bleed under the concrete barrier and into the woods.

Here, the manor feels removed, far from reach. Birds grow bold with their long-beaked stares, as if ready to peck out an eye at the slightest disturbance.

I pull my jacket hood tighter around me, the drizzle nearly a full downpour, but I need to see it. *Her.*

There's a charge to the air. A flash of lightning in the distance. I count the seconds and the cloud is still enough miles away to lend me time.

Turn back.

A sharp look over my shoulder, but nothing's there. The wind forms words I can barely make out, but there's a strangeness in the taste of them.

I see the shed, and across the way are the vines concealing the door. I'm so close.

Steps crunch behind me. I whirl around. Nothing. I thought maybe I saw a flash of red by the trees, but there's rainwater in my eyes.

When I part the vines back, the door isn't there, and I feel every inch of me go cold and numb.

MAYBE I'M ONLY supposed to go with Jamie. Maybe she doesn't want me to come alone, or I wished for the wrong thing and now I'm banned from going back. I didn't heed Roman's warning.

Make the right wish!

I checked a few more places, but I couldn't find the round garden door anywhere. The thought of never seeing the cavern again sends a bolt of cold-searing panic down my throat, as if the missing door means that all of it isn't real.

I leave my boots by the kitchen's back door. Now the weather seems to be behaving, conspiring against my entire morning. I want to scream, but I stuff it back. From the kitchen's open crank windows, I see shadows moving inside. My mother's voice drifts out along with a man's, so I press against the wall.

It's the guy with the motorcycle. Her old friend. I sneak a peek through the glass to find Gabriel by the sink.

"You really don't remember any of it?"

I inch closer to get a better listen.

There's the soft thud of something being placed down. My mom's voice: "I don't want to talk about this anymore."

"Is it your migraines?"

"Yes," Mom hisses back.

"I think being here is making you remember. Those dreams you're having—"

"Stop."

"You're remembering him." His voice softer now. "It's all right."

There's a hint of a shadow moving into view. She's moved closer to him, her voice lowering. "I can't. I don't want . . ."

Come on, speak up! I reposition, trying to catch what Gabriel says next. I grab on to the sill. The tower of ceramic flowerpots comes crashing down. A cacophony of sound killing any chance of me hearing more about whatever, or whoever, Gabriel's trying to get my mom to remember.

Fighting against the ivy sticking to my clothes, the kitchen door swings open, producing their startled faces.

"Jesus—you scared me." Gabriel releases a nervous laugh.

Mom's mouth drops before the volley firing of questions. "What the hell are you doing out here? *Are you sneaking in?* Were you out all night?"

"No!" I glower. "God."

She whispers, "Sleepwalking?"

"No," I say again, wedging past them up the step and into the kitchen. "I went for a walk this morning. Why's he here?" I gesture to Gabriel, whose brow lifts at my bluntness.

"Rude," my mom says, flouncing back in behind me. I say flouncing because it's the only way to describe the ruffled exuberance of her crop jacket.

Gabriel tries smoothing the moment with a half smile. "I just brewed some tea if you want a cup."

I eye him. "Thanks. I can get it," I say when I see him reach for a mug.

Mom tosses him an apologetic look. "Be nice. Gabe here just spent the entire morning solving our little issue."

"Oh, yeah?" I can't get to the tea without passing him, and I watch as the bitter steam rises from his cup. "He got rid of those bugs you found in your underwear drawer?"

My mom's eyes widen while Gabe plays off a choked sound.

"No," she says, gnashing her teeth. To him, she explains, "those were just errant moths."

Gabe reaches to the top shelf where the mugs are and hands one to my mom, who's been struggling to reach. She smiles at him and she's actually blushing! I've never seen her blush. Certainly not with a man. Watching her around her husbands, she's always seemed more like an overly doting secretary than a besotted lover. Then again, none of her exes looked like *him*.

"I fixed the Wi-Fi," he says, sliding a slip of paper over my way. "Here's the network name and password."

This pauses the whirl of questions in my head. "Wait, really?"

"Yeah." He laughs again. It's a warm, rich sound. "I tested it out and it's good to go."

I plug the information into my phone but catch the shared glances and awkward maneuvering of my mom and him in the kitchen.

A quick check, but there's no sign of my wish come true yet. My inbox is still empty.

"So," I say, putting down my phone, which chimes with a few messages. I see Jamie's name pop up and my insides lighten. Another from Anthony came in days ago but I plan to ignore that until the end of time. "You two have known each other since high school?"

Another shared look, and Mom smiles with a fondness I haven't seen before. "Way before that," she says.

"Back when I was a ten-year-old pimpled nerd."

Mom snorts. "You were not that bad."

"Please!" he says. "In case you forgot, I'm quoting you." Gabriel turns to me. "This one got mad at me for tripping over her art project, which she left lying around between our seats."

"It was drying!" she says in what appears to be an old argument.

"I could've died," he says. "I went flying right into Wayne." Again, he glances at me. "The kid could've been in WWE by that point. But, I spent every day after trying to make it up to her."

Another blush.

My phone keeps lighting up with messages. A few from Letty, another Miami friend who often used to play the mediator between Christina and me, but I'm distracted by the conversation happening in front of me. The question is, who is my mom remembering?

The two of them keep trading old stories, and I'm fascinated with the way they interact. My mom looks so . . . relaxed. She's using her normal voice and everything—the one that creeps in with an accent. I almost feel bad for what I'm about to ask, but now that Gabe's here it may be the only way to get an honest answer out of her.

"What about high school?" I say, and they stop, looking at me like they forgot I was there.

"What about it?" Mom asks.

"I'm guessing you knew the Sevilla boy that went missing. Roman?"

The change in her is instant. Her face goes stark pale, and the mug tumbles from her hand, shattering onto the floor. "I—" She trembles, pressed against the counter.

"I'll get that." Gabe goes for the broom and dustpan in the corner.

Mom stares at me. "God, Cecilia." She glances around as if remembering where we are and that my questions were bound to come. "Yes," she says, swallowing thickly. "I knew him. Everyone knew Roman. It was tragic."

"Were you close?" I ask. "Is that why you bought this house?" Mom knows it's unlike me to keep pushing. To ask too many questions. To not simply accept defeat. But I need to know. Like the manor, I've been empty for so long that even the smallest whisper of something more has stirred me awake in a way I've never felt before.

Gabriel and my mom share another uneasy look, but he's the one that answers. "I actually bought this house as an investment years before your mom did. Thought I could spruce it up and resell, but the market plunged and I made some other bad investment choices." He laughs in self-deprecation. "Your mom bailed me out, so I've been looking after this place as repayment."

But something about the spiel sounds rehearsed. "I see. So you weren't friends with him either?"

"I wasn't," Gabriel says seriously, and it's the only thing he's said that actually sounds honest. Abrupt, even.

"What about you?"

"Barely. He was years older than me." Her voice is quiet. "I barely knew him."

But her expression is distant—fractured—and I know she must be lying.

AFTER MOM MAKES a hasty exit upstairs, I ask Gabriel for a ride into town, where I'm meeting Jamie. When we get outside, I'm disappointed to note he hasn't brought the motorcycle, but then again, he probably wouldn't have agreed to the ride if he had.

We both silently get into his jeep.

There's no telling whether Mom's being honest. Whether Roman was a stranger or something more. Maybe she truly doesn't remember. A tragic event she repressed from memory. Or maybe she's as untouched by the event as she claims.

I also wonder if they'd ever gone to the well together. But I doubt it. Why would they ever abandon the well once they'd found it? That would be like tossing a treasure back into sea.

I just hope I didn't squander my wish if I'm only allowed a predetermined amount, if that's even how this works. If it even works at all.

More distracting than the jeep's rattling shake and Gabriel's nervous tapping on the steering wheel are the multiplying notifications on my phone screen. I have a terrible habit of clearing messages before reading them because the notification icons rocket my nerves to another level.

I open the one from Letty first since it's strange that she'd text me at all.

omg did you see this???!!!

The message is followed by an image that's refusing to load since we're out of range.

Gabriel's tapping ramps up. "So . . ." He elongates the word. "You made friends here already. That's good."

It's the first words he's said since I got into his car.

I consider the silent treatment. The preferred method of interaction with any of my mom's boyfriends when they're trying to get to know me, but I try a different tactic instead. "I guess I have. He's newish in town, too, so we have that in common."

He nods seriously at this.

"He's really nice to look at," I continue, resting a casual arm on the door. "Maybe we'll rent out one of those shady motels by the hour. Know any around here?"

He clenches the wheel. "N—no, I do not."

That seems to have exhausted his supply of conversation starters. Despite his languid coolness around my mother, I have the feeling he'd be easy to crack. "Can I ask you something, Gabriel?"

"You can call me Gabe."

"Okay, Gabe. What's the real story?" He turns onto Main Street going a little faster than he was before. "Why'd you really buy the Sevilla house?"

I expect backpedaling, what I don't expect is for him to start laughing. "You know, you're a lot like your mom was when she was your age." He raises a brow in my direction. "She was a pain in the ass too."

A backbone, I was definitely not expecting.

Gabe continues, "Look, like a lot of people did back then, your mom admired Roman. Even though I knew the guy was a creep. He was always taking things too far, pushing people too much. If you ask me, disappearing was the best thing he could've done."

My eyes flash to his, but when he parks, Gabe doesn't turn my way. Instead, he stares out the dash window. The bitter truth in his expression sends a spike of ice down my spine. He really means it. He hated him.

"She looked up to him? Or she liked him?" I ask, and his jaw tightens. "Were they . . . together?"

When Gabe glances at me, he startles as if remembering who he's talking to.

"None of it matters anymore." He unlocks the doors. "Trust me, some things are better left buried."

14

THE CONVERSATION IN GABE'S CAR still has me reeling as I walk over to the grocery store. Is the Sevilla legacy that they're all assholes? Or is Gabe's hatred a little biased? Maybe based on the fact that my mom apparently had a crush on the guy. Roman must've been at least four years older than her though. Not unheard of by any means, but definitely icky, especially if it was reciprocated. But would that mean that Mom knew Roman when he disappeared and she's being deliberately secretive about their shared past? I don't understand. I don't get why we're living in the manor. Or what my mom is refusing to remember or acknowledge, and what it all has to do with her connection to Roman.

The image of his screaming dead face crops up in my head like a faulty film roll. I can't unsee it. Asking me to make the right wish. But right for who?

Because I made the one that was right for me.

Maybe Jamie will have some insight. He should be getting off his shift any minute now, and we'd agreed to meet so he can show me *around town*. Even though town consists of a few blocks of psychic shops and delis, and the school that I'm already plenty acquainted with. I think we just wanted a chance to find out if the wish came true together.

I still don't have any emails, and my phone's clinging onto a single bar of service. At least the image Letty had sent me has finally loaded, and it's a screenshot, followed by a few more.

I gloss over the blocks of text on some Instagram posts. My gaze snags on Cristina's handle. She'd left comments on a few posts made by this art page with like ten followers. My eyes widen. Her critiques are . . . strongly worded. Hateful and excessive. Her thoughts on this person's art page are ones she'd expressed to me on more than one occasion about others, but I never would've expected her to actually post this for the world to see.

She got over 178 responses with only the first two showing up in the screenshot, but it's enough to tell me what they're saying to her.

Troll, *hater*, among other things.

Letty's other screenshot is of a TikTok where someone has Cristina's profile photo under a giant red X. The video's title being "Art Community Beware."

"Oh my god." Could this be random? Cristina's always been terrible, so why is she getting caught up in this now? There's a deep ruthless part of me that revels in vindication but there's something else there too . . . something that tightens my throat.

This isn't my fault, though. It's her own doing. Why Letty thinks I should see this, I have no idea.

I'm so caught up in the drama of it all that I almost run smack into a shopping cart.

I make it to Major's Depot and spot Jamie by the electric doors, but he's talking to someone. There's a man bearing down on him. Thin and drunk enough to blow over with a strong gust of wind. His skin is the splotchy red of a rooster's neck. But it's Jamie's expression that makes my chest lurch. Stoic. His signature uptilted mouth is nowhere to be found, as if it never existed. The man keeps trying to pluck a set of keys from Jamie's hands, but Jamie's got a firm grip on them.

The world is filled with bullies, and here's the proof.

Jamie suddenly looks up and meets my eyes, a shadow of embarrassment running through his expression. I want to tell him he doesn't have to be. I make as if to go over and help, but he gives me a discreet signal to wait. So I do.

With each whispered word between them, Jamie becomes impossibly smaller and smaller. And despite the man's rough appearance, I see the similarities right away. The telltale sign of genetics.

His father finally gives up, twisting his mouth to form more ugly words only Jamie can hear, and it makes me think of conversations with my mother. The way I shrink back and curl in.

Abuse isn't always loud or physical. Sometimes it's a barbwired whisper.

And yet, I can't do anything about it. He asked me to wait, and I have. My throat aching and tight. Once his dad leaves, Jamie hangs his head, then wipes a palm down his face as if clearing away the moment.

Another employee comes out from inside the store and pats him on the shoulder as he passes in a half jog.

"Don't worry, kid, I'll make sure he gets home," the man calls back.

"Appreciate it, man. There's a house key under the mat."

The guy takes off his work apron and gives him a salute before dashing off in the direction of Jamie's dad. There's people in this town looking out for him. Used to this kind of thing. As if it happens all the time.

Once we're alone, he looks over at me and there's the hint of a smile there again, clouded in hurt but there on the edge of his mouth. I know I'm not the friendliest face in the world, but I hope at least he doesn't see any judgment because there is none.

I walk over to him. The store's outside fan flutters his hair across his forehead and I have the distinct urge to settle the strands with my fingers.

"I got you something," he says before I can say anything. Before we can talk about what just happened, the pleading look in his eyes tells me to drop it. Jamie crouches down to dig through his book bag with a neatly rolled grocery apron sticking out of it.

I point at my chest. "You got *me* something?"

He produces a Dunkin' Donuts cold brew from the depths of his bag and places it in my hands. The bottle is cold, shining in the sunlight like a lost magical grail. Holding the sweet nectar of the gods.

"Went all the way to the Wawa for it."

I must be getting my period, because I feel a sting form as if I might cry. "All the way to Wawa?"

His smile is back to its full bloom, those changeable eyes every spectrum of brown and green. "All the way."

I gulp down the emotion where it can die in stomach acid and I can regain some control.

"You didn't have to do that," I say.

He tips his head toward the sidewalk so we can begin our tour of the town. "Oh yes, I did. I couldn't keep watching you drink the sludge they sell here. You were seriously freaking me out."

My mouth drops, and I smack his arm. "Then why would you keep bringing them to me?"

"Why wouldn't you admit they were terrible? I think Myra uses the coffee as paint thinner." He produces a Nerds candy rope and tilts it in my direction. I take a bite. "I was getting worried you were a cyborg planted here to infiltrate the town or something. Only sustained by the equivalent of battery fuel. Kind of like Bender and beer."

"Because of course that's the only explanation," I say around a crunchy mouthful.

"Exactly." He gives me a faux side-eye. "You would tell me wouldn't you?"

I go for another bite. "If I was a cyborg spy? Definitely not. I wouldn't blow my cover for anyone."

He squishes the candy to his chest. "You wound me, sexy robot lady spy. And here I thought we *shared* secrets. Speaking of which, any sign yet?"

I don't miss the *sexy* part of the description, but I show him my phone as proof that my wish has yet to manifest. "Nothing. I don't know what I was expecting. I got a rejection letter from them already. It's not like they were going to email me back with 'Oops, we made a mistake. Your work is actually remarkable and refined and we'd be lucky to have such a young prodigy.'"

I clench my teeth.

"I'm sure your art is all those things, whether they acknowledge it or not."

I wish it were that simple. But you can't get by in life without recognition. Not in the art world. Not in the real world either.

Jamie casually changes direction when we're coming up to a bar with blaring country music. There's a familiar truck wrapped in camo paint parked haphazardly in front of it. A man leans on the driver's side, smoking a cigarette. I can feel his leery gaze on me even from a distance. It's the truck that almost ran me and my mom over on our first day in Santa Aguas. The day I met Jamie.

Around town, there are missing posters everywhere, weathered and aged but never taken down, as if in memorial. They're all of men.

I point to one of them. "Think these are la Cegua's doing?"

Wariness eats at his expression. "That's the rumor."

I glance back at camo guy, he spits something brown and disgusting onto the parked car beside him. If he's not careful, maybe la Cegua will make a meal out of him.

Jamie steers us away from the bar, going down a quieter block with storefronts in a rainbow of colors. He has us stop in a colorful tortilleria, where a woman with big, strong arms and terracotta-brown skin comes to crush Jamie in a hug, giving him a free bag of tajadas—long strips of fried sweet plantain, and an orange-flavored Jarritos soda for each of us. The ladies behind the glass serving station wave at him as if he were a visiting pope. Apparently, he takes good care of one of the women's grandmothers at the nursing home.

"Wow, you're like a full-blown celebrity here."

Jamie shrugs. "People just want someone to care."

And he seems to care a lot because it goes on like this with each store. They all seem to know him. He makes time to give each person his singular focus.

The Santa Aguas community is a close-knit and eclectic bunch from what I'm gathering. We visit an apothecary that sells natural soaps and deodorants where everything more or less smells like sage or eucalyptus. They have an entire made-to-order menu for natural remedies that cure everything from warts to depression. An old man sagging under the weight of his oversized glasses takes one look at me and gives me some rose hip tea for period cramps.

We pop into a salt cavern spa next. They claim to revitalize the body and soul with only a two-hour visit, but the owner lets us peek into the room, and it's literally a collection of salt lamps with a lounge chair. Jamie finds my reaction to this incredibly funny.

The next stop is a sad little building with stripped paint and a flickering PSYCHIC sign on the window. Jamie says, "And the pièce de résistance."

"A psychic?" I raise a brow. "We passed like ten of them on the way here. What makes this place special?"

He looks overly pleased with himself. "*I* haven't been here. So we can explore it together."

I watch him for a moment. "You live for this kind of stuff, don't you?"

"Don't you?" He opens the door, eliciting a little trickle of music meant to feel mystical. "You're the adventurer."

"I've been called worse," I say, which is true, but no one's ever called me an adventurer.

I'm not sure the psychic is used to receiving customers because she comes running from the back room followed by a trail of cigarette smoke she tries dispel with a hand.

"Hello, hello. Welcome."

I pause inside her store, my skin feeling as if it'll peel back.

She has the mustard seeds by the door like everyone else, but she also has . . . la Cegua. The same grotesque horse-faced Cegua I saw at the pawnshop my first day in town. This one, however, is dressed in a pearly white gown, a gossamer veil over the horse's sinewy face.

Jamie openly gawks, and I have to pull his shirt sleeve to snap him out of it.

"Uhh—" he starts. He points to the flickering neon sign. "I know someone who can fix that for you. Usually it just needs a hard shake."

"Oh," she says. "That'd be wonderful, thank you. Sit, sit." She clears off a stack of newspapers and food cartons from the small velvet-draped table. "I'm Claritza. Are you here for a joint reading, or maybe palm? I can bring out the crystal ball if you'd like." She laughs.

It takes effort to rip my gaze away from the Cegua, but I manage to sit across from the psychic. Jamie and I share a glance.

"A joint reading would be great."

She claps her hands together. "Excellent. Let me get my cards."

The card reading is nothing new, and despite the initial shock of the horse effigy, I've already gotten used to its presence. It's not as frightening as it was in the pawnshop. Here, in the bright store, it feels like it's radiating with energy. And not necessarily in a bad way.

The woman uses a card deck I've never seen before. Clubs and daggers and cups.

She draws the two of cups.

"Ohh, a strong relationship. You might be young but the cards recognize love when they see it. Expect a grand affair with two children!"

I gape, and this is what makes Jamie laugh.

"I don't even like kids," I whisper.

Jamie taps a fist to his mouth to hide the grin. "Too late. The cards have spoken. Barefoot and pregnant before you know it."

I flick his arm.

The psychic flips another card. Seven of swords.

"A lawsuit. But for an older woman. Perhaps a relative," she casually mentions, and this one makes me sit up. The accuracy of it. Another card. A nine of swords. The card makes her pause and tilt her head.

She *tsk*s and draws out a few more, growing more agitated. "Oh, oh, oh."

"That doesn't sound good," Jamie mutters.

"I see . . . a discovery." When the psychic looks up, her gaze lands heavily on me. "You've awakened something dormant." She leans forward, and a living fire flares in my chest.

I shoot a quick glance at la Cegua's statue, but as I turn back to the psychic, her eyes are murky white. She grips my wrists, pulls me to her. She reeks of salt and mud. "They claim a curse is what they seek to break, but it is I whom they wish to see crack and crumble."

I scream. The woman's eyes are clear and brown once more. Jamie has a hand on my shoulder.

"Ceci, what's wrong?"

My chest heaves. I can't swallow air fast enough. I couldn't have imagined it. Claritza eyes me warily and I back away from the table. Jamie gets up, too, pays the woman, watches me with concern.

La Cegua's message was for me. And for me alone.

JAMIE'S CAR CRUNCHES over the rough gravel of the manor's driveway. My mom's car isn't here, meaning she probably went back to visit the lawyer. Pretty soon, the nightly visits will become weekend trips, then monthly, and then pretty soon we'll be living in some other rich asshole's house.

He puts the car into park, turning to me. "I'm sorry. I meant for today to be a fun distraction but that pretty much backfired."

"No," I assure him. "No, it was fun." It was, at least before an undead witch decided to deliver a message. The Sevilla curse. Is that the curse she was referring to? Is she saying they've tried to break it before? Could that be what Roman was trying to do?

Jamie continues, unaware of my spiral. "If you think about it, what Claritza said could apply to anything. Awakening something dormant could be like saying you've tapped into your hidden potential. Not, you know . . . brought someone back from a dormant state of death."

I wince. "If you say so. I'm not sure we awoke anything. The wish didn't even work, so that's one less thing to worry about." I haven't even mentioned the door that wasn't there this morning. I get out of the car, and Jamie comes around to walk me up the steps to my front porch. I mean to say something along the lines of thanks for putting up with me and sorry for being such a downer, but he beats me to it.

"We'll go back to the cavern soon. We didn't imagine what we saw, and it's still ours. It's still pretty fucking cool. *What?*"

I try to pinch my smile shut with my hand.

"*What?*"

"You just sound funny when you curse."

He's surprised. "Because I'm . . ."

"You're perfect."

He notes how I immediately suck in a breath, wishing I can take back the words. Jamie rocks on his heels, searching the dark, as if whatever he's holding himself back from saying is spelled out in the bruising sky.

He runs his fingers through his hair, but steps closer, so close. Half his body shaded from the wall sconce's light. "I'm far from perfect, Cecilia."

My throat goes tight.

And because he's perfected the ability to catch me off guard, he asks, "How do you feel about prom?"

I take a step closer, too, because the darkness at this time of night lends itself to boldness. "That depends. What's the scenario?"

His mouth pulls to the side. "A dress. A corsage. A suit. Some awkward poses, maybe a spiked drink or two. A date."

"Hmm." I pretend to think it over. "God, that sounds painfully suburban." I make as if to go inside. "Guess I could always ask my lab partner what he thinks—he seems pretty willing."

Jamie places his hand on the door, preventing me from opening it. He's smiling but there's a wolfish hunger now that wasn't there a second ago. "How about you go with me instead?" he asks finally, assertively.

I raise a brow, his face is inches from mine. All it would take is the slightest of movements. A ghost of a kiss.

I pull back. "Fine. I'll go with you. But my rule still stands," I say because I need the reminder too.

His hopeful expression slips a little. "No relationships?"

I shake my head. "Nope."

"Friends?"

And I bridge the gap, kissing his cheek instead, lingering for what might be too long. Even if I've never been really good at it, I say, "Friends."

I FALL ASLEEP waiting for the sounds of the front door. For the clip of my mother's heels up the creaking wood steps. It never comes. But I dream. I dream I'm carried into the woods as if I were a child. Cradled in the scent of ancient dank dwellings and rain-sodden earth.

I lie on a cold chest with no beating heart. Together we go through the blue garden door, open to reveal a forgotten path to a forgotten place.

I'm wanted here. I'm called and needed.

La Cegua walks until the light of the sun touches my skin. Until we delve into the yawning mouth of the well.

What do you wish? What do you desire?

And for the second time, I tell her what I want. I want it so bad. And it might not be the right wish that Roman wanted, but it's *mine* and mine alone.

15

DI PULLS OPEN THE DOOR to a small art studio, daintily folding away her pastel umbrella. Myra hoists her threadbare tote bag up higher, and we cram under the fabric awning to keep out of the rain.

"On the weekends there's a ton of classes," Myra says. "Mondays they do ceramics. But on Tuesdays—"

Di opens her arms wide. "Free studio space."

I shake off some of the water from my shoes before entering. There's a woman sitting in front of a table loom weaving brightly colored thread in bold geometrical patterns. She doesn't stop to look up from her work, and all the way in the back of the room, another woman with a braid all the way to her knees waves at us as we come in but quickly gets back to whatever she's working on behind the easel.

Myra introduces her anyway. "That's Minerva, the owner. If you ever want to use this place by yourself, just bring in some of your own paints and you're good. Sometimes, if you're lucky, people will leave supplies in the locker by the bathroom."

I weave through the incense smoke, stopping in front of the wall of displayed art and textiles. Bold-colored landscapes and urban collages. Bright mosaics and expertly woven patterns. What ties it all together is its indigenous Central American style. A modern reinterpretation of ancestral art.

"I made that one." Myra points to a self-portrait of herself where each quarter of her face depicts a different layer of her. There's a Chicana art style on the upper right, and the dark gothic on the upper left. The bottom half is cut between scarred and smiling, and sinewy raw muscle and frowning. It reminds me a bit of the Cegua. All the parts that tell an incomplete story.

All the aspects we have to juggle to present as someone put together.

"It's powerful," I say, wrapping my arms around myself. It's art that speaks. All of this is, I realize. A connection to self I'm terrified I'll never uncover.

Myra bumps her shoulder with mine. "Thanks. My mom and I worked on it together."

I stare at the piece one last time, a knot in my throat, and whisper, "That's great."

We spend about an hour in the studio. People weaving in and out with the same air of creativity that's infectious. I use my sketchbook, working on small pen drawings of the cavern, of la Cegua. And of Roman.

I'm thinking about my wish. About the messages Letty keeps sending me of Cristina's downward spiral. Those vicious comments she left on that person's art page have gone viral. It started with just screenshots being passed around between the Miami art crowd but it's slowly snowballed into something bigger. This morning, I was forwarded Cristina's apology video. The apology itself was brief. It wasn't even directed at the person she'd bullied to begin with. But it was what she said at the end that made my heart drop to my feet.

If the Dorset Academy could find it in their hearts to forgive me . . .

Which meant, they let her go. Her spot is open, and I can't stop wondering if it's my fault. If it's because I wished that I could go instead. Those were my exact words, after all. *Instead.* I hadn't even realized I'd said it until that apology video. Had I always meant to go instead of her?

I get a notification on my phone. I expect it to be another app reminder or maybe another message from Letty, but it's my email account.

I jump to my feet, making Myra and Di flinch.

The message refuses to load. I swipe my bag from the floor. "I have to go to the café."

"We'll come with you," Di says, and they pack up their stuff.

I'm practically sprinting down the street toward Tully's Café, not caring that I'm getting soaked, or that I haven't explained to Myra and Di what's going on. The door's bell peals when I come in. And it takes way too long to pull the email up on the ancient computer after plugging in my email password. But once it loads . . .

I feel a hand on my shoulder. Myra asks, "Are you all right? You look like you've seen a ghost."

I can't tear my gaze away. It's exactly how I felt the first time I got an email from them, but now it's a completely different message.

"I got in," I say, my voice sounding strange even to my own ears. "I got into Dorset."

Myra and Di let out a squeal of excitement, earning looks from the other patrons. They both surround me in a warm, crushing hug.

And though I want to feel the surge of relief too. The explosion of excitement. All I get is the hollowed-out ache of dread, and I know I need to talk to Jamie.

"Can you guys give me a ride somewhere?"

JACARANDA RETIREMENT HOUSE sits stately by a small bay off the Gulf Coast. Only ten minutes from town but it might as well be in a different world entirely made up of marshes and wide-rooted cypresses.

I thank Myra and Di for the ride, and pull my jacket over my head as I run under the portico and out of the rain. Piano music trickles from inside the moment I walk up the creaky porch steps, foregoing the metal ramps on either side. The retirement home looks like something out of those old Civil War movies with weathered plantation shutters and wraparound porches. Jamie had told me to walk right in but it feels odd, like it's someone's private residence and maybe I should knock.

On one of the porch chairs, there's a nurse feeding a middle-aged man wrapped in a blanket. I try not to stare, but there's a sleep mask over his eyes, and the nurse has to practically bury the spoon into his lifeless mouth.

They don't notice when I walk past and enter the foyer that smells like baby powder and industrial antiseptics, but I do make sure I give my rain-soaked boots a good wipe on the welcome mat.

After a quick check in the entry mirror and pointlessly trying to tame the frizz, I follow the sound of music down a hall and into a large recreational sunroom. In the center of the room is Jamie at the piano, and my mouth almost drops until he turns around, hands off the keys, and the music continues to play from a corner speaker. Not that his fake performance seems to faze the five elderly women sitting in their wheelchairs facing him as if they were attending a live concert. They applaud as he stands, cutting a bow and doing a cute wink that they totally eat up.

Catching sight of me, he jog-walks over, a breathless smile overtaking his face. "Hey, still pouring out there?"

My makeup must be a mess. Instinctively, I try smoothing my hair again. "Yeah, it picked up on the way here."

"Come." He reaches out for my hand, walking us to the elderly before I can protest. I get the same hesitant hitch in my stomach that I do around babies, not that I have any experience with those either. They just seem so fragile that I never know how to act around them—what's safe, what's appropriate.

But apparently they don't have the same hang-ups.

"This is the *not-girlfriend*?" one of them dressed in flashy bright colors shrills, hair dyed to a soft purple. She gives Jamie a hard no-nonsense look.

"Oh, she's pretty!" the one in the middle pipes up. They *mm-hmm* in unison but the sassy one grabs Jamie's arm, pulling him close. It seems she's wearing all the jewelry she owns and it rattles with her movements. "You better hurry up and make your move, Jamie. My Harold snatched me up just in time—I'd almost eloped with his brother."

Jamie pats her arm, his expression a little panicked. "Not helping, Martha."

She releases him and waves this away.

"Is it time for dinner yet?" an especially tiny one says from the corner.

"I swear if she asks one more time—" Martha snaps at her. "You just ate, you old bat!"

"Huh?" The little one tilts her ear closer but shrugs.

This sets off another one. "At least she can eat. I've got gallstones the size of Connecticut—"

"Ladies," Jamie pleads. "Behave. I'll be back in a few minutes."

I wave and most of them respond with cheeky smiles, except for Martha, who simply glares, tapping her wrist at Jamie as if he's running out of time. I notice she has the all-seeing eye tattooed on her wrist.

Jamie walks us toward the hall again, and I'd imagine that if I were to touch my fingertips to his face, his skin would be steaming.

"Sorry about them," he says. "They're convinced I'm not living my life as a teenage boy should—gallivanting and breaking hearts. Their words, not mine."

I press my mouth, holding in the tug on my lips.

He goes on, having to explain himself. "It was either confess I have a prom date or I was about to be set up with Martha's niece, who's a divorcée mom of two boys."

"Oh, well, if you already have a date. Who am I to be a home-wrecker?"

He narrows his eyes at me. "Too late to back out now, she's getting remarried in the spring. *Not* to me. Plus I already aired out my dad's old college suit and had it dry-cleaned. "

"Mmm," I say. "Sounds so appealing. What could I ever find to compliment such style?"

He rests an arm against the wall, mouth slanting. He enjoys this playful match as much as I do. "I'm sure whatever you wear, you'll be beautiful."

This cinches my throat. It's not the compliment itself, but the way he says it. The way he means it.

The weight of different sets of eyes draws our attention back to the room where Martha and her cohorts are straining to catch a glimpse of us. Jamie's smile is wryly amused, but we both step farther away from view.

"What's with the guy outside?" I ask, effectively switching the subject. His brow furrows, and I explain. "He had on an eye mask."

Understanding dawns on his face. "That's one of our resident psychiatric patients. He—um. They say he's one of the Cegua's victims. One of the ones who came back. He freaks out if the mask is off."

My skin goes tight. The man couldn't even feed himself. He'd go the rest of his life in the dark.

"How long has he been here?"

Jamie thinks it over. "I think he's one of the oldest residents. Around twenty years."

Twenty years . . . since Roman went missing.

Jamie's voice lowers. "So your text . . . the wish really worked?"

I blink at him, forgetting for a second what I'd come here for in the first place.

"It did," I say. "The email said that I'd been accepted after a *recent and unexpected opening*." As if this is the ultimate proof.

His jaw tenses as he stares off to the side. "Wow." He swallows. "And you think this is because your old friend got in trouble? How do we know she made those comments of her own free will?"

We don't. We could never know for sure. "Because it's completely like her," I say, and I'm not entirely sure it's a lie, but I also hate how defensive I sound. How much the uncertainty truly hurts. "Cristina . . . is not a nice person. I know this. I was friends with her knowing this. Granted the timing is weird, but it's not surprising that she'd get herself into trouble this way."

His eyes soften. "Okay. I'm not judging you. Really. I'm happy you got what you wanted. You deserve that spot." He's sincere. He's so damn sincere. "When should we go back?"

Go back. It's a relief to hear him say it. Maybe it's been on his mind as much as mine—the hunger. But I pull back before I show exactly how much I want to test our limits, how much I need to see what else the cavern will grant.

"First," I say, "like you said, we should wait for any other consequences. If there are any. It seems to work fast so maybe a day or two?"

Jamie suddenly looks back over my shoulder.

"What consequences?" a voice says. When I turn around, I come face-to-face with Adel, holding tight to an old woman who has the barest remnants of red in her graying hair.

Jamie stammers. "The consequences of gentrification in Santa Aguas," he says so seriously that I almost choke. "City council is thinking of opening up a commercial Froyo shop on Main! What's next? Major's Depot into a Walmart?"

"Jamie." I clear my throat, which stops him from talking but not from making the exaggerated face of a disgruntled eighty-year-old who just found a bike gang going through his yard. A face that says, *What is this world coming to?*

Adel's flawless brow arches.

Jamie shoots me a panicked look before turning his attention to the elderly woman Adel walked in with, "Let me get you a chair, Ms. Hathaway."

We stand there awkwardly as Jamie hurries into the sunroom. The old woman's glassy eyes wander about the hall until they settle on me as if just noticing I'm there.

"You're new," she says, her voice frail and soft. "Have you met my daughter?" She pats Adel's hand with affection.

Adel's eyes widen as if caught off guard. "Granddaughter," she says, correcting her. "Your granddaughter, Nana. And, yes, we've met."

The old woman peers up at her. Her papery thin skin wrinkles further. "Are you sure?"

"Positive," Adel asserts, but it sounds pained. Odd. "Here we go. Let's get you back to bed. It's been a long day."

The woman stares out at nothing. Along with Jamie, another caretaker helps get Adel's grandmother into a chair and wheeled away.

"I didn't know Ms. Hathaway had family," Jamie says.

"I've been out of town." Adel's tone is clipped. "So." She tunnels her focus on me. "I've been meaning to talk to you."

I almost ask why but manage to swallow it back. "Really?" I say instead. "What's up?"

"How are you liking the manor? I bet it's full of surprises, like most old places."

"It's fine," I say. "Not as scary as everyone thinks."

She seems to find this amusing. "Of course not. Most people are afraid of their own shadows." She eyes Jamie, who is now stamping his lips together to prevent talking himself into a deeper pit. "Anyway, I thought we could hang out, just the two of us. Get to know each other more. As the new girls in town."

The new girls. Even though she's "come back" to Santa Aguas and seems to know a lot about the Sevillas, Adel is hiding something. Call it a gut feeling, a hunch, but I recognize the subtle shades of a big secret. And for some reason, she wants me to know it.

"Sure," I say, ignoring Jamie's wide-eyed stare. "Maybe sometime this weekend?"

"Friday," she says with finality. Adel picks a piece of lint off her blazer. As usual, she's dressed impeccably rather than like a high school girl, as if she raided a closet that's not her own.

I remember my plans. "I'm actually going dress shopping with some friends on Friday since we have the day off. Maybe—"

She cuts me off. "Oh, that's right. It's a teachers' planning day. I have loads of dresses—black-and-white is this year's theme, right?" As if she's hardly bothered by some high school dance. "I'll bring them over to your place. I promise they'll be way better than anything from around here. I'll be there around eleven-ish?" She leans forward, kissing my cheek before I can answer. She gives Jamie a flat smile and walks past us and out the door.

"What was that about?" he asks.

I stare after her. "I'm not entirely sure," I say. "But I guess I'll find out on Friday."

A sharp whistle comes from the sunroom. Martha is glaring in our direction, the light beaming on her like the single actor on a stage.

Jamie and I share a glance, but we go see what she wants.

Once I'm close enough, Martha pulls me to her with a grip stronger than I thought possible.

"Something's off with that girl." Martha looks in the direction where Adel had stood. "She's covered in the stench of water rot. Algae and old mud. I smelled it all the way from here."

The all-seeing eye on her wrist seems to wink from her crepe-paper skin. She pulls my chin to peer at me closer.

Her eyes narrow. "I can smell it on you too."

Wanted.–

Santa Aguas, FL

Practitioners of the occult, mediums, psychics, curanderismo. Seeking EXCEPTIONAL individuals to attend to a respectable family. Must have spiritual knowledge of America-based mythos. Must be willing to relocate to Santa Aguas. Transport and full accommodations for family and person included. STRICTLY sober, reputable applicants only.

16

MY MOTHER'S GIVENCHY SNEAKERS plop over the sludgy leaves of the greenhouse, sending the two crows I was using as subjects fleeing. I shut my sketch pad before she can see what's on the page next to it—the sketch of Roman. Underwater. Screaming.

"I've been looking everywhere for you. Ew." She ducks under a massive spiderweb.

I watch her with only the slightest bit of fascination. My mother, in her outlandish outfits, could make any place feel like a photo shoot. Even this one that's meant to seem casual, ready for a day of housework. It's her cleaning outfit, complete with the pin-up head scarf.

"What's up?" I ask.

She sighs using her whole body, and I know I'm going to have to do something I don't want to do.

"I need your help today."

"I have plans," I say quickly. Though I don't really. I'm just in limbo today. It's been two days and I still haven't replied to Dorset's email. And I can't sneak off to the cave until the weekend, when my mom's gone and this incessant rain is due to clear. I can't go tomorrow either, even though there's no school and a 40 percent probability of sunshine, because Adel invited herself over. Ignoring the thick welcome packet from University of Miami on my bed was also an incentive to get the hell out of the house.

"Well, too bad," Mom says, glancing around and hugging her arms to herself to keep from brushing up against any dirty surfaces of the greenhouse. "You need to help us with the garage. It's a disaster."

I lift a brow. "Us?"

Us turns out to be her and Gabe, whom she's had stuck in the garage since the butt crack of dawn. She practically shoves me into the detached four-car square filled with boxes, wheels from broken bikes, old equipment and furniture, and dusty antiques before announcing she'll go to the kitchen and make lemonade! As if she's not just going to grab a premade jug from the fridge and find somewhere to hide out while we do the work. Typical.

Gabe stares after her with a mixture of exasperation and affection. I know the look well, and it throws me off to see the expression reflected on someone else's face. But he smiles, and so do I. The situation should be awkward considering our last conversation and the fact that I hardly know this man who's currently rifling through our meager possessions, but it's not. Gabe, I've come to realize, does not mind long silences and slips through tense situations like a ghost—as if he's not even there and is used to being overlooked despite his obvious good looks. But judging from my mom's old stories, he had a major glow up and the confidence is still a work in progress. Made obvious by his ill-fitting gingham shirt.

"We've already gone through most of the boxes on this side," he says. "I placed a few things by your door. Some bags of paint I thought you might want."

"Thanks," I say, feeling mildly guilty about judging his shirt. I heft up one of the boxes to the velvet surface of an old pool table cluttered with more junk, like an old telephone with a rotary dial. The box has rows and rows of rolled-up, ancient-looking blueprints like some forgotten straw dispenser. I bring over one of the garbage bags and billow it open. "I didn't realize we'd brought so much stuff with us."

"You didn't. This was already here, so watch out for any rat nests."

I immediately remove my arm from the fathomless depths of the box, and take another look around. "This was already here? Like it's my mom's old stuff?"

He nudges another box out of the way and dusts off his hands. "Yup. Some of it anyway. There are also some . . . relics left over."

"Sevilla family relics?" I ask.

He smirks, but instead of answering, he gets back to work, and I take that as confirmation enough. The rain picks up and clatters against the metal roof. We work in companionable silence for a while until he plays some classical music on his phone and hums, as if it's an actual bop.

I raise a pointed brow and he laughs. "What? Where do you think all your music got its inspiration from?"

"*My* music? Oh, I'm sorry, and here I thought you were at least under a hundred years old."

Gabe pauses, eyes looking a little dazed. "Damn, I do sound like an old man."

I turn back to the box, taking out books and magazines and throwing out the ones that are crumbling apart. "It's fine though," I say. "I listen to this stuff, too, when I paint. I can't do lyrics."

"Too distracting, huh? I'm the same when I'm writing."

"You're a novelist?"

He smiles at this. "Not as glamorous. I'm a travel journalist." He tilts his head. "Which I guess still sounds more glamorous than what it is."

I stop what I'm doing. "Wait. You travel around the world and choose to live *here*?"

He shrugs. His voice goes dark. "Some places you just can't get away from for long. You done with that one?" He points at my box with his chin.

I nod, and he takes it and breaks it down. "I wonder if any of this stuff is worth anything. Some of it looks like it belongs in a museum."

"Tell me about it." He pulls a drape off a weird stand with a peculiar kettle pot and spigot. "I believe this was a milk churner to make butter back in who knows when."

"Wow," I say. "Think it works?"

He builds up a sweat trying to move the stiff crank but it doesn't budge. "Maybe if the Hulk gave it a go." He misses when I roll my eyes at his corny dad joke. But a soda cracker tin falls from the top of the churning contraption, rolling toward me and spewing the papers that were inside. Except it's not paper, but photographs.

I crouch down, gathering up the pictures, careful not to crumple some of the flimsy Polaroids.

"What'd you find there?" Gabe asks.

I turn some of them around, gripped with instant wonder at the muted sepia tones of unfamiliar faces. "I'm not sure. Pictures, but I don't know of who."

There are some of a dark-skinned woman with beehive hair, posing in a beautiful lavender dress and cradling her big baby bump. In another photo she's sitting on a rocking chair, bed hair flat and sweaty against her face, a wrapped bundle in her arms. Her sweet heart-shaped face is beaming.

I flip to another picture but it's no longer the same woman. They look similar but this one's face is made up of severe lines, a harsh, thin mouth. She's clutching the hand of a little girl in a pristine white dress and waist-length hair of ebony silk. The little girl is also frowning.

Gabe stands next to me to look. "Oh."

"Oh?"

"That's Marina," Gabe says, startling me. "Right before she moved from Nicaragua to Florida with her aunt."

I cut him a glance. "My mom?" And I see it. The little girl has the same fine, upturned nose as mine. The big dark eyes that tilt down at the corners. I flip through the others and they're of Mom, too, at various ages. "Why did she always look so miserable?" I show him a particular one of her scowling, her wet hair in the middle of being untangled by her aunt with what looks to be a formidable comb. I actually really do look like her in this picture.

He breathes in deep. "Well, you didn't get a chance to meet Tita Vela but she was . . . a tough woman. After your grandmother passed, she took full custody of your mom. And she wasn't what you would consider to be the most nurturing mother figure. Though she was an excellent cook. She'd call your mom Mari knowing your mom hated it." He looks down at me, considering. "Your mom had to grow up a lot sooner than she should've."

He keeps taking me by surprise. It's weird to have someone answer your questions. To at least be somewhat honest. My mom's past, our past, has always felt like a puzzle with missing pieces. Like a water-stained letter obscuring the most important words. Having this glimpse into the past is a bit startling, because it makes my mom come into focus just a bit more, but the more she does, the less it feels like I know her at all.

Lately, I hardly know myself. Those weird sleepwalking daydreams I've been having since getting here. I never thought myself particularly intuitive before, but maybe that's changed.

"What about that whole spiritual emigration thing? You know, the Sevilla guy who brought in a bunch of psychics and mediums to town?"

Gabe's brow quirks. "What about it?"

"Did they—my mom and aunt—come here because of that?"

Gabe stacks the photos, neatly rolling them back into their capsule. "Hmm. I actually don't know. Why don't you ask your mom?"

The resulting scoff is involuntary, because there's no way. Even if it were true, Mom would never admit to it. She's always thought psychics are scammers and people who believe in that stuff, gullible idiots.

Gabe's giving me another scrutinizing look and I turn away, facing the door that leads to another part of the garage. "What about what's in here? Do we have to clean this out too?"

Before he can finish his sound of protest, I'm opening the door. It takes a moment for my eyes to adjust to the total darkness; the only light comes from behind me and illuminates the wisps of dust. After fumbling for the light switch, I see a single, shiny car. It looks like something out of a dream. What you imagine coming toward you on a dark, foggy highway rumbling the night awake.

"Whoa." I put my fingers on the sleek hood.

Gabe lumbers inside with little enthusiasm, whistling out a sigh. "Well, it's still in good shape, that's for sure."

I walk around the car, opening the driver's door. "It's like a muscle car and a pickup had a baby."

"It's a Chevy El Camino. They don't make these anymore."

I'm examining the dash, the ragged leather seats. The big dials and cassette player. It looks so . . . old. When I look up, he's staring at the car with a far-off look. "Who'd it belong to?"

Instead of answering, he gestures for me to get in. And I do. He slides into the passenger seat, pulling open the glove compartment and jingling out a set of keys. There's a triangular key charm with a monogrammed *R.S.*

He turns on the ignition and we're both quiet as the engine roars to life, just as I'd imagined it would.

"It belonged to Roman," I whisper, my heart clashing behind my ribs.

Gabe's face confirms it.

I grab hold of the steering wheel as the car gains an even grander significance. I marvel at it again. "How is it still here?"

He shrugs and scratches at his close-cut beard. "Want to take it for a ride?"

I sit back, letting go of the wheel as if it were on fire. "No, thanks."

This makes his brow quirk. "Seriously? I figured you'd want your own ride if you're going to be stuck in this town."

I bite my inner cheek. "I don't drive."

"*You don't drive?*" he repeats, and he turns off the car so we don't asphyxiate in a closed garage, which I hadn't even thought of until that very moment, making it all the more clear I shouldn't be behind the wheel.

The familiar hollowness spreads through my stomach, the grip of immobilizing anxiety. "I'm not good at it, okay?" I tried and failed, and didn't see the point when I could just call for a ride when I needed one. Some people were just good drivers, some shouldn't be allowed behind the wheel. Some could go on to become artists and have families and be successful and find the love they talk about in movies, others . . . aren't meant to.

He sits back, quiet for a moment. "What happened?"

I gnaw at my lip. "I crashed. Ruined the whole front end." I cross my arms. I remember I'd just gotten a frantic call from my mother's coworker, who said Mom was arguing with her boyfriend outside the restaurant and it was getting physical. I'd just gotten my permit, and Mom had left her car at home because the jerk-face was supposed to bring her home after her shift. I left in a panic, took a wrong turn, and got on the expressway. I tell Gabe,

"I couldn't stop in time when a car cut in front of me. My reflexes just suck." I clear my throat, my voice having risen. They had a kid in that car. I mean, nothing happened. But it could've. People don't understand the things that could've happened, they only focus on what didn't, and that's what makes them repeat mistakes over and over again. I don't want to repeat mistakes.

"I see." Gabe drums his fingers, brows furrowed. "Well, this is Santa Aguas and the nearest interstate is like twenty miles from here. There's only two lanes and rarely any other cars unless you count tractors. I think maybe you can give it another shot if you want and I can be there to guide you." He pauses, smiling. "I promise I have really good reflexes."

I give him a droll look, but, at the same time, this would be a perfect car to take with me to college. I could drive myself to school, I could—and then the thought pops into my head, the beacon of realization that I don't have to play by the rules anymore. I could wish to never crash again. I could wish to be the best damn driver in the world if I wanted.

And this time, the wish wouldn't take anything away from anyone.

I grab hold of the wheel again and Gabe nods, pressing the button clipped onto the sun visor that opens the garage door with a shrill squeal. The rain has stopped, and bright light cuts across us as my mom stands there with a look of complete horror. She moves aside, and I pull the gear lever to idle forward.

Gabe hunches so he can talk to her from my window. "We're just going for a quick drive, Marina."

"Gabriel—" she starts, stopping to swallow hard. Then a realization cuts across her expression because her gaze drops back to me. "You're going to drive?"

I shrug. "You wanted me to practice, right?"

She touches two shaky fingers to her lips. "Right."

"We'll be back in no time," Gabe assures her.

She gives him a hard look. "When you get back, we need to talk." She wavers uncertainly. "Drive careful." And with that, she bounds back to the manor.

I suck my teeth. "Oof, you're in trouble."

He smirks. "Shut up."

We drive for an uneventful hour, listening to the radio and driving straight as if trying to reach the edge of the horizon. We pass about three cars all heading in the opposite direction, and I don't have to use a turn signal, not once. Well, maybe once. But the car drives sure and smooth, bulky and sleek like a majestic sea creature riding a current. I'm in love with it by the time we get back, and it isn't until then that Gabe notices the gas meter hasn't budged.

"So it's busted?" I ask.

"Nah, just a quirk."

"But it makes you think the car's always half-empty."

"I prefer half-full."

"Of course you do." I purse my mouth just as the manor's gates come into view and we pull inside.

"Still," I say. "That isn't exactly safe. It's running a gamble each time you leave your house."

I park, and he gets out, peering back inside, his face lit and challenging. "Life's a gamble, kid. But you still gotta play. I'll take a look at it later. By the way, you did good today." He raps his knuckles on the hood wearing a self-satisfied grin and makes his way inside.

I stay in the car for a while, staring at the gas meter's needle right in the center between empty and full. When I pound a fist over the dash, seeing if that'll get it to move, the glove compartment flops open instead. I reach over, fumbling inside until my hand closes around something. I come away with a black leather-bound sketchbook.

I handle it like I did the car, with the sense that it's something more than simply what it appears to be. Maybe the cavern has taught me to prepare for the unexpected. When I run my fingers across the worn cover, when I unravel the leather strap holding it closed, I realize it is so much more than just a random sketchbook.

It's his. It's Roman's.

And maybe Gabe's right, at least for today, some gambles do pay off.

AFTER HAVING A GLASS of Mom's bitter lemonade, I sneak Roman's sketchbook upstairs, taking the steps two at a time. The worn Moleskine notebook is an ember burning a hole through my back pocket.

I flop onto my bed, crack open the sketchbook stiffened by time, and fall back into the year 2000.

Hours go by as I study every page. Every insight, absorbing the sketches until the light outside goes dark. There's so many of the cavern. Of la Cegua. And though it's startling to have it confirmed, it's not surprising to uncover that Roman's been to the cavern.

He might've even died there.

A lot of the drawings are of the same girl, always her side profile. Always with the same tumble of dark hair. Like most artists, he struggled with drawing hands. There's several attempts on multiple pages, and in each one, there's a ring on the subject's index finger. A plain band that could be gold, silver, or anything.

My own ring is brass, and it slides on my thumb, barely staying on since I lost the chain in the cavern.

I pause on one of the last pages. There's a sketch of a cliff's edge. A single figure left standing on the precipice looking at something down below. I run my finger along the figure's wide back, smudging the pencil shading. The sketch moves beneath my fingertip as if alive.

A chill creeps across the floor, over the mattress.

I keep tracing the lines of the sketch. Finding the areas where extra care was placed. Like the tree line behind the figure and the wisps of dark hair on his head.

Vertigo makes the room go hazy. My eyelids close as if there were tiny weights on the lashes, and wind rushes across my ears, into my nose, strong enough to imagine myself standing on the craggy edge.

Like back in the cavern, everything dissolves around me until I'm not in my room at all, but hundreds of feet in the air, looking out over everything through a gossamer screen of white.

The wind no longer prickles my skin. There's no relishing in any of it anymore.

I watch the boy with his friends. His face like his father's and the one before. Eyes obscure like the bottom of a storm-ravaged lake. I detest those eyes.

The hunger is always there like a genetic disease.

Only two of them remain standing on the jagged point of the cliff's edge. Wind whips across us, so loud all they can hear is its wail. The rustle of my dress quiet against it. Still as a frozen lake.

"Come on, Roman! Just leave him alone!" the girl he calls Marina yells from the waters down below, a strain in her voice when it was meant to be light. Already, being near the Sevilla boy is changing her. She bobs in the bay, waiting, her long black hair pooling around her like a spill.

Roman stands at the edge, high above, hand latched onto a gangly boy's shoulder. The boy is covered in sweat, face screwed tight in fear. Only the two of them have yet to jump.

"I—I don't think I can do this," the small one they call Gabriel says.

"Hey, look," Roman reasons, voice dispassionate. "I'm only trying to help you out here." He leans forward, whispering into Gabriel's ear, but I can hear the words, as if they were spoken into my own. "If you want her so bad, at least show her you're not a pussy."

Gabriel whips his head around, wide-eyed. "I—I swear it's not like that."

The boy is a little lamb.

And Roman is the wolf. "Not for lack of trying, am I right?" His hands tighten, curl like claws. "If I'm going to win the girl, at least don't make it so easy on me."

And he shoves Gabriel off the cliff's edge, watching him sail through the air, silent as a stone.

When Roman looks over his shoulder, his gaze finds mine through the trees. Sees past the veil to the bone-mask beneath. The wretched boy smiles.

"It's not like you expect anything else from a Sevilla." His face hardens. "Isn't that right, Soledad?"

17

I WAKE UP THE NEXT DAY with Roman's sketchbook clutched to my chest. The page open on the cliff. The vision still clings to me. A scream bobbing in my throat like a buoy. My mom was there. Her connection to Roman solidified because I know it was real. I don't know why or how I know, but I'm certain the dream was a memory—a point in time drawn vividly to life for me to witness.

It doesn't make sense. I don't know if I'm seeing these things now because of the town, the manor, or the cave. Or have the visions always been there simmering under the surface, only waiting for me to access them?

I'm also not sure why it hurts to uncover he'd been cruel. That the simmering sharpness in Roman's dark gaze I'd recognized so well went beyond anger. It was danger.

It's no wonder Gabe hated him. *If you ask me, disappearing was the best thing he could've done.*

Sitting up in bed, I tug the sheets that have tangled around my legs, then run my fingers over another one of his sketches, shutting my eyes tight as if that might take me into another memory. I wait a few seconds. A few more, bracing for the wave of vertigo, but nothing happens.

I flip to another page, this one blank. The page before it had been torn out. Seeing it with daylight filtering in from the windows, I can make out the imprint of words left behind. I swallow down the metallic taste from my mouth—blood pooling after I bit my cheek in my sleep—and grab a pencil from my vanity.

Gently, I brush the charcoal tip over the indentations until words start taking shape.

Curandera Lupe. I scrape faster. Beside it, underlined—an address. A local address.

311 Montego Rd.

The entire book has been littered with nonsensical words, the name Soledad reappearing more than once. The name he'd called la Cegua in my dream. But this is what he tore out. An address?

A knock comes at my door, and I quickly shove the sketchbook away.

Mom barges in a moment after. The long black hair from the dream now cut short around an older face. I watch her like I'm seeing someone new.

She sniffs at the room, at my discarded paints and canvases strewn all over the place. "Uy, Cecilia. Como tienes chunchadas." I think being back in Santa Aguas has made her pick up on her Spanish again, and it startles me each time. Mostly 'cause I don't understand half of it since she was so determined I perfect my English first and foremost.

Before I can ask her what that means, she announces, "I'm leaving." But we already had this conversation yesterday. She has a trip to take to Miami for a hearing. And the more-than-flirty lawyer is meeting her halfway at that *adorable bed-and-breakfast* they went to last time. Gross.

This was all discussed between our many instances of awkward silences at the dinner table.

"Fine," I say.

But she goes on as if she didn't hear me. "Cecilia, I told you this hearing is a huge deal. I mean"—she takes on an odd look, picking at the dresser's peeling paint—"you don't watch the news, do you?"

I lift a brow. "No."

Her faces loses its tenseness. "Good. It's a long, tedious process."

"It's fine, I get it. I'll see you Sunday, right?"

She blinks back at me, expecting a remark, a cut, anything—the classic *I don't care*, but I need her to go. Not only is Adel scheduled to arrive at any moment, but I need to get back to the cave. I need to convince myself it's still there. That *they're* still there—the statue and Roman. Everything has been leading me back, and I can't wait any longer.

She seems to relax, placing down one of the crystal frogs I used to collect as a kid, but she still lingers by the doorway.

"Was there something else?" And I don't mean to sound rude but impatience creeps into my voice.

She rests her head against the doorframe for a split second, as if whatever she has to say is too hard to get out, and I notice then how tired she looks. The headaches she's been complaining about wearing on her. "I . . . I wanted to tell you that I'm proud of you."

My heart squeezes with the words, wrung dry like a rag.

"I know how hard yesterday must've been—driving again." She swallows. "If you want to keep the car . . . I don't have any objections is all I'm saying."

There's a crushing pressure in the back of my throat but I manage to say, "Okay, sure. Thanks."

She nods at this, and I think she might leave but again she hesitates. We always leave so much unsaid between us, so many read-between-the-line moments. There's an impenetrable layer to my mother I've never been able to pierce, no matter how prickly I've been. But since we got here, so much has spilled out, as if this place held on to pieces of her, hidden for me to find. There's so much I want to ask her, so much I want her to tell me. And she's right there, lingering.

"Mom?"

Her tone is soft, almost hopeful. "Yes?"

But I know how fast that door can close, lock, and shut me out for good. I've been left outside those walls too many times. So I shake my head, and say, "Never mind. Good luck at the hearing."

MYRA:

You want more info on Soledad?
As in Sevilla numero uno's wife?

DI:

Don't spiral on us, Ceci!
That freakky ass house is getting to you.

MYRA:

Who cares! There's nothing wrong with
a little research rabbit hole.

DI:

Says the girl who spent two weeks
looking up Disney subliminal messages
and almost failed chem.

MYRA:

DI:

But I love you for it!!! 

ME:

Do you know where I can learn more about her?

MYRA:

YEA, as a matter of fact . . . I do. You can come to my house tomorrow and ask my mom who, as I've mentioned, has everything you can think of on the Sevillas. Legit obsessed.

DI:

And you can celebrate Myra's birthday with us.

I pause.

ME:

I'm an asshole.

MYRA:

NO, you're just new. By next year you'll realize my birthday is like chaos during mercury in retrograde, no avoiding it

DI:

Meaning, you can only play the newbie card once. You're officially stuck with us

This makes my heart lurch. I'm staring at the message when the doorbell rings and the phone jumps from my grip. Jamie chimes in while I'm making my way downstairs.

JAMIE:

I have tomorrow off

MYRA:

a miracle!

JAMIE:

I could come pick you up, Ceci,
if you need a ride to Myra's

I type out a reply just as I'm getting to the door.

ME:

Be here at 1

MYRA:

You heard the woman, Jamie.
And don't be late!

JAMIE:

Copy that.
Wouldn't dream of keeping her waiting

Dork.

There's another message outside of the group chat. A private one with Jamie. The one before it was a screenshot of the address I'd found in Roman's sketchbook.

JAMIE:

We're still on to check out that
address later today?

I swallow. Yes. I need to find out why Roman had gone to visit a curandera. What answers could he have needed from a psychic. If he was looking for answers about the cavern, about the wishes, and the magic, I need to know too. I need to understand how it works, and figure out how far the consequences can go. Maybe Cristina losing her place at Dorset was inevitable, and I just sped up the process. Or if I continue to wish, will the magic eventually run out? How much can I truly get out of this?

There's another impatient knock at the front door, and right as I open it, Adel stands there with a dainty fist raised. Her other arm weighed down by a pile of garment bags.

She tilts her head, tail of red hair swishing from her ponytail. "There you are."

"Sorry—" I start but she's already walking in, devouring the house with her gaze.

"Come on in," I whisper too low for her to hear. She sets her purse down on a settee by the fireplace. Takes in the impressive foyer and sighs. "Hasn't changed much."

This gives me pause. "You've been here?"

Adel walks around, appearing lost in thought, her fingers tracing over everything. "A few times. My mom brought me. She was *really* close to Roman. Wanted me to see where she'd spent her time growing up." She looks at me then. "It's why she moved us away. The memories were just too painful."

"Oh," I say, twisting the ring around my thumb, so curious to know what stories she's heard of Roman, but not sure how to ask without sounding like I'm interrogating her.

"You said your mom was also close to mine?"

She shrugs. "Not really. You know how high school is."

I swallow this information down.

Adel clears away the awkward silence. "Anyway, I can't wait to see you in these dresses." She stops at the foot of the stairs. "Lead the way."

Once in my room, Adel drops the clothes on my bed, already striding to my windows. She pushes back the sheer blinds and peers outside.

She doesn't seem to find what she's searching for, because she turns away from the window with a frown. She crosses her elegant legs and sits by my vanity, giving the pile of clothes a sweeping gesture. "Try that first one on top. I think it'd look amazing on you."

My eyes dart to the vanity's drawer close to where her elbow rests. Where I hid Roman's sketchbook. She arches a brow.

I do as she says and unzip the first garment bag. The dress that unfurls is inky black—a corset bodice with a beaded A-line skirt. It looks like a starry night sky cascading over my hands. Like it belongs in a dream.

I glance back at her. "This is gorgeous. You sure you want to let me borrow this?" I leave the rest unsaid—it looks awfully expensive, chic-antique even, and we barely know each other.

She makes an impatient sound, getting up to take the dress from my hands. "Don't stop to think if you're worthy of a gift, Cecilia. Worry that the gift is worthy of *you*. Let's see how it fits." There's no irony in her words, just that intimidating confidence.

I know what she's waiting for, so I shimmy out of my jeans and puff-sleeved sweater.

If she's not going to turn away, then neither will I. Whatever allure she can pull on other people doesn't work on me despite my entire flushed body saying otherwise. I take the dress back from her and slip it on, adjusting the bodice and running a hand to smooth down the beaded tulle. I stand in front of the mirror and suck in a breath.

"Stunning," she says, right over my shoulder. And for once I can agree with the compliment. The dress is something magical.

"It goes so well with your skin tone."

I stiffen. Her hands go to my neck, pulling the hair back from my face, nails sweeping my skin. My eyes shoot up to meet hers through the mirror. She smiles.

"What happened to that necklace you always wear?" I feel her breath brush past my ear.

My hands instinctively go up to grab it, but of course there's nothing there. The ring now rests snugly around my thumb.

"I lost it swimming," I say.

"Swimming?" she asks, eyes lighting. Her fingers still linger around my skin, pressing a little firmer than before. A waver of shivers flow up my legs. "I used to go swimming all the time at the springs. Where did you go?"

I take a step forward, bringing some distance between us. "Some lake. A friend took me."

Her hands drop to her side, eyes narrowing. "Sounds fun. Maybe you can take me to this lake sometime."

"Sure."

She saunters back to the window, peering intently toward the woods. "Have you explored any other places since moving here? You know, like Crystal Springs, the Sumner Quarry?"

"What's the quarry?"

"One of the highest points in Florida. Kids go there to cliff dive or make out." I bite my tongue, thinking of the cliff from last night's dream.

Adel stops in front of me, blocking me from unzipping the next bag. "What about caverns? We have so many caverns but only the rare few are truly special." Her sea-glass eyes peer into mine and I swallow. "Seen any of those yet?"

I'm already shaking my head. "No," I say, forcing a hoarse whisper.

She stares for only a moment longer before shrugging a thin shoulder. "That's too bad."

Adel knows.

She knows about the cave. She knows I've been there. But how? And why can't I bring myself to tell her the truth? I give an internal snap of the fingers. I need to find out something about her. Turn the tables. And I remember that no one seems to have known her until recently.

"You know a lot about this place. How long have you been gone?"

Her gaze sharpens, something cracking at the edges of her expression.

"I hardly know anymore."

And the words are so haunted, so hollow, that I can't think of what to ask next.

She stands back, lifting my arms to take in the dress that seems to have melded to my skin, some of that fiery light reenters her eyes. "This is the one. Don't bother with any of the others. Do you have any matching shoes?"

I withdraw my arms and cross them. "My mom does—I'll be right back." And I escape the room, hurrying to my mom's room on the other side of the manor. I need a moment to gather my thoughts, catch my bearings.

I need to tell Jamie that I suspect Adel knows about the cavern, but I left my phone in my room. At least the screen is locked.

This side of the house looks much more lived-in. Rooms repainted in airy white with modern beds and hardwood flooring. It's no wonder Mom would pick this side. But no matter the renovations, the house moves with you, whispers decades' worth of secrets in just the creaks and sounds, and I imagine she hates that. There's no changing it to something that it's not.

I reach my mom's chambers—really the only way to describe the space given the double doors and suite-like design. This room is carpeted in a lush, cream fiber. The walls pearl white with golden trims. It's a room befitting a queen, and the closet is no exception. Funny how she gave me such a hard time for packing all my art supplies when she seems to have kept every single outfit she's ever owned, including the gowns she'd worn with David to high-society galas.

As if she had no doubt that those days would come again.

I find the shoes I'd had in mind up at the very top of her closet in a sealed plastic box. Her black Vera Wang pumps that she probably won't notice are gone. Maybe. I grab them in a hurry to get back to my room. It was stupid of me to leave Adel there alone with all my stuff—my sketchbooks of the cavern, Roman's notebook, and my phone.

As I'm hurrying out, something flashes from beneath my mom's pillow. A glossy book spine partially stuffed away from view.

My brows knit. I move toward her bed, and get hit by the familiar scent of her—a combination of expensive perfume and rose oil that I've always secretly loved.

I withdraw the book from under the pillow and find that it's actually a yearbook. A Beckmann High yearbook. One I've never seen before.

It's so weird to think of her in bed looking through it, reminiscing about times way before I was born. It feels like every day I find more clues to my mother's past. Like finding the edges to a puzzle, but the center pieces are still missing and none of it really comes together. I place the book in front of me with a quiet reverence.

It's been looked at many times throughout the years. Worn edges and scuffed pages. Like the books that I've reread over and over again, the yearbook has some pages that are wavier than others. A crack in the spine and a dog-eared page that demands the book be opened.

I open it to reveal the bookmarked page. And it's not my mother's senior photo like I expected but Roman's. And just like they did in the cavern, his dark eyes bore into mine. The heaviness of his brow coupled with the flinty fire in his expression make it impossible to look away. Unlike the personalized quotes from the other students, the words below his picture read: "In Memory of Roman Arturo Sevilla-Beckmann." I flip to another page—at the end of the senior class photos there's an entire page dedicated to his memorial, but his isn't the only one. There's another for some kid name Dominik Nowak. Strange, two deaths in one year.

I flip to the next page. It's a collage of candid photos with a large banner that reads: CONGRATS, CLASS OF Y2K! The class of 2000. It's the same year Roman went missing, his senior year.

One of the senior candids draws my eye, and it takes me a second to place her. But it's the smile that gives her away, no matter how many years have passed. My mom's long hair is braided back. She's wearing a crop top, low-rise jeans, and magnetic blue eye shadow. I recognize Gabe beside her, scrawny as a vine. She's pressed tight into someone barely in the shot but his face is buried in her hair. I can still make out who it is. It's Roman. An arm clamped around her.

Wait—my heart is beating so loud, it makes it hard to think. The year 2000. She looks seventeen or eighteen in this picture. She's in the *senior* candids. But that's not right. Can't be right. She was eighteen when she had me, and I was born in 2005. I run the math quickly in my head. Then again for good measure.

The year 2000 was twenty-three years ago. If she was a senior, it means she'd have to be turning at least forty-one this year, but Mom only just turned thirty-six last month. A thirty-six-year-old in the year 2000 would've been *thirteen* years old.

Either the dates are wrong or she's lied about her age all these years.

It'd be just like her, pulling something this elaborate for the sake of vanity. But I've seen her license before. It doesn't make sense. Unless Roman was dating someone vastly younger and she just looks older in this picture. But there's no way. This is not the picture of a thirteen-year-old. I flip through the senior photos organized alphabetically, stopping at the Ns. And there she is. Marina Navarette.

But why go through all this trouble to lie about it? Why keep all these secrets?

Unless—no, it's too absurd to think about.

Did she have something to do with his disappearance? Could she be the reason Roman went missing? I mean, if she is, it could've been an accident. Something that's haunted her ever since. And that's why she skipped town. Why she's never mentioned him before coming here, and why she keeps lying to me at every turn. Something else is nagging at my thoughts, but my head is too much in a jumble to form the connection.

Since we got to this town, she's been so jumpy. Her migraines getting consistently worse. She's been fearful, and Marina Navarette is never afraid.

Maybe it's because she can still get caught.

Something else snags my attention back down. At the corner of the candid collage page, there's a black-and-white picture of a row of cheerleaders. I peer closer to the one in the middle—the queen bee—her arms are thrown wide, pom-poms in the air. But the cut of her jaw, the arrogant slant of her mouth. It's impossible. If she weren't in my house right this second, I'd swear this was—

"Find what you were looking for?" Adel's voice comes from the doorway and I jump, almost falling right off the bed. I knock a pillow onto the open yearbook and swoop the heels I'd left propped on the nightstand.

My throat is dry as blanched bones but I force myself to move in her direction. I hold up the heels but her flawless face has lost some of its amusement, giving way to something colder and impatient.

"Wonderful," she says finally. And I lead her from the room, down the stairs, and to the kitchen like I'm running on mechanical parts. After some stilted small talk, where she asks me a lot about my mom and me, Adel runs up to get her garment bags. We say goodbye, all while I'm trying not to release the scream in my head. Could it have been her? Not possible. Could be Adel's mother and they just have insanely strong genes. That's not unheard of. I mean, she did look a lot like her grandmother at the nursing home.

Either way, I was dying for her to leave so I could go back up and study the pictures closely. Except when she finally does go, and I run up the stairs, bursting into my mother's room—her bed is neatly made, the window is blown open, and there's no yearbook in sight.

18

"SO YOU THINK ADEL stole the yearbook?" Jamie keeps a tight grip on the steering wheel, maneuvering the car on the narrow road. Signs every so often warn of road flooding or wild hog crossing. Swamp water is nearly level with the asphalt, and there's no guard barrier preventing the car from falling in should he make a sudden jerk to the left. The address I managed to reveal in Roman's sketchbook is leading us to the middle of nowhere. Cutting through a nature reserve with glimmering marshlands as far as the horizon.

"Who else could've stolen it?" I say, gripping my seat as Jamie cuts a sharp turn. "I mean, she was the only one there. She could've easily sneaked into my mom's room when she went up to grab the garment bags."

I was careless. I should've gone up with her, but she'd insisted.

Jamie follows the spotty GPS down a dirt road, and I worry it's misdirected us again. The cloudy marsh looks a drop away from spilling across the street. "She could've. But I don't get why."

"I'm telling you, the picture looked exactly like her. Adel was in that yearbook, and she caught me looking at it." I settle back in my seat. "Maybe she's a vampire."

He pitches a brow. "All right, Bella, calm down. Wouldn't someone who's lived here all their lives recognize her?"

I shrug. "Would they? Ever since she 'moved back to town,'" I say, using air quotes, "it seems like she's kind of flown under the radar. Myra and Di go blank whenever I bring her up."

Jamie's expression pinches as if trying to think back. "Yeah, I guess they do. And you think that's why Adel seems hung up on your mom? Because she knew her? Like back when they were our age?"

"Yes," I breathe. Though the implications are too much for my brain to comprehend right now. Because it would mean Adel's been around for ages, and her questions about the cavern could mean her . . . affliction stems from there. I think this entire town is plagued with a secret that not everyone's in on. And my mom, Roman, Adel. They're at the heart of it.

The car bounces along the hole-ravaged road, and just when I'm about to declare we're lost, a two-story ramshackle house comes into view, the only building for miles. But the GPS confirms it: we're here.

311 Montego Rd.

More surprising is the camo truck parked up front. It's the same dirtbag from town. Jamie parks behind the old beat-up truck with a loose license plate, leaving enough space that he doesn't block it or us, should we feel the need to get the hell out of here. Chickens scatter from around the car as we get out, clucking in offense, and beer bottles pile up on the porch's railing like forgotten Christmas lights.

I can tell Jamie's making an effort not to cringe at the amount of work this place needs.

"You really think Roman came here?" Jamie asks.

I'm about to respond when the door to the screened-in porch bangs open and the leathery man comes ambling out, barely dodging whatever is thrown out after him. He yells back an obscenity, and the woman inside responds in kind.

Jamie unnecessarily takes a subtle step in front of me, acting as a shield.

The man, only half-dressed, jumps when he sees us. "Jesus Christ," he says. "What the hell you kids doing out here?"

I step past Jamie. "We're looking for Curandera Lupe . . . does she still live here?"

He snorts. "Oh yeah, the mighty curandera's inside. The old witch will outlive all of us, I tell you." He looks me up and down, then makes for the van but calls back to the house. "Perla, you got people out here looking for your crazy má. Good luck," he says to us.

"I know you took it!" Perla, I assume, yells back, coming to the door. "That money's for the mortgage, you piece of shit!" A sandal poised to throw. She brings the weapon down when she sees us, but the hard frown on her face doesn't ease. She's got the sunken eyes and pockmarked skin of a woman who's led a hard life. It makes my heart ache, though I don't know her, and she probably wouldn't even want my sympathy.

"What do you want?" she barks.

I debate telling her to forget it, we made a wrong turn, but I have to know why Roman came here. What information he was trying to glean before disappearing.

"We're here to see your mom," I say. "Curandera Lupe? I want to ask her about someone who might've consulted her a long time ago."

The woman crosses her arms, leaning against the doorframe. "Good luck with that. Má can't remember the last thing she had for breakfast. And even if she could, you know that was all bullshit, right? Má made shit up all the damn time for big-pocket out-of-towners." She picks at her teeth. "But she had the flair to sell it, that's for sure."

"Please," I say. "I just want to ask her, see if she can remember anything at all."

The woman takes her nail out of her mouth and looks me over again, raising a brow.

Jamie pulls out a twenty-dollar bill. "This is all I brought. Just for a question," he hedges.

The woman smiles, moving aside. "All right. It's your time you're wasting."

She pockets the twenty. When we follow her inside, every inch of my skin recoils. The woman's a hoarder. There are trinkets upon trinkets, clocks, plastic bins, and disassembled washing machines piled in stacks that reach the ceiling. Perla leads us through the junk like a tour guide through a maze. I almost think it's a mannequin when we get to the recliner and see the old woman staring blankly out a window.

"Má, your psychic services are needed." Perla winks at us and leaves the room.

The old woman's face shifts slowly in our direction. Her skin so thin and dry I'm afraid it'll crack with the movement.

"Curandera Lupe?" I ask.

The woman blinks. "Sí?"

She only speaks Spanish. Great. I'm rusty, and it always makes me self-conscious when I have to stumble through words. Just something else I can't nail down right.

I clear my throat, switching to Spanish. "Hello, I was hoping you can tell me something about Roman Sevilla."

Her eyes still have the glaze of fog. I try again. "A boy looking for information on la Cegua." I'm not sure if that's right, but it *feels* right.

Having mastered the language, Jamie tries, "It would've been around twenty-three years ago."

"La Cegua." The old woman stares right through us, muttering low under her breath, but something deep in her expression lights with recognition.

"A girl born under a lucky star, blessed by la Virgen de Candelaria."

I lean forward. "Is that Soledad?"

Her attention remains fixed on a distant point, but she carries on as if reciting an old story. "Weave and weave, wash and dry, she'd feed the birds, by la laguna's eye. Until a merchant came on his gleaming boat, with unbridled spirit and an ambitious gloat. A dormant part did come alive, in the silly girl's heart, when he stood by her side. Some tender song her mother would sing—of hope and longing, and terrible things. Caution, my child, take care, she said, for what is it that first brought him into your bed?"

Jamie and I exchange an uneasy look.

The rocking chair sways. "But little warning did the young girl heed, despite his demands of fortune and greed. The power she had to grant him desires, would soon earn her a cage built by a liar. The lucky bird destined to drown would bear the burden of death's crooning sound."

A shiver combs over my skin. The woman goes silent. Her story was familiar and strange all at once. A lullaby told to frighten young girls from trusting pushy men.

Jamie tries again. "What about the boy who came looking for answers? Roman?"

"Roman Sevilla?" We turn to find Perla standing behind us with an assessing gaze. "That's who you're asking about?" Her brows lower, scrutinizing us with a new suspicion that wasn't there before. She sighs. "Follow me."

Once again, we get up. Curandera Lupe starts the story from the beginning, her voice trailing behind us like a shadow. A girl born under a lucky star, an ambitious merchant, a cage built by a liar. We follow Perla into the small kitchen of peeling paint and unfinished cabinets.

"So he did come here?" I ask.

She nods. Jamie and I lean against each other as Perla searches through a cupboard. She uncorks a small bottle of whiskey and pours it into an old Valentine's Day mug.

"Do you know why he'd come to her specifically?"

We watch as Perla stuffs the bottle all the way in the back of the cupboard, hiding it from view before turning to us.

"You mean why choose my mom when the town's riddled with psychics?" She shrugs. "Má's from Villa del Sur, rumored to be where la Cegua's from. Witches." She twiddles her fingers like it's all nonsense.

Where la Cegua's from? Does she mean where Gerardo's first wife was from?

She leans her hip on the counter. "What are you two getting mixed up in? Roman Sevilla is long gone—way before you two were even born."

Jamie fidgets under the woman's glare. If I say something like a school project, she won't give us the time of day, but maybe if I'm a little honest.

"I live in the Sevilla Manor," I admit. "I've . . . found things that make me think there's more to his disappearance than people assume. I want more answers."

Her eyes narrow, and for a moment, I think I've said the wrong thing.

"Má didn't trust him. Told me the kid was rotten to the core, but I went to school with his ass so I already knew." She tips the mug back, taking a long swig before leaning forward. The whiskey's scent envelops us until my eyes prick. "You're the second one this week to come sniffing around here for that Sevilla kid."

I meet Jamie's widened eyes. "Second one?" I ask.

She sets the mug down. "Yeah, that's right. Some snooty rich kid came trampling through here not two days ago acting like we owed her something."

"It was a girl?"

Perla scowls. "Mm-hmm. Some redhead with old eyes, if that makes sense. Something not right about her."

Adel. She has to be talking about Adel. Why would she come here asking about Roman? After she was digging for information about the cavern?

"She wanted to know everything we knew about Roman. And I'll tell you exactly what I told her, I don't know nothing about his disappearance, all right? Let's get that straight."

I nod, encouraging her to continue.

"But before he vanished and this town became a zoo of cops and reporters, he went to see us in town. Well, went to see my mom. Looking for a way to break his curse. The infamous Sevilla curse." Her brow lifts at my expression. "Oh yeah, we all know about it. La Cegua has it out for them. All of them. The kid was a little asshole, just like his daddy, and the granddaddy, and those before him, I'm sure. He came looking for a quick fix, and that's just not how it works. Got real upset with us, making threats, all that nonsense. But if my family curse was fast ticking, I guess I'd be pretty desperate too."

"What was the quick fix?" I ask.

"He was trying to trap the one who cursed him."

"La Cegua," Jamie breathes.

Perla purses her lips in a disbelieving gesture. "Yup. Got it into his head he'd be the one to cheat death. If you ask me, the entire family just had bad genes. So after he refused to leave, Má spewed that honeyed BS in his head that if you had a witch's bones and found her heart, you could trap her with mustard seeds and blood, but I think she was just trying to get rid of him. A Cegua lives off vengeance. The only way to put the Cegua to rest is for the Sevilla to die. Or give up what they most desire—that part seemed to get his attention. Guess we'll never know what happened there, because he's gone."

Except maybe he's not. La Cegua is still here, though Perla doesn't know that. Why would she still be out for blood, if all the Sevillas are dead? If Roman is trapped in the cavern, could that mean la Cegua's still free to roam? Because something went wrong with his plan and he couldn't control her?

"Well, time's up," Perla says. "Hope you found what you were looking for. Next time try shaking a magic eight ball instead."

But I did get what I was looking for, so I thank her. Because we now know what Roman was after. To trap la Cegua, but there's no shortcuts. What I don't know is what la Cegua wants now, and what she's trying to get me to understand with the things she shows me.

We're led through the maze again, and I almost miss the old woman standing stock-still in a dark corner, staring at me clear-eyed and alert.

Perla puts a hand to her heart. "Jesus, Má. Scared the shit out of me."

Curandera Lupe ignores her daughter, staring in my direction. Gaze glacial clear and ripe with awareness. "Find it behind the wall. The shred of her humanity and her bones. Seal with the blood of her enemy and she is bound. Wish wisely, girl. Your fate depends on what she finds in your heart."

Perla turns to us, eyebrows raised. "See what I mean? Nonsense."

19

I LACE UP MY ANKLE BOOTS, this time prepared for the trek through the woods with mosquito repellent and long, sturdy jeans to keep the pinchy hitchhikers from scraping my skin. I'm also wearing a bathing suit underneath. Something simple I slipped on right after our visit to the curandera.

I don't know what to expect when we get to the garden door. How I can explain to Jamie that it wasn't there the last time I checked, as if the door were sentient. That it disappeared on me when I tried to go again without him.

But when he moves aside the vines, the weathered blue gate appears, as if it'd always been there. A quiet sigh of relief escapes me.

"What do you think she meant by that?" Jamie asks. "The bones and heart stuff?"

Curandera Lupe's words from this morning echo in my head, making my stomach churn. "I think it means I need to start looking for these hidden rooms Adel claimed Gerardo built."

Jamie moves aside a palm frond so I can walk ahead. "Maybe whatever Roman was trying to do to control la Cegua got him trapped instead."

I hadn't stopped to think that maybe he'd trapped himself in the cavern. Maybe there was some truth to the ritual but in reverse. It captured him instead. From what I've learned about him, he was a lot of things, but he didn't sound gullible. If he bought into this ritual, if he attempted it, he must've had more than one curandera's word to go by. After all, he came to them first looking for answers. But something must've gone wrong. Maybe he didn't have her bones, or her heart.

The footpath is sludgy after the days of rain, so we hold on to each other purely for the sake of not falling.

Jamie reaches for my elbow before I can slip on a particularly mushy patch. "Maybe it was a scam, but she still seemed to know what she was talking about. She said *wish wisely*."

Again that squirm of doubt from him. From what we're doing and the cavern. But I'm not ready for it. I'm not ready to step away from something as magical and inviting as this. Not when there's still so much to gain, so much to learn. I'm not Roman. I'm not seeking to trap anyone. On the contrary, I want . . . freedom. From everything that's held me back and kept me afraid. La Cegua's visions, the feeling I get by being at the manor, in the cave, in the woods . . . the feeling of *rightness*.

It has to count for something. Plus I'm not a Sevilla, and I'm a woman. I have nothing to threaten la Cegua. As for Jamie, he's . . . Jamie. She has no reason to hurt him.

I stop, just as we get to the clearing with the well. Like before, the electric charge fills the air, thick as humidity after a storm. Thick enough to cup and take a bite of. The tiny hairs on my nape stand. An enticing shiver unfurls beneath my skin.

We both approach the well cautiously. Now we know it's not just a place to explore—but a numinous space containing a presence that may or may not welcome us again.

The scent of cool, damp air hits me first. The soft water drips and our shoes crunch rock as we descend into the pit. Like before, the cavern light springs up from the deep and dank, and it still takes me by surprise. The rays fall toward the spring in multiple cascades. A hollow echo of undisturbed spaces.

And she still stands in the middle of it all. The veiled woman of the woods. As beautiful and serene as when I'd first seen her but with her untenable, ethereal watchfulness.

Did Roman want to trap you? Are you really responsible for so many deaths?

We make our way down to the bank, placing our bags on the ground and expecting . . . I don't know. I don't know what to expect this time. Maybe I'm asking too much of this place. Of her.

"Hello, Cegua," I whisper, but still my voice carries. And maybe, if the suspicions are correct, I should be calling her Soledad, but I don't want to say it out loud and have it be real, conjure her like a kid would Bloody Mary in the mirror. Jamie dips his head at the statue in a show of respect, and I think part of him fears the same thing.

"I feel like we should've brought her something," he says low. "Some offering. Or a gift. Think she likes Ghirardelli?"

I shush him, bumping his shoulder with mine. "Have you thought of what you want to wish for?"

He doesn't move away. Instead, he stays very still so our arms remain touching. The warmth of his skin spreads down to my feet.

"Sort of." His voice is gentle. "I don't think I should."

This catches me off guard. "But we waited . . . Cristina will be fine. There's been no other consequences."

I say this, but I have yet to answer Dorset. Each time I've tried, my throat seems to swell.

"No, it's not that." Jamie shrugs. "I just . . . I don't know. The things I really want have to be earned, I think." And his face tilts to mine and we're entirely too close, his mercurial eyes changing colors like a mood ring. His usual brown irises shadow to amber with a forest-green rim, like a woodsy tunnel you can't help but step into and explore.

There's a hint of mischief in the color.

"Wait," he says, mouth slanting. "You didn't think I meant *you*, did you?"

I feel my face go hot. I backhand his stomach. "Shut up."

"Oh god, you did." He steeples his fingers. "Listen, I like you as a person, but . . ."

I roll my eyes. "Haha. *Fine*, suit yourself. I'm making a wish, though." And when I start unbuckling my jeans, the teasing dies from his face, and he's quick to turn a shade of red, turning around to give me space—ever the gentleman.

The water feels exquisite against my burning skin. The mugginess and sweat I'd worked up on the hike get washed away as I dip my head underwater. When I come up for air, Jamie is still at the bank's edge, filling a test tube.

"Figured I should get a sample this time. Make sure we're not going to die of cholera down the road." His goofy grin withers to a grimace when he notices my expression. "Kidding, kidding. Well, I mean, sort of."

"I'll make sure to keep my head above water from now on."

He points a finger at me. "Probably for the best. So what are you going to wish for?" He zips up the tube in his backpack, whips off his shirt, and tiptoes into the water in the most adorably childlike way that's so at odds with how formidably he's built. Whatever jobs he's dabbled in have made him cut in all the right places but not enough to trim away the sweet curves of being young. It's a reminder he's not at all like the people I've dated. If you can call it that. The singular focus of my attraction was because they'd been hot and available at the moment. But I've never looked at someone and thought they were beautiful in the same way you would stare after something you covet, something you long to keep by your side.

He wades over to where I am, careful not to splash, to keep his body as unobtrusive as possible, but each ripple is like a tiny explosion against my skin. He sinks low in the water so that we're face-to-face. "So Cecilia Navarette—" I give him a warning glance about my name but he responds with a devilish grin. And if I'm being honest, I don't hate the way he says it.

"What do you most desire?"

Family, my brain supplies immediately. Because I do want that. But you can't wish for a family. I have no idea what that would look like. If the cavern would make someone come home to me who never wanted to be there in the first place. Or if it'd make moments happen between my mom and me that I could never trust.

My arms stretch as I float, staring up into the veiled woman's hidden face.

I shut my eyes tight, and what I say instead surprises even me. "A birthday party." The words carry and multiply against the cavern walls. "With balloons, streamers, cupcakes, and a ridiculous theme. Maybe pony rides and a piñata filled with all the cheap candy."

Jamie comes closer, until I'm floating beside him. "You've never had a birthday party?"

My head hits a wall, except it's Jamie's chest, and I open my eyes to find him looking down at me, his expression tinged with sadness. "Like I said, I moved around a lot." And maybe it's being here in this isolated place, and seeing that his sweet face holds no judgment that makes me go on. "I never—I was afraid no one would show up." I told my mom it was childish when she'd offer. I was embarrassed of kids coming over and noticing the cracks on the pretty picture I'd painted—the one where I was just overly independent, didn't need my mom picking me up or coming to school functions. I didn't want a dad to dance with at the Quince parties. One look at my empty bedroom, and they'd quickly realize I was nothing more than a lonely girl too afraid to put down roots. "So, I told everyone I didn't like birthday parties. I lied."

His hands frame my face. "Of course you did. Who doesn't like birthday parties?" His thumb runs across my cheek. "I'd be honored to be your first guest."

"Who else would I invite in this town?"

The way he beams does something horrible to my heart.

"Myra and Di, too, of course," I add.

"Of course. Let's see if this place knows how to throw a party then."

I smile, and make the wish, barely finish the words when everything flickers.

We're both church-quiet as the cavern goes blindingly white, as the spring shrinks down to size and the floor becomes concrete hard. We're in a pool, outside, hundreds of miles from where we started. Specifically, we're in the community pool that used to be right outside my window as a kid. One of the times my mom and I had lived alone together and she'd work until 2 a.m. bussing tables right before meeting some financial advisor and starting one of the many flings that led to her first generously substantial alimony. I used to sit on my bed and watch kids play in this pool all the time, throw parties. I'd see their parents handing out burgers and hot dogs, drinking a beer on the plastic chairs while the kids splashed and dunked and raced from one side to the other.

The pool is calm, it's only me and Jamie in the center of it—our eyes roving wildly across the vivid sky, across the plastic chairs with people I'm positive aren't really there. It's like being in one of those panoramic museum rooms that show you an aerial view of mountains and rivers and canyons. Except I can smell the sunscreen, can feel the breeze and heat of the sun on my face coupled with the airy magic of the cavern.

Kids run around the pool, and there are streamers and balloons everywhere but in black with skeleton and ghoul prints that sing to the most core part of my being. I love it. Jamie's lips are shaded in blue, as if he'd recently bitten into a cupcake. We laugh, struck with wonder, because I'm sure I probably look the same. There's a hat tied to my head with an elastic band, and it's the most absurd thing about this entire moment.

"Happy birthday," Jamie whispers, awed. And just as he says it, the lights dim, the water dissipates and I'm sitting in an ornate chair wearing a constricting party dress in the dining hall of the manor. There's a flower pinned to my dress. A rose. When I touch it, a tiny thorn pricks at my fingers, making blood well and drip onto the floor.

The room is shrouded in dark wallpaper with prickly vines that seem to move as if caught in a light wind. The long dining table stretches fathomlessly into the dark. Jamie sits to my right, eyes wild, gripping the edge of his chair. To my left are small children chattering, but I can't see their faces. The shadows pull at their features until they're indiscernible—ghosts. The disquieting sensations grip my throat until I can barely squeeze out a breath. On the other side of the dining room, from the door that should lead into the kitchen, two people step through the dark threshold. Again, their features are obscured, their silhouettes visible only because of the lit birthday candles on the cake they carry. I push back into my seat.

Happy birthday to you.

The figures step closer, swaying side by side, singing as if from a distance. I lean forward, ice encasing my spine.

Happy birthday to you.

It's a man and a woman. My mother's familiar lilt high on the notes, and his . . .

Happy birthday, our dear Cecilia.

The man leans forward and places the cake on the other side of the table that feels impossibly long and far away. I can almost make out his features . . . I can almost see who he is . . .

Happy birthday to you.

The cake slides across the table toward me. I catch a glimpse of my mother's face before she's gone. Poofs from existence. The only one left standing there is Roman. He slams his hands against the table, sending a rattling pulse up my arm. His skin is a grotesque blue, the irises of his eyes filmy like curdled milk. My lungs constrict. I don't have time to scream—I can't—

"Find it," Roman urges, glancing over his shoulder. "Behind the wall! Where a Sevilla belongs. Find it!"

Fear gusts through my mind like a cyclone. I try standing, leaving, but I can't move. My heart is a tangled root of knots in my chest. "F—find what?"

His frantic urgency pauses, his ghastly face twisted in tender pain. He looks my age, dead so young, but the weight of his gaze is decades old. It's otherworldliness tinged in a very human emotion—longing. A splinter of loss infects me with that look. "Cecilia . . ."

From the shadowed darkness, a long-nailed hand clamps onto Roman's shoulder, and this time I do yell. I can't stand. I can't help. "Make it right!" he pleads. "Stop her! Wish . . ." He's sucked into the darkness as the room dissolves, and I scream until that's all that exists. Until it's only the echo of my voice playing over and over in the void.

When I open my eyes again, when the scream subsides, I'm on the cavern's bank, and Jamie is there gathering me to him like I'm a child found wandering alone. Jamie presses me tightly to his chest, as if he could stuff me into the cavity of his ribs. His hand runs over and over my hair, soothing the tremors as he murmurs softly.

"What happened?" he asks. "You disappeared. I got so scared, you just disappeared."

I pull back, pressing a fist onto my stomach until the ache subsides. "I—you didn't see him?"

Jamie's brow furrows. "Him? No, it was just your mom. She gave you a cake, told you to make a wish, and when you blew out the candles, you disappeared. Is that not what you saw?"

I sniff, blinking up at him with aching, fractured eyes. Again, Roman didn't appear to him. He's only shown himself to me, but I don't understand what he wants. What's he leading me to, and what or who is holding him back from saying more? La Cegua showed me what's in Roman's heart and I didn't like what I found there. Still, la Cegua is a supernatural creature meant to hunt and lure. Trap. It'd be unwise to trust either of them, but what I do know is that I'm drawn to this. I belong to this somehow and I'm going to figure out why.

It's the returning retreat in Jamie's expression that makes me say what I say next. Because I'm not ready to give this up just yet. And I don't want to do this alone.

"It was nothing," I say, steadying the pounding in my chest. "I must've just stayed in the vision longer. I thought I saw someone else there, but it was only a shadow." Just a ghost.

20

I'M HIT WITH A FIT OF COUGHS as I unroll yet another blueprint. Dust settles all over the velvety fabric of my blouse, and I won't have time to change before Myra's party. But I remembered the box from the garage, the ancient-looking blueprints and documents.

If I'm supposed to find something where a *Sevilla belongs*, getting as close as possible to a map of the manor is my best bet.

Roman had said to find *it. Behind the wall.* Curandera Lupe had used the same words, said that's where I would find la Cegua's heart and bones. Roman could've meant the same thing. He must've had her bones somehow, obsessed with finding a way to break his curse. But could he have found whatever embodies her humanity—her heart? And why would Roman want me to find it? I don't have the blood of her enemy, or any desire to trap her. Not unless she tries to hurt us. But how the hell am I supposed to know where a Sevilla belongs? I'm not even sure if I should help him.

A shadow falls across me from the garage door and I startle but it's only Jamie.

His fist is poised on the wall as if he were about to knock.

"I didn't want to scare you." He takes in the piles of blueprints around me, the dust no doubt streaked on my face. "Am I . . . too early? You said pick you up at one, right?"

I puff out my cheeks. "I got a little sidetracked."

"I see that." He sits cross-legged on the ground beside me, reaching over and wiping a casual thumb across my forehead, as if it's the most natural thing in the world. I thank him and turn away before he can see the heat rising up my neck. I explain what I'm doing, excluding some details since he still doesn't know Roman appeared at the well yesterday.

Jamie picks up a leather-bound journal I hadn't noticed inside the box. "So you think Roman might've had secret rooms around the house like Gerardo?"

I shrug. "Maybe Roman just repurposed them."

Tendrils of hair fall across Jamie's brow. He doesn't notice since his hyperintense focus is on whatever he's reading inside the journal. His increasing frown makes my stomach dip.

"What is it?" I ask.

He finally looks up, then flips the pages over so I can read too. It's a diary, handwritten in severe cursive. A date on top reads 1946. The signature at the bottom is Percival's. As in Percival Sevilla, the religious fanatic who brought an influx of psychics to Santa Aguas.

What's strange is that the journal is bookmarked with sticky notes and marked with highlighter. "I'm pretty sure highlighters didn't exist in the 1940s," I say.

"They didn't." Jamie points at one of the marked passages. "Someone made note of this for a reason."

The Angel of Death came to me again in a dream. Told me where to find her bones.

I suck in a breath.

"Look at the other highlights," Jamie says, flipping a few pages.

I fear I've angered her. Have I not been pious enough? I made the cavern her temple. I hid her bones in the manor house as she commanded. I've guarded her heart. What more can I do?

The sticky note over the page is in familiar handwriting. The same scrawl that was in Roman's sketchbook. *The last piece. Are the letters her heart? Her connection to Villa del Sur?*

"The letters . . ." I say, looking up at Jamie. "He must've found the bones and what he assumed was her heart. He thought he had everything right for the ritual to control her."

Jamie rubs a hand over his jaw. "But he was wrong."

He must've been. The rest of the journal stops at the year 1949, devolving into frantic, nonsensical prayers and scribbles. If the Sevilla curse took hold, then Percival must've died before he could turn thirty.

I go back to the blueprints, tracing a finger over the hand-drawn lines of the manor when it was first built. A map of young bones and cartilage to house the infamous Sevillas. The blueprint in front of me is dated 1891. Additional rudimentary drawings are layered over the original design on yellowed tracing paper. Extra closets and bedrooms.

I'm careful flipping through them. There's a room under the staircase that I already learned now holds the electrical boxes and central air conditioner. A few jotted designs over the bathroom and kitchen for plumbing and fixtures.

Some of the rooms are labeled. My mom's room is labeled the "bridal suite." There's a few with "guest," and I find mine simply as the "sewing room."

I tap on it. "Look at this. It says the sewing room, but that's actually my room now. It's pretty big for a sewing room."

There's a brief moment where my sight loses track of the blueprint and instead goes deep into the lockbox of dreams. Or visions. I think of Soledad on the grass, her cheek tender, her husband building the door, and a meticulously embroidered flower on her dress. A white sacuanjoche—a tropical flower she might've stitched on herself.

"Maybe Soledad used my room. Maybe it was special to her." A place made to create.

I catch the scent of Jamie's cologne. It's soft and smoky, and curls in my chest like invasive roots straining to take hold of hard dirt.

His eyes are wide. "And you think that's where she wanted Percival to hide . . . something?"

"Maybe." I stand. The rest of the blueprint is just technical jargon, and no sight of the supposed "groom's room," assuming Gerardo had his own.

On a hunch, I grab the crowbar and hammer on my way out, aware I look like a serial killer storming through the house. It's time to really start looking, even if that means taking a sledgehammer to it all.

Jamie follows after. "You have a very scary glint in your eye right now, and I have to say it's kind of hot."

I roll my glinty eyes but smile. Whatever he's seeing is only a fraction of the rampaging chaos inside my chest. And it's such an odd sensation to be filled with so much at once. To be overwhelmed with emotion. With this impulse to do something, *solve* something. When for so long, the emptiness felt endless. You could drop a coin inside me and never hear it reach the bottom.

AN HOUR LATER, I'm army crawling out from under my bed. Jamie and I have knocked on every wall panel, lifted carpet, moved dressers, and I've broken two nails trying to find a wedge in the floorboards. I officially have to change before we leave.

Jamie's jeans have seen better days, too, and I feel mildly guilty that I wasted so much time.

"I never thought the first time you'd invite me into your bedroom would be to tear it apart." Jamie is plopping down on the window seat with an exhausted puff of breath when I lean against my closet door and feel it. An electric pulse so subtle I can almost dismiss it for my imagination. I whip open the door and the pulse becomes a shrill in my ears.

"The sewing machine," I breathe.

Jamie helps me wheel it out. I look inside and under the attached pine wood cabinet, wiggle the foot pedal, but don't find a thing. Except the static that digs under my skin is still there, and I know something's hiding. When I run my hands over the cold metal of the sewing machine, some of the stenciled veneer peels off and I notice the entire contraption is loose from its wood base.

Jamie comes back with the crowbar and hands it to me. Sweat beads on my forehead. I jab the bar under the metal base and lift. The sound of it cracking away from the wood reverberates across my molars, but there's no going back now. When the entire machine comes off, I stare into the hidden nook.

"There really was something in here," Jamie says in disbelief, as if this entire time he's merely been going along with my destructive rampage for moral support.

There's a booklet on dress patterns, including one for a Ladies Outing Jacket. I open a red velvet case with sewing needles, a few embroidered linens with the same sacuanjoche flower.

And then a metal case.

I bring it out, the edges sharp with rust, then carefully open it.

There's a doll. A ragged little thing, delicate as a spider's web. The hair is made of dyed black thread. The white dress has a bold

Nicaraguan pattern riddled with sewing pins. When I pick her up, small seeds fall from her pockets. Red and black seeds.

"Are those . . ."

"Mustard seeds," I say. The floor shifts beneath us like the rocking of waves. The entire room swims in my vision the moment I bring the doll close to my chest.

Again I'm traveling back. Hurtling through time and space until hands that aren't mine are grabbing hold of the doll's soothing figure.

Mama looks at me like I'm already lost to her. I can't stand to see the pain in her eyes.

"Para qué recuerdes siempre de dónde vienes."

A cold tear slips down my cheek. "Mama, I will always remember where I'm from. This isn't goodbye. Gerardo will bring me back whenever I wish it. He promised."

My mother's smile is pain filled, her eyes telling me she doesn't believe this. But I need her to. I can't leave home without her knowing that I will be back. This place holds my heart.

My sisters hug me one by one, their smell of wildflowers and sugar water tight on their skin. They tell me to write to them, and I promise. I promise I will.

As the horses are brought around, I feel each one of my doll's needles press into my chest.

Jamie's voice wrenches me out of the vision. "I can't believe the doll's been hidden here all this time. Do you think it was hers?"

I feel as if I've traveled across oceans, across time, but it must've been a single moment. Private, for me to see. There's a sting pressing into the backs of my eyes, and it takes me seconds too long to figure out whose skin I'm in.

"Yes," I manage. "It's hers." Her heart. The shred of her humanity Curandera Lupe cautioned me to find. It wasn't letters. It had to be this.

Jamie's typing on his phone. "Myra wants to know if we're almost there. What should I say?"

I put everything away, except the doll, leaving her propped against my nightstand. Out in the open where she belongs. "Tell her we're on the way."

21

JAMIE KNOCKS ON MYRA'S DOOR. "You sure you're up for this?"

I'm staring blankly at the tchotchkes on the porch. The sun-and-moon terra-cotta figurine on the wall that spells out the duality of every warring emotion running through me. I don't know what to feel.

"It's been a long day," I say instead, but I give Jamie a half-hearted smile and he's gotten to know me well enough to know that it's the most I can muster.

I fidget as we wait for the door to open, looking down at the birthday bag that feels a stone too empty.

"She's going to love it," Jamie says, reading my mind.

A woman who looks exactly like Myra opens the door, and she rushes me like a linebacker. I assume she's Myra's mom. Short and fierce like her daughter, with thick arms meant for suffocating hugs. A brief flash of a memory runs through my mind—my mom flexing her arms, calling them brazos de molenderas. Arms made for rolling out tortillas and kneading breads. It was such a rare thing for her to say—to express something about Nicaragua without anything other than annoyed detachment.

"Oh my god," Myra's mom rambles, pulling me back to take a good look. "I have so many questions for you."

Funny, because I have so many questions for her. The Sevilla expert.

"I'm Carolina. It's so nice to meet you!"

She rushes at Jamie next, fixing a stray hair that'd been sticking up on his head since we demolished my room.

"Hola, Señora Casador," Jamie intones in his adorably practiced Spanish, straightening as if waiting for a gold star. Carolina speedily asks him how his day has been in her singsongy Mexican accent, and he just as easily responds, with a sidenote in my direction that he took three years of Spanish in school and practices Duolingo like a religion (his words). The fact that he takes an interest in learning the language, my language, even if I rarely get the chance to speak it anymore, makes an unsettling warmth spread through my chest.

I hear Myra call for her from inside.

Carolina's smile is wide, and again I see Myra in her features. "Come in, come in."

Di has an arm around Myra on the couch when we come in, and their faces both light up. And Jamie was right, Myra loves the gift. A little goblin duende figurine I'd found in one of the manor's rooms with covered furniture.

"You shouldn't have given me anything! It's your day, silly."

I don't have time to ask her what she means, because Carolina peppers me with questions about the manor all through dinner.

"So your mom bought the house but you have no connection to the Sevillas?"

I shake my head, accepting the offered plate. "None. My mom used to clean the manor with her aunt, and I guess it stuck with her."

Carolina plops down on her chair. "Who could blame her? That place is . . ."

"Terrifying," Di says, cutting off the crispy corners of her brownie.

"Magical," Myra adds, around a mouthful of yellow rice.

"Yes," her mom agrees. "Magical. When they had their first estate sale, I wanted *everything*." She seems to realize something. "I swear I'm not a tragedy chaser. I wasn't there for any of Roman's things like everyone else."

"I didn't think that," I assure her.

She smiles, a little embarrassed. "I just like collecting antiques. I'm a history professor; it's an occupational hazard." Carolina gets up from the table once we're done with dinner and dims the lights. I'm mentally preparing for the birthday cake that no doubt will have me reliving that scene from the cavern.

Myra's mom comes back in with the cake. Black frosting with little fondant skeletons. I'm about to join in on the song, on the clapping, when I realize everyone's staring at me.

Carolina places the cake in front of me.

Happy birthday to you.

No. This is all wrong. I meet Jamie's gaze and he's just as shocked.

Happy birthday, dear Cecilia.

This party . . . it can't be for me.

Happy birthday to you.

They're all waiting for me to blow out the candles. Myra's expression elated. But this is her birthday. I took her day with my wish.

When I blow out the candles, I ask for things to go back to how they're meant to but of course it doesn't work. This isn't the cavern, and all I can do is go along with it.

AFTER WE'VE HAD our fill of cake, where I'm too embarrassed to meet Jamie's eyes, we filter into the living room. Jamie offers to pick up the dishes, and Carolina gives his arm a grateful squeeze, but he steps up beside me first, whispering so the others don't overhear.

"It's not your fault, okay?"

I finally look at him. "Of course it is. I wished it and now . . ."

He holds my hand for a brief moment. "And now we celebrated, all of us together. We'll make it up to Myra." He smiles. "You know her. She would've shared her day with you anyway."

I swallow thickly.

"So, Mom," Myra says, coming up beside me. "Ceci wants to know a little more about Gerardo and his first wife. I told her you'd be the perfect person to ask." Myra inclines her head, signaling that now's the time to segue into my original purpose for inviting myself over, before I knew it was Myra's birthday, and now that I'd hijacked it completely, I feel even worse.

But Carolina's eyes alight with the same kind of spark Myra's get when she delves deep into history.

"Ah," she says. "Soledad Valeria de las Raíces."

My heart ignites at the name.

"We'll let you nerds get to it," Myra says, tossing a wink my way. She walks behind my chair and gives me a hug. "Thank you for the duende. I love him. Even if it is your birthday."

My stomach gives a squeeze and Carolina ushers me and Jamie into her office. A small messy room with warm lighting and floor-to-ceiling books ranging from ancient to old. But it feels cozy, just like the rest of the house.

"I don't think I've ever been in here," Jamie remarks.

"That's because I know you, Jamiesito. You'd feel the need to rearrange my books and papers, and then I'd have to kill you."

Carolina misses Jamie's pout because she's turned to her shelves, scanning through a stack of old magazines in their sleeves.

"There's not a lot on Soledad, and considering the town wouldn't even exist if not for her"—she plucks one of the magazines out, removes the sleeve, and lays it in front of us—"it's a travesty."

"This," she says, "is a profile written by a frenemy of Gerardo's after his death—a eulogy turned diatribe, if you will. You should read some of the old society columns that came out shortly after; people were not happy with the article. But basically it boils down to the fact that Gerardo was painted like a villain. And people just don't want to hear that about their town's founder, despite the fact that he did plenty to earn the reputation on his own."

Carolina opens the magazine to an old reprinted feature. A picture of Gerardo Sevilla stares out from the page. A serious mouth and those dark, piercing eyes Roman must've inherited from the generations.

She points to a small, highlighted section. "This is the only part where he mentions Soledad, but it sheds some light on the superstitions that spread through town."

Jamie and I lean in, both of us reading.

After living a stint in Granada, Gerardo followed his golden nose to Villa del Sur, where fate would lead him to his very own witch.

It was through one of these drunken rallies that he confided in me his reason for setting his sights on Villa del Sur. There were whisperings of a family of a most unusual nature. Witches, to be frank, who could heal small ailments or make a man go bald with a single word. What interested Gerardo was word of their most prized, Soledad Valeria de las Raíces. She was said to bring those in her favor quite the fortune, their heart's desires, and as luck would have it, she fancied Gerardo enough to leave her family behind and condemn her town to its new fate of political patronage.

A witch able to grant desires. It's her. I think of the doll. The goodbye between her mother and sisters.

"What does that mean?" Jamie asks. "'Fate of political patronage'?"

Carolina perches at the edge of her desk and sighs. "That's a lot to unpack, and again, there's little info on what really happened, but I have done some digging, and I can pretty much sum up the rest of that article. The author had a propensity for circling the damn point. What he meant by political patronage is that when Gerardo went looking for his meal ticket in Villa del Sur, he wasn't only looking for a witch. He was looking for a town with little political power. Nicaragua's coffee bean revolution was only beginning. There were plenty of rural cities still run by the indigenous population that had been there for centuries. When the political system changed, rich patrons ran to appropriate the land of those who had neither the means nor the knowledge to retain their property."

"So they just took the land and displaced everyone?"

Carolina's nod is world-weary. "Pretty much, or they'd take them on as the labor force. In the case of Villa del Sur, households and land were almost entirely owned and run by women. Widowed women, and even women who'd never gotten married. That was extremely rare during that time. But then—"

"Gerardo," I say.

"Gerardo." Carolina sighs. "He'd amassed a bit of land in other parts of Nicaragua because of his affiliations, but wasn't satisfied. He wanted somewhere closer to Granada—the political epicenter. When he learned of Villa del Sur, I don't think he was as concerned with the supposed witch magic his new bride had to offer, but the territory that came with it through her family's land rights."

Centuries-old anger boils through my veins. "But she went with him? She left and came here, and stuck with him." My anger feels displaced. I know it's not her I should be angry with, but the man who put her in that position to begin with.

Still, I can't shake it. I think of my mom. I think of all the men she's let trample through our lives. I don't understand why being alone is such a terrible option.

"Oh, darling," Carolina says, "it was a very different world back then. Even before the property laws changed, women could run a household but couldn't afford to maintain it. They'd still have children because contraception was nonexistent, and they had no bodily autonomy."

My shoulders sag. "Did anyone else write about what happened to Soledad, once she got here?"

Carolina handles the magazine with care, placing it gently back in its sleeve. "Only that Soledad became depressed, took little interest in town politics or appearances. She was branded insane and forgotten. It was said she left one night and was presumed to have died in the wilds."

Typical. The woman who started it all was erased from history. And I have a feeling she wasn't going to let them get away with it. I understand now why Roman and the rest of the town reached the conclusion that they did. Soledad is la Cegua. She's haunting Santa Aguas so she won't be forgotten.

My legs are restless, the prickling waver beneath my skin that I usually get near the well comes creeping back, standing my hairs on end.

Some change in my expression must be noticeable, because Jamie slides his hand over, long fingers engulfing mine. This time his eyes shine a crystalline gold from the lamplight. A color so lovely I've never seen it on a palette.

"And . . . I'm out," Carolina announces looking between us. "I'll give you two a moment."

"Oh," I say. "No, it's—"

But she's already backing out, hands raised. "It's all right. I was a teenager once too."

Heat floods my face. I almost feel the fire on my teeth, and it only gets worse when I look at Jamie's more-than-amused expression.

"She thinks you're hot for history."

I smack a hand over my eyes, which only makes him laugh. "Oh my god. Anyway, back to the Sevillas—"

Jamie's expression sobers. He checks down the hallway to make sure we're alone, but for an entirely different reason.

"You think his first wife was haunting him?" Jamie asks. "Maybe because she didn't really disappear but instead he . . ." He runs a finger across his neck.

"You think he killed her?" I pull my sweater tighter around me, the smell of Carolina's old books reminiscent of wood rot.

Jamie shrugs. "Maybe. That would be the recipe to a vengeful spirit in the woods. La Cegua is a creature born of tragedy and abuse, fueled by revenge."

My mind whirls with thoughts. "The fact that he used her for land would also be enough to make her vengeful."

Why not stop after Roman went missing, though? All those missing posters around town. The superstitions that still live on and keep everyone afraid. Her work here feels nowhere near finished. Maybe because people continue to be shitty.

Jamie's expression clouds with worry. "We're messing with some dark stuff. La Cegua, or Soledad, or whoever she is—she's not exactly known for being benevolent."

"After everything they put her through, who could blame her? I mean, what if the stories are just that—cautionary tales skewed to fit some patriarchal bullshit angle? I mean a bogeywoman designed to stop men from straying?"

He winces at this. "Yeah, I mean, I'm not saying I fall for all of it, but the town does have a history of—you know."

I cross my arms. "Finding jerks on the side of the road nursing a raging hangover?"

His face goes dark. "It's more than that. She doesn't just gently return these guys—she destroys them. Leaves them empty. Myth or not, she's earned a pretty real rep around here."

"But haven't most of them been assholes anyway?"

He rears back, and I think maybe I've hit too deep. I've said something I can't take back. He looks down at his lean hands, kneading each finger. "That doesn't matter. They're still people, and . . . I mean, they have families. People who care about them."

I think of his dad that day outside the grocery store. The way he talked down to him because he was wasted. The way Jamie's perpetually smiling face was drawn tight, shuttered with pain, and I hated seeing him that way. Now I realize what he fears—that his dad could easily become one of those men. Become one of her victims.

"Jamie . . ." The apology is there, right in my voice, and he looks up at me, long-lashed and vulnerable like the damn poster boy of innocence. It tears a spike through my lungs. "I wasn't thinking. I'm sorry. You're right. Whatever's out there is dangerous, and we should—we should be armed with as much knowledge as we can. We should be wary."

His smile is still hesitant, like watery sunshine peeking through after a storm, and I don't want it to be like that between us. I don't want him to feel like he needs to please me, or agree with everything I say. I don't want to be just one more job, another thing for him to fix.

I grab hold of his hand, and it surprises both of us.

"I don't know why, but I feel a connection to her."

His eyes soften.

"I don't often trust my instincts, but I'm trying to do things differently. I'm trying . . ." Our hands tighten, and I don't know how it's happened, but he's tugged me toward him enough that his breathing and mine are almost one.

"I'm trying to *feel*."

He nods, like he gets it. But I'm not even sure I do. All I can think about is his hand moving to my waist. The fact that I brought it there. The way his fingers are curling into my shirt, pressing into my skin.

A clatter of footsteps comes crashing from down the hall, driving us apart.

"Ceci!"

I'm still panting when Myra comes barreling into the room, grabbing hold of my arm and pulling me with her into the living room. "You guys can make out later. It's your mom! She's on the news!"

22

I'M WEDGED INTO THE TINY SOFA beside Myra's grandmother and Jamie, watching the news, but I might as well be on the other side of the world with how distant I feel from my body. Every part of me is numb.

The infographic scrolls by at the bottom of the news anchor's face. "Latina Wife Switches to the Defense in $15.7 Million Scholin Case: Is It Love or Promise of Payout?"

I don't see what the hell her being Latina has anything to do with it or why they found it necessary to call it out, but it's not surprising that they would.

Jamie shoots me a worried glance. I can't look at him right now. I can't look at anyone.

Scholin is David's last name, my mom's ex-husband. The news report is about the fraud charges against his online pharmaceutical company. The news anchor skims quickly over the trial, the investors that were called in to testify, the company employees that are being countersued by Scholin in an effort to redirect blame for fudging the numbers and falsifying prescriptions. And then I see her. Her name big and bold, because this is the winning journalistic piece the news media is after: Marina Navarrete. An image of her in one of her signature widow hats in chastity white is frozen at the top of the screen.

"Is she okay?" Myra asks.

"She's fine. Just perfect." The news station plays the recording they must've taken earlier in the day. My mom's being escorted to a black town car by a security detail. So poised and shiny you'd never know she'd spent the last few days pawning off her stuff. And if you didn't know her, you wouldn't be able to tell that she's hiding the exhaustion from her eyes, the darkened rim underneath. From the camera's angle, all you see are the reporters' graspy little hands clawing for my mom's white suit, as if they were venerating a saint. "Ms. Navarrete! Ms. Navarrete! Will you be overseeing Scholin's corporation? What about the money that's owed to investors? Will you be moving back to Mr. Scholin's home?"

In the video, my mother steps into the back seat of the town car, closing the door and bringing all questions to an end, but then she rolls down the tinted windows. She leaves her giant glasses on her face, no doubt to hide the emotionless mask behind it. I have a throw pillow in a choke hold.

"My daughter and I will be moving back to *our* home. That we share with Mr. Scholin. We'll wait for him however long it takes."

We'll wait for him. The clip ends there and devastation floods through me. A familiar ache so frigid it burns off nerve endings until I can't feel anything at all.

Mom's reconciling with David. He might be released. All of it has been televised like some damn reality show. But she can't be serious. Mom can't go back to him. Back to the same man who stole from us. Who would introduce her at times as his "exotic" wife. Who, on more than one occasion, had called me a vacuous bitch behind my mother's back.

"You think it's true?" Jamie's hand twitches in my direction, as if he wants to comfort me.

"I don't know," I whisper, wiping the sleeve of my shirt over my mouth. "I don't know."

He keeps glancing at me, afraid I'll break down. Afraid I'll cry. I can't remember the last time I cried. I don't even think it's possible at this point.

I've thought about it more than once. That I might be broken. That the rivers of my veins are more ice than blood.

"She could've just been saying what the lawyers asked of her," Di offers. "Maybe it's just to hold back the press."

It could be, but I don't know. I don't know.

I meet Jamie's worry-filled eyes, and I don't even have to say it out loud. He nods, gets up. A task given in just a glance, and it's his nature to respond.

He pretends to stretch. "Well, it's getting late. Mind if I take you home a bit early?" he asks me. "Sorry guys, I have work tomorrow."

This sends a wave of groans through everyone, except Myra's grandmother, who fell asleep a few minutes ago, curled up like a little mouse in her blanket.

I thank them all for having me and appreciate that no one asks whether I'm okay. I'm fine. Just fine.

I'm quiet for the ride. We're halfway to my house, my mind a million miles away. We keep the windows down and the air is warm and pine filled. The car's speed makes the wind sharp as a needle's point.

Jamie keeps darting his gaze in my direction, too busy gauging my mood to realize someone's standing outside in the dark. I scream. Dig my feet into the car's floor. There's a man in the middle of the road, trying to wave down the car or stumble out of the way. Jamie cuts the steering wheel to the shoulder just in time, and along with the seat belt, the weight of Jamie's arm slams against my chest as he breaks to a full stop.

"Holy shit, are you okay? Are you all right?" Jamie glances back at the man in the road. "What the hell is he doing?"

"Jamie," I say, giving a pointed look down at my crushed boobs and his forearm. But he doesn't have time to be flustered, because he's out of the car running toward the man, who I now recognize as the same guy outside of the grocery store that day. His dad.

As soon as Jamie opens the back door and starts helping his father inside, I get a waft of sweat and beer.

"What were you thinking?"

The man makes a groaning sound in response and takes up the entire back seat to lie down. Jamie slams the door and comes back to the driver's side. I take in more of the fresh air from outside because the smell is overwhelming and lean forward as the man adjusts himself, kicking the back of my seat. Jamie rests his forehead on the steering wheel for a full minute, and I don't say a word, giving him as much time as he needs right now.

Finally, Jamie lifts his head. "I'm so sorry about this—he's—he gets caught up with work and forgets to eat before he drinks, and with all the sinkholes he's been investigating—"

I place a steady hand on his arm. "You don't have to explain. It's okay."

His expression doesn't budge—a bleakness that can't be masked—and it cinches my lungs. "I'll need to take him back home, though."

"I know. Just drop me off and we'll meet up at school on Monday."

He opens his mouth as if to say something but his dad lets out a whimper of pain. I glance back to find that he's barefoot, tiny rocks embedded in his skin. Jamie puts the car into drive and we leave in silence. The more time that passes, the more agitated he becomes. His hands tighten on the steering wheel in a white-knuckled grip. I stare outside to the flickering wall of trees, the pressure in the car building like a noxious fog. My mind keeps replaying the same image of my mother, not from the news but from right before she left for the weekend, when she'd stood at my door and told me she was proud of me. The same soft-spoken lies she'd given the reporter.

"This really sucks," Jamie says, cracking the silence. His chest rises and falls. "We had plans. He's always going on about how *I'm* drifting. That I don't have direction, but look at him." Jamie glances back at his passed-out father, who's breathing fitfully in his sleep. I do look at him, and I can tell they're nothing alike, despite their common features. Jamie's voice grows quiet. "I mean, what if she takes him? La Cegua? The town drunks, the wanderers. They're always the ones to disappear."

A knot forms in my stomach. "We're going to figure this out before anyone can get hurt, okay?"

Jamie slouches. "Sometimes I don't know why I choose to stay with him."

"He's your dad," I say, hearing it sound as hollow out loud as it does in my head.

"Well, he hasn't been a really good one." He wipes a hand down his face, glancing back at his dad's sleeping form. "He wasn't a really good husband either."

"I wish I had some wisdom to offer, but—" I wave my hand as if that were explanation enough, which I guess in a way it is.

"Yeah." Jamie gives me a relieved look. A relief I was unfamiliar with until lately. It's one of understanding. Knowing you're not alone in the world.

"Maybe one day we'll have our own kids to traumatize as we see fit." It's meant to sound sarcastic, but the words come out with more fear than humor.

"Or, we can be the ones to break the cycle."

I swallow. "Maybe."

Jamie turns onto the manor's street, past the open iron gates.

Once in front of the empty house, my anger comes sweltering back. Jamie leaves the car running for his dad and walks me up the steps. We hover at the threshold, staring at each other in silence. The air is so dense between us, I could mistake it for water. I could pretend we're somewhere else.

Sometimes there's an understanding between two people that's too great to put into words. A silent exchange that's louder than anything spoken. When Jamie reaches for me, gathering me into a hug, I know instinctually what to do. I know where my head should rest, and where my hands can touch to make us fit.

With his face buried in my hair, he whispers, "Please, don't go to the cave. Wait for me." I don't say anything. "Don't wish for anything rash . . ." he adds, as if he suspects the truth.

I pull away. Place a hand against his chest and push back, breaking an embrace that felt too much like home. "I won't," I say, regret cloying my throat. "I'll wait." But the moment I say it, I know it's a lie. One I deliver soft-eyed and earnest like I learned from my mother.

THE SKY AT DUSK looks like a watercolor painting, the sun rays painted with a smudged thumb over the clouds. My ankles grow cold with mud, and I don't care if my mom shows up at the manor only to find it empty. Only to not look for me at all.

I expect to feel afraid as I plunge down into the dark pit of the well, but the pervasive ice inside my chest doesn't let fear take root. I think about what I want to ask over and over, reeling the thoughts back in when they seem to go too far. I wish she'd stop thinking of herself. I wish we could stay in Santa Aguas longer. I wish she'd stop being such a money-hungry bitch.

I wish she'd want me. Would, for once, choose me.

It feels different here when I'm alone, darker and more foreboding. When the stairs end, the cavern opens up like an alligator's maw. Drips echo around the domed cavern, and there's a deep frequency in the place, as if a meditation bowl had been rung with a mallet.

I take off my sodden boots, the scratch of sand and tiny rocks scraping along my feet before they hit the water.

I don't know what I'm doing. If this is right. I don't know who I should be asking.

"Roman," I try, whispering it like you would whisper *I miss you* to a grave. An eerie echo sweeps through the cavern but no answer comes. I can almost feel the air recoil. So instead I try, "Soledad," and a silvery sheen ripples across the cavern walls before everything goes still and quiet. With a groan of rock, the marble statue's face tilts up, and I fall back, scrambling over the hard ground until my back hits the cavern wall. She doesn't move from her pedestal. But I know I'm being watched. Being heard.

A downpour of warmth spreads down my body, that welcoming sensation of home. Of love. Because deep down, that's all she was, until it was twisted into something bitter and cruel.

My throat is bone dry as I say, "Help me. I'm not ready to leave yet." And I don't have to go on. I feel the change in the cavern air. A tightening release, as if the presence here had let out a held breath. I realize then it's not about the words of the wish.

It's always been about the intention.

23

A PHONE VIBRATES and I startle awake. Sunlight beams on my face. My neck is stiff as I sit up and hit the steering wheel. The steering wheel? I look around—I'm in Roman's car. How the hell did I get in here? Was I sleepwalking again? Gabe had left the car out to fix, but I don't remember climbing in. In fact, I can't remember anything past the cavern . . . and my wish.

My wish. *Shit*. I didn't even stop to consider the wording, or all the possible consequences. I didn't stop to think of anything at all besides myself.

Outside the garage, there's a trail of soggy footprints on the pavement leading to Roman's car, and I can't tell if they're mine.

My phone vibrates again. It's somewhere under me. I dig my hands underneath my seat, hand roaming clumsily before my fingers wrap around my phone. I fumble with it. There's a series of notifications on top and a local number I don't recognize, but I answer the call.

"Hello?" I clear my throat.

"Oh, thank god. Ceci, it's Gabe." He sounds so rattled. "I don't know if you got my messages, but I'm in the hospital with your mom."

I CAN HEAR my own heartbeat pounding in my ear. The fretful drive to see my mother too reminiscent of the last time I drove by myself, but somehow I was able to make it here without crashing this time. When I get to the hospital, the smells make something inside my chest wither. I know everyone says it, but the stench of hospitals is a visceral reminder that the world isn't safe. That no one is free of sickness or death. Or wish-induced accidents.

My stomach hollows as I let the emergency room nurse know who I'm here to see, and she opens the doors leading to the curtained triage rooms. Immediately I see Gabe outside one of the cubicles, pinching the bridge of his nose. He looks up and spots me.

"Oh good, you're here." He takes a deep breath, a placating hand going up. "Like I said on the phone, she's okay. Just a sprain, a few bruises. She's fine—"

"I'm not fine," my mother cries from behind the curtain. "I'm in agony and these people won't give me anything stronger!"

The curtain is thrust aside and a nurse stomps out sweaty and scowling. My mom is propped up on way more pillows than I think a hospital usually provides. There's a bag of her colorful clothes beside her, a drippy ice pack, and about five different cups of apple juice and coffee. But her wrapped leg is propped on a foam wedge and there's gauze on her forehead, making my throat tighten.

Did I do this? Is this really because of my wish?

I sit on the chair beside her. "How'd this happen, Mom?"

My mom's bronze complexion darkens like she's embarrassed. "It was dumb. I was crossing the street toward the salon this morning, when that same damn camo truck didn't look where they were going and slammed into me." She makes a pitiful noise reaching for her juice so I hand it to her.

It was camo guy. Gabe clears his throat, and Marina scowls at him. "What? It's the truth!"

Gabe raises a brow and says, "Bystanders said you ran out in the middle of the road to catch your flyaway scarf and dove out of the truck's way before it could clip you."

That sounds more plausible, but still my stomach is in knots.

"It's still the guy's fault! He's a complete menace!"

Gabe's face darkens. "That's for sure. That guy needs to be arrested."

I remember the disturbing force of that man's blurry gaze. But Mom getting hurt right after last night is too much of a coincidence to not have something to do with my wish, and when the doctor comes in, she basically confirms it, because I don't think we'll be leaving Santa Aguas anytime soon.

"I'd say a few days of bed rest and as little pressure on the ankle as possible for at least two weeks. If you have stairs, I'd avoid them for the time being. Have someone bring up food and such. Is there someone at home that can help you around for a while?"

All heads turn to me, and I realize I'm going to have a lot more time with my mother than I bargained for.

BEFORE MOM'S DISCHARGED from the hospital, I'm going through the vending machine options in the lobby when Jamie walks in with a bundle of flowers looking particularly frantic. He catches my eyes, and relief sparks through him.

"Hey!" He's shushed by the receptionist and hunches as he makes his way over.

"What are you doing here?"

He lifts up the flowers. Carnations. "Heard from some people in town your mom was hit by a tractor trailer. Is she okay?" I roll my eyes. Small towns.

"She was *nearly* hit, and not by a tractor." But I swallow because it could've been so much worse. "She's okay, though. Are these for her?"

"Yeah. They didn't have roses."

I grab the flowers from him. My mom hates carnations, but I don't tell him that because I think it's incredibly thoughtful of him.

"How's your dad?" I ask, and he shrugs. Answer enough.

I feel I should say something. Maybe tell him that I broke my word and went to the well. That I wished something would happen to let us stay, to make my mom take notice of what I wanted, and now this happened.

But everyday accidents are normal, right? I close my eyes, and I can clearly picture the shimmering cavern walls, la Cegua's marble face shifting to peer at me. My heart begins to pound, an avalanche of guilt, worry, and fascination filling every cavity of my chest.

A sudden commotion by the emergency room doors catches us off guard. Jamie and I move off to the side to let a gurney and a pair of EMTs pass.

They hover over a man staring vacant-eyed at the ceiling, his mouth open, contorted in an unnatural angle. His hands curled to his chest like a dead animal on the side of the road. I almost don't recognize him. His leery gaze is no longer bloodshot and carnal. In fact, I don't think he'll ever see again.

It's the man with the camo truck—the asshole who nearly killed my mother.

A fleet of triage nurses take the man to another hall and they disappear. The EMTs that first wheeled camo guy in linger by the receptionist desk, visibly shaken. I know how they feel, I can barely hold myself up as we wander closer to overhear the EMTs whispering to each other.

"—mustard seeds in his pockets. I'm telling you, man, it's the Cegua again."

Jamie's hand slides into mine and I squeeze it back tight.

Perla comes in a moment later, wearing sweatpants rolled up on one leg and an inside out purple shirt. Mascara runs down her face.

"Perla!" I say. She's looking for her wallet to show the security with shaky fingers. She looks up at me.

"Did you see where they took him?" Her voice cracks, and we point to the double triage doors. The security guard stops her from going forward, so she dumps the rest of the contents over his desk, then digs around until she finds her ID.

"Is your mom home alone?" Jamie asks. "Do you need someone to watch her?"

Perla rips her gaze from the security guard to face Jamie. Her face a mask of angry grief.

"My mom's *dead*." Her tone drips sarcasm. "But thanks."

Dead. Curandera Lupe died?

"I'm—I'm so sorry."

It can't . . . it couldn't have been la Cegua, could it? I mean, Lupe was elderly but could someone have hurt her? Jamie and I lock eyes while Perla finally gets cleared to go through the doors.

There's a wisp of cold air that rushes forth, the muddy scent of the cavern, and then I see her.

Adel's leaving one of the hospital's corridors, heels clicking on the reflective floor. Perla shrinks back, keeping her distance as they cross paths before she disappears down the hall in search of the man who will never be the same.

Adel finds us and smiles at me on her way out, as if we're just running into each other at a party.

"Unfortunate, isn't it? Someone should really put a stop to this."

My heart is beating wildly. "A stop to what?"

"Come on now," Adel says, an unstable gleam entering her eyes. "There's no need to pretend with me, little Navarrete."

She keeps walking toward the doors, holds a finger to her lips, then points at me, her hand shaped like a gun.

"Let's just see who finds her bones first."

24

ADEL'S LOOKING FOR LA CEGUA'S BONES. Maybe she wants to control her like Roman did. Because it wasn't Adel's *mom* who was really close to Roman. It was her, back in 2000. And maybe now she needs to finish what he started. Maybe she wants out of her own curse, or wish gone wrong.

Whatever her reasons, I need to find the bones first.

The EMT's voice still echoes in my head from yesterday. La Cegua's making herself known, and it's all my fault. It has to be my fault. And yet . . . I want to go back. I want to see her. I think maybe she was helping the only way she knows how. But what does that say about me? To sympathize with someone who can do these terrible things? To trust something no longer human.

I nearly trip on the first step. I make the thousandth trek from the manor's east wing, down the unnecessarily long steps to the outdated kitchen, to fetch my mom another snack. She's had me running up and down these stairs, bringing her cookies, gluten-free sandwiches, or whatever strikes her fancy, as if I were an elite athlete training for a world record. Though we spent all last night watching movies and old reruns on her king-size bed, wearing robes and face masks—which I'll admit, hasn't been all that terrible—that doesn't mean I should make another wish. Mom may be mostly whole, but Jamie was right. It's too dangerous.

I fall back down on her bed with a sigh, sinking into the mountain of pillows, and grab my sketchbook from the night table. The news is on and the local reporters are still talking about the sinkhole that swallowed a farmer whole on the outskirts of town a few weeks ago—and the ones that are cropping up all over Santa Aguas, taking trailers and livestock with them. Sinkholes are common enough, but you don't often hear of so many at a time, as if the earth itself were in an unforgiving rage.

Mom *tsks*, lowering the TV. "Same thing was happening years ago."

I point to the news. "The series of sinkholes?"

She bites into a chip and nods. "Yeah. Like when I was in high school. People were freaking out just like they are now, but the sinkholes eventually stop."

In high school. Like when Roman went missing? Was it because he was messing with the cavern? Making wishes?

"What are you working on?" Mom asks, ignoring the TV, and, surprisingly enough, peering at the open pages on my lap.

The change in topic surprises me, takes me a moment to answer. "Just dumb stuff," I say. "Scribbles."

Her mouth presses to the side. "That doesn't look like scribbles. That looks really good." My heart does a funny leap. "Can I see them?"

When I look sideways at her, a disarming sight with her short hair in disarray and her leg still wrapped in bandages, she seems harmless, but I know what her words can do. How they can whittle you down to a splinter. Still, there's this sincere honey to her gaze, and I recognize the olive branch for what it is.

"Sure." I hand her the notebook. One that's free of any drawings of Roman, la Cegua, or Adel.

Last night while Mom slept I'd drawn Adel. Her expression had made a cold spike of ice shoot through my spine. I don't know what she was doing at the hospital yesterday, or who she was there to see. But I heard the threat loud and clear.

I bite my lip so hard I nearly draw blood while Mom flips through my sketchbook.

"Wow." She stops at one drawing of a rotting fruit, spotted and dented over a pristine kitchen counter. My heart screams in my ears. "Morbid, but still, Cecilia, this is impressive. You've gotten so much better." She keeps staring at the sketch as if scrolling through a million different meanings behind it. I love when art does that. I especially love when it has that effect on someone like her. Someone who's usually too busy or preoccupied to be pinned down by such trivial things as finding meaning in the abstract, in the mundane.

I don't mean to take advantage of her in her weakened state, but it's unusual for her guard to be down. Now would be the perfect time to get some information out of her.

"Mom?"

"Hmm," she says, still studying the pages, turning the sketchbook to get a view of different angles.

"Did you know someone named Adel, or Dominik, in school?"

I see her knuckles blanch, but she keeps looking down at my sketchbook. "Mm, sounds familiar, why?"

I tuck my leg under me, making up an excuse. "Myra's mom, Carolina, mentioned them. Said they were Roman's friends."

She almost tears off a page and I flinch. "Right," she says. "That was—they were a tight group."

I pick at my nail. "She mentioned that she might've seen you around them too?"

Mom scoffs. "She's mistaken. I knew of them," she says, missing my glare because why is she still lying to me? I checked her license again the other day and it still has her right age. She should've been thirteen when Roman went missing, but the yearbook pictures suggest otherwise.

She pinches the bridge of her nose. "I think . . . I think Dominik lost his brother or something. It was all over the news. His little brother went missing then Dominik . . ." Mom's eyes go cloudy with pain. "He couldn't handle it."

I shouldn't keep pressing, but I have to ask. "What about Roman? How well did you know him?"

Color crawls across Mom's neck. "I—I'm not sure. I might've talked to him a few times before . . ." Mom's face contorts in pain. She doubles over.

"Mom! Are you all right?"

She winces. "It's just my head. It's pounding."

I wish we would've thought to tell the doctor about her headaches. The migraines have been coming on more and more frequently, and I hadn't wanted to tell her, but she was looking . . . sickly even before the accident.

She hands back the sketchbook gingerly, taking a deep breath like she's readying to say something else. Something vulnerable or profound. I find myself leaning in. She stares into my eyes, the words nearly there, nearly spelled out in that look. A sadness perforates through the intention. Then she shuts her eyes tight and the words are gone, compressed like a fist.

"I just need some rest." Mom pats my hand, swallowing whatever she'd been about to say. Her breath is deep and rattling as she lies back down and drifts off to sleep, making small, pitiful noises as she dreams.

THERE'S SOFT FRENCH MUSIC playing throughout the manor because my mom says the silence creeps her out, and if she's forced to stay in this godforsaken place, she might as well make the most of it. Honestly, I prefer the quiet. I don't see how the haunting sounds of French vocalists are helping. Before running upstairs again with a steaming cup of tea, I linger at the library. If la Cegua is back, if I somehow agitated her by venturing into the cavern, by making wishes, then I need to figure out where Roman could've hidden her bones before Adel does.

The library's the most modern room of the building, remodeled by the last Sevilla resident after a fire broke loose. There's a framed blueprint displayed proudly on the walls, remodeled in the year 2000. A busy year. The furniture is still dark cherry wood like the rest of the house but it looks polished and new, free of any scratches and dents. Only one wall is filled with books, encyclopedias and volumes with old, dusty covers, making it look more like a showroom for academic libraries than something that actually belongs in a home. I've already pulled out every book, hoping to trigger some kind of Murphy door and reveal Gerardo Sevilla's hidden office. Even tugged at the rifle hanging over an aerial view of Santa Aguas, but that didn't budge either. Though there is one place I haven't looked.

There's a behemoth mahogany desk in the center of the library room with a red Persian rug underneath. I place the tea down and move the heavy desk, barely an inch, muscles straining. Next is the rug, but I don't need to roll it up all the way to know there's no hatch in the floorboards. Not unless it was covered up during the remodel.

"What are you doing?" Gabe stands at the doorway, carrying a container of soup. I jolt up, smacking my head under the desk. "Shoot," he says. "Are you all right?"

I rub my head. "There's two of you now, and I don't think I can take it."

He's learned by now when my sarcasm doesn't warrant a response.

I get up from the floor. "You brought her soup? She hates soup. And she's not sick."

He lifts the container, swirling the specks of vegetables floating inside. "What are you talking about, girl? This sancocho is for me. I got you and your mom's food in the kitchen."

He helps me nudge the table back to where it belongs. Gabe's become a steady fixture in the manor lately, bringing us food from our favorite places. He even slept over last night and helped me clean up. I haven't minded it as much as I thought I would.

"So what was going on here?" He gestures back at the desk as I grab the tea and follow him out.

I wave this off. "I thought I saw something crawl under there. Wanted to kill it before it laid eggs or whatever. Could've been poisonous."

He raises a brow. "Right. 'Cause the logical thing to do when faced with something poisonous is to go after it."

"It's better than it sneaking up on you when you least suspect."

The smells wafting from the kitchen are making my stomach grumble, and I've already decided which movie I'm going to force them to watch this time, but before I help Gabe carry everything upstairs, he stops and taps his head.

"Wow. I almost forgot to tell you: Jamie is outside working on the yard."

My treacherous stomach tightens for an entirely different reason. "Did he ask for me?"

Gabe gives me a playful look. "What do you think?"

NO MAN COULD EVER COME between me and food, so after I eat, I head out to the garden, where I find Jamie taming a particularly unruly shrub with shears.

He's wearing the same short-sleeved shirt I met him in that says, HAVE YOU BEEN HELPED TODAY? The sleeves are rolled up to reveal his lean muscled arms, tan from the sun.

I know how easy he is to scare, especially dangerous when handling pointy objects, so I make sure I crunch heavily on the crinkly leaves to announce my presence.

He turns around, his grin taking up half his face. His mood-ring eyes as green as the lit-up forest tops.

I find myself smiling back. "Heard you were asking about me?"

His face reddens. He puts the shears down and uses the edge of his shirt to wipe the sweat from his face, lifting it enough to reveal his stomach.

He catches me watching and his embarrassment disappears. "I might've."

Damn him. It's cute when he's flustered but it's unbearably hot when he challenges me back.

"In all seriousness, though, I found something I think you might want to see," he says.

This makes me sober up, and I follow him past the shed to another overgrown path within the trees, a few paces on the left of the manor. The way it was hidden behind shrubs and the encroaching woods, I could've missed it. Dismissed the clearing for a dead patch, a forgotten tilled garden.

If not for the stones sprouting like fingers from the dirt, laid side by side.

"A graveyard," I breathe.

"Not just any graveyard," Jamie says. "It's a family plot. All the Sevillas are buried here."

My skin chills as I make my way through the once ornate headstones with chiseled angels now caked in dirt. I stop in front of the last one. A grave that feels . . . empty. Nothing at all like the electric pull of the cavern with the presence I expect to feel here. Because Roman, beloved son and Sevilla heir, was never found.

But still. It's where a Sevilla belongs.

Find it. Where a Sevilla belongs.

Jamie's already reached the same conclusion. "Think her bones could be hidden here?"

I glance over to the plot with a large cross—Percival Eugenio Sevilla.

"I think we might as well check."

Jamie hangs his head, but says, "I'll go get the shovels."

25

I GLIDE A HAND OVER the obsidian beadwork of Adel's dress and wince. The blisters from the night of useless digging still haven't healed. Roman's plot was empty as expected, and Percival's was . . . I'd rather not think about it. But judging by the clothes, the bones were his.

I stare into my reflection. Prom day arrived quicker than expected, and guilt spreads inside me like an oil spill. I should be staying home, watching Mom, but instead she's sending me out to celebrate this ridiculous rite of passage into adulthood like everything is normal, when the last thing I feel is normal.

Yet, it's hard to stay grim when I catch the light shimmer of my dress, and it looks like I'm dipped in stars. Whatever she is, Adel has great taste.

There have been no more run-ins with her. She hasn't been at school or anywhere around town, according to Jamie. But I know she's around. Waiting and searching. The lock to the back door was broken into, and the plant my mom takes to every single house we've lived in was knocked over. Gabe replaced the locks but I always get the prickling sensation that someone's been in here.

My gaze flickers over to my open laptop—to the multiple tabs of the *Santa Aguas Tribune*, articles ranging from April to August 2000. Even though Santa Aguas had a lot of newsworthy events in 2000, nothing really trickled out to the main news channels. But the local paper gave me what I'd been looking for—the weird occurrences. Random sinkholes, including one on Sevilla grounds and another at the school. An eighteen-year-old kid winning the lottery—though the name was redacted for their protection. Missing boys. A suicide. Petrified men on the side of the road. All this in a period of a few months. All of it starting right before Roman went missing.

These could all be the products of wishes gone horribly wrong. And now with the Cegua growing bolder, with the reemerging sinkholes, and my wishes coming true, I might've started it all over again.

The laptop light goes dark and I shut it, grabbing the sheer shawl from the back of my vanity chair.

I check my eyeliner and stuff my bag for the after-prom campout with my phone, keys, an extra set of clothes, and the smallest Moleskine I have, because I never leave home without a sketchbook. I wish I had mace or some kind of weapon to pack. Even a letter opener would suffice at this point.

As I make my way to the stairs, something makes me pause by the wall of portraits.

A breeze sweeps through the windowless hall, an errant wind that snakes its way beneath my dress and runs across my ankles like cold water. I move toward the end of the hall, closing in on the imposing portrait of Gerardo Sevilla, past the photographs of Roman and the others with their stern mouths and infectious dark eyes. The air is still circulating here, cold and damp, making the hairs on my arms stand on end. There's no air vent and the wind doesn't seem to be coming from the attic space above. It seems to be emanating from the walls.

I feel something take over, a heavy drape dictating my movements, an ethereal pull bringing me closer. My fingers reach up to touch the portrait of Gerardo, his penetrating eyes stare into mine—sharp and unforgiving. The buzz in my head shrills.

Come find me.

A muffled yell draws me away and I shake off the disquieting sensation radiating off the walls. Having heard this particular yell nonstop since my mom's accident, I register her distinct pitch: she wants something. I take a last lingering look at Gerardo's portrait and bring the shawl tighter around myself.

Closer to the stairs, I can make out what she's saying. "Did you hear me? Bring me my phone for pictures!"

"I heard you!" I call down. I'd told her not to forget anything before Gabe and I carried her down earlier. I sweep into my mom's room and go to her nightstand, where she keeps her phone plugged into the charger. The screen is lit up with a text and I just glance at it, but my eyes snag on the word *visitation*.

I look toward the door and unlock her phone; the passcode has always been my birthday. The messages are from someone at the law firm. Telling her they'll meet her at the prison and prep her for the press, listing visitation hours for this Saturday, tomorrow.

She's going to go see him. My fingers clench around the phone. I can't believe this.

Everything from my wish and her accident was for nothing. Did any of this even happen because of the wish or was it just plain luck? And what I thought was a change in our relationship, an actual moment of us growing closer, was it actually just a detour in her route back to our old lives?

A lump forms in my throat.

From downstairs, I hear Mom call my name again and as much as I want to shake off the sudden dark cloud over my head, I can't. I text them back. Tell them to go to hell and that I've found representation elsewhere, capturing my mom's haughty tone, then block them—not that it'll do any good. Because a part of me wants to be vengeful. I take a few steadying breaths, the rattling emotions in my chest too much to handle right now. I will my mind to quiet, to regain some of that hollow emptiness from before.

I almost succeed, almost feel nothing, but from the top of the stairs, the first person I catch a glimpse of is Jamie, and he looks so heartbreakingly beautiful that the hollowness sloshes with something more unsettling. He's talking to Gabe, and the moment Jamie's eyes catch mine, they brighten as if a lantern were lit inside him.

The hair, for once, isn't blocking his face. It's slicked back and recently cut, accentuating the hard lines of his jaw and cheekbones. He's definitely not wearing his dad's old suit either.

Behind Jamie, Myra and Di look beautiful in red and gold dresses clasping each other and smiling happily when they see me come down. Neither of them whisper under their breath, exchanging some catty remark like my old friends would've. Like I'd come to expect.

My hands almost slip along the waxy banister. Gabe has his phone out taking pictures and a blush blooms through me. Even my mom's expression as she waits on a wingback chair makes it hard to stay mad at her. They look so . . . admiring. I can't say I entirely hate it. I can't admit that I don't care, and I really don't understand why this moment is making me so choked up.

Jamie comes to the end of the stairs and grabs my hand. "Can I say something corny?"

I swallow down the knot of emotion. "Can I stop you?"

He shakes his head, smiling and leans in to whisper close to my ear, his breath warm on my neck. "You look like a wish come true."

My throat tightens again because when Jamie pulls away, there's a seriousness to him that's even more rattling.

"I want to hear what he said!" Myra calls, but Di shushes her. I try to break the thread of heat before I embarrass myself and cry for no reason. "You did warn me it'd be corny."

"I did." He laughs, grabbing something from Gabe. It's hard to tear my gaze away from Jamie's face, but the dark velvety purple flowers of a corsage in black tulle draw my eye as he slips it onto my wrist, leaving his fingers on my skin for a beat too long. There's a matching flower on his lapel.

"Figured you're not a baby's breath and roses kinda person."

I give my wrist a little admiring twist. "You would assume correct."

A bright flash momentarily blinds me as my mom stands on one wobbly foot and takes a candid using Gabe's phone. "Oh, that's a good one. Let's get a group one now by the fireplace."

I hug Myra and Di, standing beside them, and take a moment to chat about their gorgeous dresses, glad they broke away from the boring prom theme.

"What can I say, I'd rather die than conform." Myra's striking a dramatic pose in her scarlet siren dress with black bodice, and Di's beside her wearing a silky gold dress with her braided hair in a sleek high ponytail. She's working hard to keep Myra from tipping over in seven-inch heels. "What she means is we're too broke to buy anything new."

Myra sticks out her tongue.

Everyone's so excited, but there's still a weight keeping me from feeling the same levity. There's a few rounds of photos where Mom pressures me repeatedly to do a "real" smile, and when she zeroes in on my hand, I know it's going to be another complaint.

"The ring doesn't match," she says. "It's so tacky."

I pull my hand back. "It used to be yours."

She narrows her eyes at it. "Well, it's no wonder I don't remember it. Just one night—leave it home."

My teeth clench. I don't want to argue, especially not in front of others. I'm about to hand it to her when Gabe is there taking it instead. "What if I hold on to it? You know how things mysteriously get misplaced around her," he fake whispers, making Mom scoff. But he has a point. "By the way, kid. You clean up nice."

I roll my eyes.

"No, seriously, you look beautiful. I hope you have a fun time. Just don't do anything too wild."

I almost retort with *okay, Dad*, but the words die in my throat. There's a vulnerability I'm scared might escape with the joke, and I know Gabe will bring it up and try to make a lesson out of it. Turn it into some sappy moment that'll have him wanting to hug me and that'll pierce into the hard membrane around my heart, something I'm not ready to let soften entirely.

Before we go, Gabe whispers some very intense words to Jamie that seem to involve the after-prom campout and responsibility. The campout is supposed to be some big secret from the adults, but there's no way something like that will stay secret in Santa Aguas. I take the moment to talk to my mom, handing over her phone.

"Are you leaving tonight?"

Mom's face reflects the brief spark of panic before sighing. "I'll be back by Sunday. Gabe can always swing by throughout the weekend so you won't be alone. I just need to handle some estate business for the Coral Gables' house."

"You don't have to lie, you know. I already know you're visiting him. So what, you tried to move in on some smarmy lawyer and when that didn't happen you went right back to the crook?"

My mother pulls me away, the others pretending they didn't overhear. "Cecilia, have some respect—he could be dead."

"The crook?"

"No! Liam, the lawyer."

I feel myself go still, a stone dropping into my stomach. "What do you mean?"

"His firm thought he left with his ex-wife, but it turns out no one's seen him. He just disappeared off the face of the earth. And I wasn't moving in on him, *god*!"

Disappeared. After I wished we wouldn't have to leave Santa Aguas. Could him disappearing be the consequence? Forced to leave my mom alone through whatever means possible?

Mom pats my arm, and I flinch. "Besides, I'm only going to appease the press and find a way out of this hole. No need to sound so accusatory." She takes a big breath, easing her tone. "Relax. Go have fun tonight, be young. I even have a surprise for you later."

"A surprise?"

Her smile is Cheshire sharp. "Maybe some old friends stopping through? A certain football star."

Panic crawls up my neck. "Mom, you didn't. Please say you didn't."

She *tsks*, turning me by the shoulders, practically shoving me toward the door. So much for a weakened state.

"It's not a big deal. They may or may not come. Just go and have fun," she says, and with one fluttering gesture, she closes the door on us but not before I catch the pained look in her eyes. If she were really feeling guilty, though, she wouldn't do this. She would choose me instead.

Once we're alone, Jamie jogs over to Di's car. Myra and Di are already sitting in the front seat, so he opens the back door for me and helps me slide in without ruining the long hem of my dress.

I'm wringing my hands. I don't have the brain space to think of a possible visit from Anthony. The thought that I might've inadvertently made a man disappear imprints guilt on my chest like a branding iron. But I mean, what if he's perfectly okay and just decided to take an isolating vacation? It could be a consequence of the wish but it doesn't necessarily have to be a bad one.

I'm trying to brighten up. There's no need to ruin Jamie's night. Not when he's gone to all this effort to make it so sweet.

Eventually, Di pulls up in front of the school where a cheap archway of black-and-white balloons marks the prom's entrance. A sea of monochromatic color filters into the school gym, and as we make our way to the entrance, a kid collecting tickets stares in our direction, appalled.

Myra takes out a flask from her bodice and takes a swig. "Here we go."

THE MUSIC POUNDS with the grainy low quality of old speakers. The first hour it was fine, but now it's starting to grate.

"Are you regretting coming here yet?" Jamie asks coming up behind me with a fresh drink.

"You caught me," I say, but the smile I try to smother behind my drink calls my bluff.

Sure it's a low-budget party with bad lighting and even worse music—past me would've probably walked right out—but it does have company that I don't . . . hate.

Our calculus teacher passes by us wearing a simple black church dress and pearls. She's pauses in front of Jamie.

"Hey, Mrs. Morgan," he says, using the chipper voice he reserves for adults.

"Hi, Jamie! You look handsome." She brings up a lecturing finger. "Now if only we could get the same kind of effort applied to our work." She gives him a mock-serious look before laughing it off, but I can see how it makes him flinch. His long, lithe fingers drum at his side again. He tries to play it off like he finds this funny, too, but it doesn't work. At least not to me. How could someone look down at him when he tries so ridiculously hard for others even when they don't deserve it?

Mrs. Morgan is about to leave again but pauses when words start streaming from my mouth before I can stop them. "You know, I have a friend who has this incredible work ethic," I start, and Jamie gives me a startled look. "He's smart, motivated, vocal in class. I think he even picks up some of the teachers' coffees in the morning." At this Mrs. Morgan looks uncomfortable. "But the education system in this country is unfortunately fucked—pardon my French, because some students just need a different approach to learning, wouldn't you say, Mrs. Morgan?"

She clears her throat. "Yes, well, I can do without the profanity—"

"It's a shame we don't take into account that teens, like adults, are not cookie-cutter robots. Imagine if we put effort into pinpointing the real culprit and coming up with real solutions? Like teachers being adequately compensated and not only taught to recognize the variability in learning patterns but given the freedom to implement necessary changes in their own classrooms." I shrug. "You know, for a student's well-being."

Mrs. Morgan blinks at me, mouth parted like she wants to argue but is slowly processing what I've said. She pinches her eyes shut for a moment before her expression becomes more human. She sighs and pats Jamie on the arm. "If you want to retake Monday's test, come into my office early next week. And I mean *early*, got it?"

Jamie lights up like a rocket. "Okay! Yes—I'll do that. I'll be there, Mrs. Morgan. I won't let you down."

She gives us both a wry smile. "Have fun you two. And try to lighten up. You're too young to let the crushing weight of the world bring you down just yet."

Jamie's eyes are huge once she goes. "I can't believe you just said that to her."

I wince. "Embarrassing for you?"

"What? No! No, I'm . . ." There's a softness to his face that makes some fluttery thing graze the inside of my ribs. "Grateful, and I think you might, *like-like* me."

I roll my eyes. "Let's not get ahead of ourselves."

"Cookie-cutter robots," he muses.

I push his shoulder. "Shut up."

His smile is overwhelmingly beamed in my direction and my heart catches.

"Are you sure you don't want to dance? I've heard I have some killer moves. As in I'm a literal hazard on the dance floor." His shoulders are shimmying in a way only someone truly comfortable in their body would move.

"What a selling point," I say. I glance around, the couples are breaking away from their groups of friends as a slow dance starts.

"So, what do you say?" Even with this lighting, his eyes are arresting. Disarming. I don't know how he always manages to turn a playful moment into one that makes me lightheaded and confused. It's terrifying. Because what happens when Mom decides to move us again? When the emptiness creeps back in?

"Cecilia?"

But we're both dressed up, and it's prom, and what harm could one dance really do?

We make our way to the dance floor, past Myra and Di, who sway tightly together.

His hand is hot on my back, pressing me closer to him, and the thump of his heart raging against my chest makes me forget what they're playing. If the song even requires us to be this close. By the end of the song, my nose is even closer to the soft skin of his neck and his freckles and some spicy cologne I've never smelled on him.

The entire gym could be transformed into a ballroom and I wouldn't noticc.

When I look up at him, his eyes slide down to mine, darkening before they linger on my lips.

"So this friends thing . . ." he says, voice hoarse and hopeful, longing. A mirrored longing. An aching, fervent longing.

His nose touches mine. This close, I tip into the molten warmth of his eyes. I can almost taste him, his mouth a breath away. My heart a racing bird.

An inch more is all it would take. But I shift away. The kiss lands on my cheek, at the barest edge of my mouth.

Movement behind Jamie's shoulder draws my gaze and I latch on to it. Needing to focus on something other than the flood of hurt on his face. Needing desperately for this moment to end before I do something I'll regret. There's a familiar banner of red hair skirting the shadowy corners of the school's gym. Prowling. Her eyes are on me with every step she takes.

"I—I'll be right back," I say, pretending like I don't notice the way his entire body has curled and slumped. Better he get used to the disappointment now, because I'm not who he needs me to be. I can't be. At any moment, I'll have to say goodbye, and I don't want it to hurt more than it already will.

I zero in on Adel, and she lifts her drink in a salute, waiting for me to draw near like she expected. "What do you think?" she says, waving her drink out to encompass the entirety of the school gym in its Party City glory. "Who'd ever want to leave with entertainment like this, right?"

I stop in front of her and cross my arms. "Have you been stalking me? Breaking into my house?"

She feigns shock. "Vain, are we?" She tips her head back and laughs. "I bet you think this song is about you, don't you?"

"Clever," I say. "But I have questions for you."

She stares at me from behind a hazy film of strobe lights. Green eyes glowing like a panther's. "It's about time. Let's hear them."

My jaw clenches. "Who are you really? Why did you take my mother's yearbook, and more importantly"—I lower my voice—"why are you in it?"

Her stare becomes an uncomfortable sear over my skin, and then she cracks an unnerving smile. "Those are some great questions." She dumps her cup into someone's unattended purse. "How about you tell me when *you* were born, who your father is, what your mother's kept from you, and what la Cegua has granted you so far?"

Her narrowed gaze peels away at my skin, revealing each tainted layer. "But you only know some of those answers, don't you? I think that's what you should really be asking."

I feel the ground waver under me, as if at any moment a new sinkhole will open up and gulp me down.

"What do you know about my father?" I ask.

She brushes past me without answering, smelling of smoke, drink, and something else. Something like cavern air. Adel goes about the crowd whispering things to others, pointing in my direction. A string of excited murmurs slithers through the room.

Jamie rushes to my side, face etched in worry. He's out of breath. "She's telling everyone to meet at the Sevilla grounds for the campout. Said you okayed it."

It's like she leaves behind a trail of grease. Her suggestion spreading through the room quicker than I can rein it back, and already students filter out. No doubt on their way to the real party. Myra and Di come up to us.

I meet the shocked faces of my friends, dread curdling in my stomach.

She's leading them into the woods. My woods.

26

"DID YOU KNOW THAT THE CAMPOUT was going to be here?" Myra asks, unloading the tent from the back of her car.

Di takes a look around the darkened woods, at the incoming clouds ripe with rain. "Seems bold. Especially since people are saying she's back."

She's not back. La Cegua never left.

"No." I keep my eyes sharp on the trees, searching for a flash of red hair or a veil of white. "It wasn't my idea. But it's too late to stop it now."

There's already an infinite line of cars parked down the road leading to the manor gates. My mom should be gone by now; if not she'd put a stop to it. I never should've ignored her warning about these woods.

Jamie carries both our bags as we make our way to the clearing, where kids have already set up a bonfire and pitched tents. There's a turbulent air of anticipation snaking through the night.

Jamie holds up his phone. "I have no service."

Neither do I. We're too far from the manor to reach the Wi-Fi, but too deep in the woods for cell service. The manor grounds include acres and acres of undisturbed trees. Whenever we've traveled the path toward the cavern, I've never been able to tell which direction it was in relation to the house. There's no telling how close we are, or if the cavern simply ceases to exist whenever it feels like it.

But it is bold to be out. Almost like a taunt. I'm not sure what Adel is up to leading us all here, if she means to draw la Cegua to us, or get me somewhere isolated. Whatever her plan is, I welcome it. I need answers. Adel knows what my mom's been hiding. She was there when everything with la Cegua and Roman went down.

"We can tell everyone to get out," Jamie says quietly. "If they don't listen, we can call it in for trespassing and underage drinking."

I take in Myra and Di, hands clasped and swinging as they make their way to a spot by the bonfire. They look so happy. I know they've been looking forward to this for a while. A night together before we graduate and everything changes. Before everyone goes off in different directions like an exploding star. I don't want to ruin this for them.

"Maybe Adel's just messing with my head," I reason. "There's a big group of us. We'll keep an eye out."

His mouth tightens. "Okay."

We join the party. Someone parked their truck with a small trailer near the clearing. A stereo is strapped to the trailer's plank, while a generator spews a faint whiff of gasoline. There's mulled cider in old water jugs and a few cases of beer being offered around. Some of the tents pushed deeper into the woods already move with bodies in them. And a fire blazes in the center of it all, pulling people toward it like moths.

I don't see Adel anywhere.

My heart leaps when a girl screams and Jamie's hand clamps on my arm—but it was just someone who'd jumped from behind a tree to scare her, and they both laugh it off. On the other side of the bonfire, a guy drunkenly howls at the canopy of forest before putting the keg hose to his mouth while others egg him on. It's all very primordial. I can see the only reason the campout is such a yearly success is the access to cheap beer and the lack of parental supervision.

The normalcy of it all makes me laugh a little. Which makes Jamie laugh too.

He loosens a tight breath. "I don't know. Should we try to have fun?"

I feign an exasperated sigh. "I guess, we might as well. I mean, the night's just starting, and this is technically prom night. Epic things should happen."

"How epic?" His eyes shimmer, but I grab hold of his hand and pull him behind me before he can read too much into it. We veer toward the congregation of sweaty drunk bodies. I lift my brow in challenge as I swipe the keg hose and bring it to my mouth for a long, strong pull that seems to go on forever. The beer is a cold river down my throat. Once I'm done, silence meets me head-on until I throw my arms up and yell like I'm in a sorority, earning an approving chant from everyone else.

"You've officially been in this town too long." Jamie cracks the biggest smile, holding on to my elbow so I don't stumble back on a tree root. His touch is tender and strong, and the adrenaline is still racing through my veins, because I want nothing more than to pull him to me and kiss that sweet, beautiful mouth. Have the warmth of him steal every bit of cold I keep locked up inside.

The thoughts must flicker across my face. The heat-seeking press of my gaze on his, because I can read it reflected back. "I don't think I've been here long enough," I say.

A bellow suddenly splits the night, a booming voice so familiar yet so ridiculously out of place, that I'm left reeling. In an instant, the beer rushes to my head and I can barely stand on my own.

My mother's surprise, I take it, stumbles into the revelry with cases of beer on his broad shoulders—Anthony, followed by Cristina. My old friends come back to haunt me.

Everyone from the party looks around in confusion. It's a small town and these are entirely new and attractive faces. The kind only money can buy through means of nose jobs and weekly facials.

"Ew, why's the ground so mushy?" Is the first thing Cristina says when she sees me.

People stare wide-eyed as Anthony shows off his football-star acquired physique by placing down the three cases of beer by the kegs. Once free of the added weight, he holds his arms up. "Heard there was a party here."

Immediately the guys gather and hail him the god of drink, asking where the hell he came from.

"Do you know them?" Jamie asks, but before I can explain, Anthony zeroes in on me like a shark picking up a bloody scent. He takes large steps in my direction with a massive grin and all I can do is stand here frozen.

Once he gets to me, he picks me up, squeezing me until I'm almost out of breath. When he sets me down, he grabs my face between his large palms and presses his mouth to mine like he'd done so many times before.

I'm ice. I can't feel a thing.

Then I see Jamie's expression, and I feel too much at once.

I back away. "What—what are you doing here?"

"We're here for you, babe!" Anthony says.

Cristina throws her arms around me. "Oh my god! Look at you—still our moody bitch. Girl, we have missed you."

She pecks me on the cheek. Neither of them find it strange that I'm standing here catatonic. Because they're used to it, and I recognize this feeling coming over me. Misery.

"We drove like forever," Cristina says. "But your mom said tonight was your prom and we had to come see you."

Anthony puts his arms around me, weighing me down, sinking me into the ground. He takes a deep whiff of my hair like some kind of animal. "You still smell so good." As if he expected me to smell differently.

Anthony pulls his face from my hair when he notices Jamie, who's just standing there looking as lost as I am but with a veil of something I can't pinpoint in his expression. Betrayal? Disappointment?

You would think I'd recognize it by now. "What's up, man?" Anthony introduces himself.

Cristina sizes Jamie up.

Jamie shakes Anthony's outstretched hand, and I notice Anthony squeezes a little too tightly. A dick move I'd ignored before when he was trying to be possessive.

"You've been watching my girl for me?"

My face goes hot. "I'm not his girl."

"Right." Jamie's voice is granite. He puts his hands in his pockets, his expression drawn and tight. He looks to me for answers but I don't know what I look like right now. I don't know if I'm even able to form an expression. The gulf between us feels oceans wide.

Anthony laughs. "I know, I know. You're no one's girl."

"Our Ceci doesn't date," Christina explains, bumping her shoulder with Jamie's. "But I do."

Finally something pierces the metal casket encasing where my heart lies dormant, but I don't know if I have a right to it. I want to scream, but all sounds are lodged in my throat. I don't know what's wrong with me. Why my body has gone back to autopilot when I had only just started taking the wheel.

Anthony takes the hose from my hand, kissing the top of my head. "So what's up with this keg?"

Jamie scoffs. "I should've known."

"It's not—" I start, but Cristina is diving into a story about the drive over through the "boondocks," unaware of the heated exchange going on right in front of her. Anthony winces, because he does notice.

"It makes sense," Jamie continues, but his eyes are soft. Not angry like I'd expected, but definitely not friendly.

"Jamie."

"I've been so stupid."

"You haven't," I say.

Finally Cristina stops talking long enough to realize something's up. "Do you two need a moment?"

"No," Jamie says at the same time I say, "Yes."

I grab hold of his hand, leading him deeper into the forest, until we're far enough away from any prying eyes.

He stops, digging in his feet, more irritable than I've ever seen him. "All this time I thought the just-friends thing ran a bit deeper, you know? But you already have someone. Of course you do—why wouldn't you? I mean look at you."

"I told you it's not like that."

"He *kissed* you. He kissed you and you let him. I was just a small distraction before you got back to your real life." He mutters again about how stupid he's been and a flare of anger shoots through me. I told him from the beginning that this couldn't turn into anything more. Even if he's got it all wrong about Anthony, I still can't give him what he wants. Not when I don't get a choice about where I go, or where I live. Even the cavern has proven that it can't change the fact that I have no say in any of it.

"Weren't these people kind of terrible to you?"

My tongue feels glued down. The disappointment in his tone is like a compressor on my chest.

He takes a step closer as if to catch me. "I wish you would've just told me."

Words spew in a flurry of heat because he's not listening. "Maybe you should've wished for that in the cave."

He grows taller somehow, hurt and temper morphing him into someone else. "I don't need a magic cavern for this, Ceci. If I thought for a second that you were excited to see them, that this guy . . . these people make you happy, I'd leave it be, but I know that's not the case. You seem cornered. Not like yourself, and I'm trying to be a good friend here."

I look back up at him. "Really? You sure that's all you're trying to be?"

His eyes narrow, glittering black in the dark. "What do you want me to say? I like you, a lot. I think you know that, but I'm here to be whatever it is you need me to be."

My hands are starting to shake. "You shouldn't have to mold yourself into what I need, Jamie. I'm not another job you can take on. I'm a lot of work even for you. You have no idea how fucked up I can be."

He throws his arms up. "Every single one of us is fucked up in one way or another. Look at me! My mom moved on without me. My dad wouldn't notice I'm there, cleaning the house, working multiple jobs, washing his soiled clothes unless I sprouted a damn beer can on my face. We're all messed up, Cecilia. But we shouldn't stop trying. We shouldn't stop searching for the things that make us happy. I don't want you giving up on yourself, letting others trample all over you. You don't deserve that. I want you to see what I see."

"There's nothing to see." My voice cracks. "I'm empty."

He shakes his head. A bitter laugh. "You're wrong. You're overflowing. I think you're so full of sadness that it hurts. But you're also brave, and passionate, and creative, and have this killer dry humor. I see it, and it's why I really, *really* care about you."

My chest is heaving. A tidal wave of emotion rushes forward and seems to inflate my heart. Until it feels like it might fail on me. But I don't know how to let myself feel it all. All my life I've worked to squash down those desires, those rages of emotions, that I don't know what to do when I'm anything but hollow anymore. He's right that it all hurts too much. Especially this—whatever this building feeling is, it's the worst of all of them.

You let people in and they disappear or disappoint. It's what people do. It's what I do.

"I don't care," I say, though it was meant to be *I'm sorry*, and I watch his expression shatter. I watch myself break him, as if this were another vision la Cegua thought I should see. The cruelty of others. I'm a terrible creature of habit, and I guess my mom and I are as alike as everyone says.

His jaw hardens but he dips his chin in defeat. "Sure you don't." And he's gone. Walked away, swallowed by the dark night. Watching the hard planes of his back disappear, I want to take back my words. Take back every time I've ever pushed him away. Because I don't mean it. I care too much. I feel too much.

I walk back to the bonfire in a daze. The final rider on a messed up roller coaster. I wonder if this is how Soledad felt. Having to keep everything hidden and unsaid. Being alone in a new place, unsure if any of your decisions were worth it.

Cristina spots me first, pulling me to her and telling everyone to hush. "Listen, listen." She tugs on the sleeve of the guy she'd been talking to. "Tell that story again—about the murdered boy who used to live in Ceci's house."

Anthony hikes a brow, glancing down at me. "Oof. That's dark. You knew that?"

"Yeah," I say, voice like a ghost. "I've heard."

Someone else chimes in. A girl in my third period. "Everyone thinks la Cegua took him."

And then people around the campfire take turns giving their two cents, adding to the story that I know is steeped in a dark truth.

But I can't hear any more of this. I get up, my heart already leading my steps even if my head hasn't entirely caught up.

Anthony stops me with a tug on my shirt. "You ready to dip?" He and Cristina dust off their clothes as if dying to get rid of the country grime.

"Come on, C," she says. "We're kidnapping you. There's a music festival like half an hour from here!"

"There's going to be some sick DJs," Anthony adds.

"Leave?" I ask again, my mind working sluggishly.

They laugh. "Are you drunk?"

I'm not leaving with them. They're the last people I want to be with. And I know Mom did this to prepare me. So we can go back to our old lives in a gilded cage. Back to the same people that made me miserable. That I'm pretty sure I made miserable right back.

I lock eyes with Myra and Di, sitting on the other side of the bonfire, and they lift their hands as if to say, *What's going on?*

What's going on is that I made a terrible mistake, but I still have time to make it right.

"I'm not going," I tell my old friends.

It takes a few seconds for them to hear me because their minds are already miles away under the strobe lights and in the smoky haze of a concert. They don't care. Or they care about so many other things, beyond me, that there's no space. And maybe I was too used to that being enough, avoiding anything more than scraps, because I didn't have anything to give in return.

Except I don't feel that emptiness like I used to. Little by little, this town, these people have filled me. Nourished me back to a human when I was nothing but a shell.

"What?" Cristina looks at me like I'm crazy. "You want to stay *here*? In this place? But we came here for you."

"Yeah, babe." Anthony throws an arm around me, but I shove him off, his entire face etched in confusion.

"I'm not your babe. I'm not your anything," I snap, then face Cristina. "And I was a pretty shitty friend to you, which is why you were also a pretty shitty friend to me. We just matched what the other could give. And I don't think there's more to us than that."

Cristina's mouth opens and closes like a fish. "I—I've been going through a lot," she says, and her eyes water. I know she has, and I know some of it was because of me—my greedy wish for Dorset. But she had other problems too. Her parents' divorce, her sister's lupus. She'd mention these things offhand, but I'd never asked for more details. I never really tried to get to know her, or help her, because I hadn't cared about anything in a really long time.

"I couldn't drop everything to deal with *your* problems," she says.

"I know," I assure her. "I'm not blaming you. I'm just giving a really shitty apology."

She's careful wiping the bottom of her eyes, eyeliner remaining intact as always. "You've changed, Ceci."

I know that too.

"Not cool." Anthony shakes his head as he passes, disappointed, but he'll get over that by the time he gets to the car, and if he doesn't, I don't really care.

When they leave, I feel lighter than I have in a very long time.

27

THE MOMENT THEY'RE GONE, I dash over to Myra and Di, who sit side by side on a log.

"What the hell?" Is the first thing Myra says. "One second we see you and Jamie inches—and I mean *inches*—away from kissing and then this big-ass guy is all over you."

"Give her a second to explain," Di says, voice so compassionate it makes my eyes sting.

I swallow hard. "I know, I messed up. I said some things—have you seen him?"

Myra and Di are up in an instant. I flinch, but they encase me like a blanket. "He'll forgive you," Di says. "And if he doesn't we have some choice words." They squeeze me tight and step back. "But I haven't seen him. His bag is still here, and he doesn't have a car so he couldn't have gone too far."

Gazing out at the dark woods, my heart beats double. Because he could've gone far. Too far.

My gaze stops at Adel across the fire. She's surrounded by other people, tipping a drink in my direction with a knowing, secretive smile.

I don't have time to deal with her bullshit.

"Want us to go with you?" Myra asks.

"No, I'll find him." I can't risk someone else out in these woods—not with the looming scent of mud and sweet cavern air filling the clearing. "Can you guys—if I'm not back soon, please go. Don't stay here."

"Ceci—"

"*Please*," I say, and they nod, reluctantly, the fear in my tone convincing enough.

I run out toward the street first, look to the pitch-black sky with stars littered like broken glass and yell his name. The only response is the silence of the soft wind. I jog down the street, my shoes crunching on asphalt as I pass all the cars parked in the dark like sentient beasts. But there's no one here.

I guess he could've tried walking to the manor. It's only about a mile away. But he could've gone to the well. There's a purple flower thrown to the side on a patch of dead grass. I stoop to pick it up and it's obvious who it belongs to. The matching one is in my bag by the campfire. The boutonniere to my corsage.

"Jamie . . ."

A billow of white shifts in my periphery and I straighten. Ancient earth and stale air.

From the woods, a white veil flutters from the trees before the rest of her materializes. La Cegua moves jaggedly, like something that long forgot what it's like to be human.

I expected her this evening. I knew she'd find me one way or another. Over her shoulder, a horse's skeletal face peers out from the woods. The exposed muscles of his nose pinching as if sniffing the air. He's grotesque and beautiful. Horrifying and otherworldly.

La Cegua pats the horse's bony neck.

"What do you want from me?"

La Cegua slants her head to the side. A barrier spread between us of language and feeling and soul.

"Do you know where Jamie is? Have you hurt him?"

Nothing. Irritation makes me stalk forward, reason makes me pause.

"I want to understand you," I say. "*Please.* I wish I could understand you."

A tug on my chest, and la Cegua turns around, moving into the dark grove of trees with the strike of horse hooves falling beside her. She expects me to follow, and I do. Time dropping away like the dead leaves of fall. We walk for what feels like hours but could very well be minutes until my knees start to ache, and a familiar trail appears.

It leads to the well.

With every step closer, la Cegua's pristine white veil fades and her skin becomes more translucent. Her horse waits at the well's rim and her fingers softly graze its back before we descend. But it's not to the well I know but from another moment in time. A vision I was always meant to see.

28

SOLEDAD WASN'T SURE HOW LONG she'd have before he showed up. She tucked the letters under her arm. The stack of letters she'd written to her family in Villa del Sur that had never been opened. Never been sent.

Her husband had lied. But that was no surprise.

He'd wrapped the letters in a bag of silk with mustard seeds—an hechizo meant to gain control and one she'd taught him to use to gain their fortune. Together.

Inside her was a war of relief and rage. Relief that the silence from her sisters and her mother wasn't out of anger that she'd left with the Californian to settle in la Florida. That they didn't despise her for her betrayal. They'd been right—her husband was a devil in disguise.

He wants you, mija, for your gifts. A power-hungry man like that desires a witch more than he needs a wife.

The rage she felt was at her own gullibility. Her yearning for something new and different that took her away from everything she cherished most. And now she was trapped with a man who only wanted to control her gifts.

She closed his ledgers. Though Gerardo would hardly care had she looked. He thought she couldn't understand what the transactions meant. But she did. He'd been funding the militia in Villa del Sur since before they left. Since before he'd claimed they were being driven out. Instead, he had struck a deal. Made profit off the revolt that took her family's land.

She heard a noise.

Soledad rushed up the steps of Gerardo's office—another secret he had kept from her. Closing the door that was his portrait, shutting away the hidden steps, she dashed toward her sewing room, placing the stack of letters where she kept most things precious to her.

She was angry, but she had to play this smart if she was to go home.

Gerardo called from downstairs. He was drunk again, and the idea of his hands on her now made her shudder.

"I will be down soon!" she called back, then went to dress for dinner.

"WHY ARE YOU wearing that?" Gerardo watched her through unfocused eyes. She wore her mantilla and the simple beaded ivory of her wedding dress. It was the only dress remaining from home. Crafted by the skillful weavers of her pueblo.

Soledad dabbed at her mouth. "Why not wear something on more than one occasion, my darling? Once you acquire something, shouldn't you use it until it is worthless?"

He tipped his glass back, draining the wine. "You are a strange creature."

"It's what you love about me, isn't that right?"

He laughed as if she had made some funny joke, but he was staring at her suspiciously, and she worried this last jab had shown her hand. She reached over and placed her palm on his, stifling the revulsion. She forced herself to smile. Little did he care about the bruise that her dress could not hide. Her dress was not fashioned to tuck away the sins of her husband.

Soledad waited until Gerardo fell asleep in the library lounger as he usually did after dinner.

Then she stole into the night. She took Caramelo from the stables, taking off her glove so the horse could eat the apple slices she'd brought to keep him silent. She had a vague idea of where to go, consulting a map that darkened as she moved deeper into the surrounding forest. She knew the journey would be long and she would not be welcomed back, but she had to try. She refused to die in this house away from her family. Away from la Laguna de Apoyo, where all others before her had been buried. Where she had always meant to live and die, had she not been so blind.

Caramelo trotted quietly as if sensing the need for secrecy. They were nearly to the manor's gate when she saw the light of her bedroom bloom to life. Even from here, she could hear her name being screamed by a man who'd just misplaced his favorite toy.

Soledad reared the horse into the forest, kicked her heels. Her mantilla fluttered behind her like a specter, threatening to snag on the thorny branches.

She heard the dogs barking now too. Gerardo's hunting dogs would soon be sniffing her trail. He'd suspected. He must've seen something in her face. Known she could no longer stand the sight of him.

Soledad tried moving faster, but she had no idea which way to go, had never been through the forest at night. In this unfamiliar place, she had no inherent sense of direction.

She could hear another horse gaining on her, the dogs closer than before.

Then a shot cursed the night.

Her horse buckled beneath her, and she went soaring through the dark.

Soledad's back somehow hit a wall that seemed to spring from nowhere. It was a watering well she'd slammed into.

Her arm bent painfully. She knew she was bleeding but couldn't tell from where.

Moving felt impossible.

A shadow loomed above her. She tried mumbling the words her mother had taught her long ago to heal, but her mouth kept filling with blood.

"Where do you think you're going?" Gerardo loomed above, looking at her broken state in disgust. "Did you truly intend to leave me? After all I have done for us? After all I've put up with from your family and your refusal to give me a child!"

Soledad clutched her arm but her body shook, and she realized it was from laughter. "Why would I bear a devil's son? My womb is sacred." She coughed. "My womb is *mine*."

Gerardo bent down, his skin flushed with fury, his dark eyes flashing with revulsion—a revulsion he'd kept hidden for some time. "You are the witch," he spat, his fingertips running across her neck like a caress. "But worse, you're a betrayer to your own. I have you to thank for our luck, and the people of Villa del Sur have you to thank for their misfortune."

Soledad felt her eyes water. "I should've cursed you . . . the moment we met."

His hand wrapped around her throat, squeezing until her vision blurred.

"Wouldn't that have been lucky?"

It would have, and her last thoughts, her last breath, was a curse. She cursed him and his children. She would come for them all.

Never would they truly be loved.

Only if someone could prove otherwise would she ever show mercy.

Gerardo Sevilla picked up his dead wife and discarded her in the darkness of the well.

29

SOMEONE'S HANDS ARE OVER MY NECK and panic floods my veins.

I won't die like her.

My arm swings but it connects with air. I sit up, scouring my surroundings, completely disoriented. I try clearing the fog from my head but Soledad's past trickles into my memory like melting snow.

I flex my arm, but it's not injured.

The well is right there, only a few feet away. Even from here, the air is ripe with its magic.

"I figured she wouldn't kill you."

I whirl toward the voice—Adel stands there, a hip cocked as if annoyed to have been kept waiting. She saunters toward the lip of the well. It's then I notice what she's tapping against her hip.

A pistol.

"You would think I'd never want to be back here." She scrapes the gun against the rough rock, a grating sound I feel in my teeth. "The prison that's kept me for over twenty years. Longer than I'd been alive at that point."

I suck in a breath.

Her gaze shoots to me. It's the first time I've seen the full extent of unsteady turmoil in her eyes—the deep well of revenge.

"I went back to fix what your mother couldn't finish. What she didn't have the heart for, and *I* was punished for it. For loving him better."

I sit on my knees, afraid to make a sudden movement. "I don't understand."

She laughs. "Oh, I know. There's a lot you don't understand. La Cegua only shows you what she wants, and truth has never been Marina's forte, to say the least."

"You made a wish," I state. "That's what happened? You made a wish about Roman and got stuck here."

The gun comes away from the well. She swings it around as she stalks. My throat seizes.

"More or less. Until you came back."

Me? Why me?

"*You*," she says as if hearing my thoughts. The gun comes up and I flinch. "You and your mother returned, and the witch thought it was time to release me. Took me a bit to figure out why."

"Why me? I never lived here. I wasn't coming back."

"Oh, but you were. You left as a little parasite and returned all grown-up." She pretends to wipe a tear from her cheek. She gestures with the gun for me to get up. And I do, slowly, my mind wrangling with what she's saying. I left here as a parasite . . . a baby?

"You never would've been born had your mom been trapped here with me like she was meant to be, had she not found some sort of loophole."

I keep my hands up. "What do you mean? What loophole?"

She laughs bitterly. "Same thing I would *love* to know. What loophole did Marina find that I couldn't? I tried talking to her at the hospital, but she didn't even remember me. And I was in theater with her so I know she can't act."

"My mom . . . she was supposed to be trapped in the cavern?"

Adel beams. "Ah, she's catching on. So here's what's going to happen next: We're not going to make a fuss. We're going down there and *maybe* we'll both make it out again, if you cooperate."

Millipedes erupt from the dirt, crawl over our shoes. I swallow down the panic.

"Why are you doing this?"

Her head tilts. "God, you really haven't put any of it together, have you? Guess the apple doesn't fall far from the tree. Didn't the old curandera tell you? For la Cegua to have her fill of justice, the Sevilla line must die or one of them has to give up what they most desire. That's how the story goes."

There's movement behind her, but she's staring down at the well with a hitched lip, unaware.

Jamie's there, raising a finger to his lips, and my heart cries out but I don't dare make any sign of acknowledgment.

I need to distract her, keep her talking, because despite her claim, if I go down to the cavern with her, I know I won't come back alive. "The—the Sevillas are already gone, though. Why is she still around? Why are *you*?"

Her eyes narrow. "None of this is over, and I really didn't want to be the one to break it to you—" Jamie's creeping closer. His feet bare. "But the Sevillas are not all gone. You're still here."

My attention is fully on her now. A truth welling up that can't align with reality. That I refuse to make sense of. She looks at me and frowns, bitter with old, old resentment. With untamed jealousy.

"You, Cecilia, are the last living Sevilla. But that"—she lifts the gun again—"changes tonight, one way or another."

A snap. Jamie lunges for her, stealth forgotten, but it's too late for Adel to react. He swings a fallen branch over her head with a sickening crunch, and she spins, crumpling to the ground.

I'm by his side in an instant. He's running his hands over my face, the tears pricking my eyes.

He's here. He's safe.

Jamie picks up the fallen gun and chucks it into the woods. And he's a complete fool.

He turns to me with a wince. "I . . . probably should've kept that."

I sigh. "I'm just glad you're okay, but yeah. Probably."

Adel's still breathing. I grab hold of Jamie's hand and we dash through the trees, back onto the path toward my house.

The more I run, the harder it is to catch my breath and the easier it is to not think about her words. We right ourselves quickly after slipping, helping each other through the muck of the watery trail.

"The moment she wakes, she'll be coming after us," I say. "How'd you even get there?"

We go through the blue garden door, sidestep the vines. I guide him toward the garage, where Roman's car waits.

"I walked into the woods after—after we talked, and I couldn't find my way back. Then I heard voices. I don't know how to explain it, but—"

"She led you to me," I finish. And he nods. Maybe Soledad hasn't abandoned me yet.

We reach the garage, slip into the unlocked door. When I get in the car, the keys are under the visor where Gabe last left them.

Jamie sits in the passenger side, gaze tracking the interior. "I don't want to be *that guy*, but this car is beautiful."

I scoff a small laugh, look at him. His smile is sheepish. Not because of what he just said, but because of the way we left things between us.

We have a thousand more pressing concerns, I know this, but I want to apologize for saying I didn't care, because it wasn't true. I care too much and when he looks at me with this incredibly tender expression, I think he knows this too.

But I don't want to leave things unsaid between us. Not anymore.

His eyes widen as I grab his shirt, bringing his face close to mine.

And I kiss him.

My mouth is over his, my grip tight on his collar, because I'm unwilling to let him go this time. His hand immediately finds my neck, fingers pressed to the wild thrumming pulse. He tastes as sweet as I've imagined. As fevered and loving as I could've dared hope.

There's a desperation in the kiss, a release we've both needed after weeks of fighting this. My chest unfurls, betraying all the pent-up desire.

I want to stay here forever; I want this kiss to go on all night, but it can't. We can't.

Pulling away, though neither of us wants to, I open the garage door and spear the ignition. The engine gives a sputter. Dead. The gas tank reads that it's half-full, but it can't be. Of course it can't be.

I hit my palm over the steering wheel. We need a place to hide. A place—

Find it. Where a Sevilla belongs.

The portrait, the hall of Sevillas. Like in Soledad's vision. I look to Jamie, his panicked eyes riddled with questions.

"I know where to go."

NEITHER OF US have our cell phones on us, but we try the house phone first. The line is dead. Everyone from the campout is at least a mile away, and there's no way I'm going back out into the woods right now. Jamie struggles to keep up as I take the stairs of the manor two at a time, fingers crossed that my hunch proves true. My vision blurs. Jamie was right. The well's magic, la Cegua, none of it was ever safe. The well comes with deadly consequences, and I'd placed my mom in danger. Adel had been there for years. Imprisoned by a wish gone wrong.

She said that I . . . that the Sevillas—

My throat feels like it's closing up. I can't think about this now.

Instead, I'm picturing the vision. Soledad sneaking out of Gerardo's office. A hidden office right under her nose. Right under mine. Hidden where a Sevilla belongs. Where a Sevilla would find it.

The pit of my stomach is acid. If what Adel said is true, does that mean la Cegua has been slowly luring me into a trap, reeling me in as a spider would a fly? That I'm meant to give up my life or my greatest desire?

The last living Sevilla.

I flinch at the words.

"Are you all right?" Jamie pants. We're almost to the hall. "We should really talk about what happened."

"Not now," I say.

"I heard what she said, Ceci. About you. About your mom."

Once we're upstairs, Gerardo's portrait glares back with his fierce eyes from the end of the hall.

"Please." I turn to Jamie. "I can't—I don't want to have this conversation right now. I know I messed up. I should've listened and not wished for anything to begin with. The curandera was right—they've been waiting for me. Soledad. Roman. Adel. Whatever they're pushing me to find, to do, will put an end to it."

"An end to what?"

I tap Gerardo's portrait tentatively, as if the painting will leave my fingers with an oily slick. "What he started."

I grab hold of one side of the enormous frame with both hands, thinking it'll take immeasurable force to budge. But it doesn't.

The air pressure makes it stick, but the frame pivots outward like a Murphy door with a bit of cracking and a groan.

Jamie takes it in. "Holy shit. All this time."

He helps me nudge the rest open, and a waft of mildewy air rushes up to greet us. A stairway leads down into the pitch black. Just like the wishing well's first steps down into the cavern.

An abandoned, forgotten place.

"We can hide in here. Eventually my mom will get home, and we can call for help then."

"When is she due back?"

I grimace. "Not until tomorrow."

"Well, all right then." He grabs my hand, no hesitation, and squeezes.

Like before, we're careful going down the steps, feeling our way and holding on to the wall until we reach the ground. On the last step, there's a dangling cord. A light switch. When I flick it on, the entire room comes into focus.

"It's so . . . normal," Jamie says. "Someone's room, maybe?"

I take in the band posters, the bare mattress on the floor, the dusty guitar. A place to escape and store the things you don't want found. What snags my attention is the wall covered with photos and notes, strings connecting one thing to the other, face-to-face, event to event. A detective's board—chaotic and telling.

"Almost normal." Jamie steps up to the board first. "He was obsessed."

This was Roman's room. He must've found Gerardo's office and turned it into his room. The old antique writing desk I saw in my vision of Soledad is still here, pushed up against the wall and cluttered with books and sketchbooks. It's where she'd found her old letters back when it belonged to Gerardo.

"Ceci—you gotta see this."

I take the last hesitant step to his side, facing the chaotic photo wall. There are pictures of Roman and my mom everywhere.

There's one of her in his car, by his side, flicking her middle finger at the camera. A date scribbled *July 1999*. An entire year before he went missing. They'd been together for a while.

An entire relationship she kept hidden. What Adel said about a loophole. Is that why her age and all the other dates don't line up? Because she was trapped here like Adel? At least for a time . . .

There's a photo of Dominik and his little brother shoulder to shoulder. A tacked note under the picture says: *First test: wished to be only child. Result: dire.*

Adel's photo. *Second test: wished for parents to get off her back. Result: successful, with wounding consequences.*

My mother. *Third test: wished for money. Result: unsuccessful, with all lost.*

"Oh my god," I say. "He treated this like some sick science experiment." My mom wished for money. Of course she would. Resulting in all lost, whatever that means. To reduce what happened to Dominik and his brother to *dire* is just cruel.

Jamie seems equally disturbed. He points to the picture of Roman in the center of the board, the final placeholder on a genealogy chart for the Sevillas branching above him. It's the same picture of him from upstairs. He's standing by the manor's woods. A cold secret in his eyes.

He doesn't state what he wished for, it simply says: *Result: Die. Or get someone you love and truly loves you back to plead for you. Even if it costs them.*

It's almost exactly what Adel said. What Curandera Lupe had warned. The only way la Cegua finds her fill of vengeance is for every last Sevilla to die. Or give up what they most desire. For Roman, I think living was what he most desired. To outrun a decades-long curse. Results: obviously unsuccessful. Adel had mentioned finishing something my mom couldn't and being punished for it. Did she try to plead for Roman's case? Had my mom tried and failed?

Jamie wears a grim expression.

On the board, there's also news clippings of sinkholes around town, dated near his disappearance. I think he was also tracking what the effects of going to the cavern were, and an uncomfortable thought forms—I'd been doing the exact same thing. Figuring out how this works, unraveling the cavern's magic as if it were composed of tried-and-true laws, and not a spirit with a mind of her own.

The rest is more pictures of my mom. So beautiful and young. Long silky hair wound in braids or hanging loose over her shoulders. She looks so happy in some. Cowered in others. Roman's arms around her waist, or neck, or tight on her shoulders like a vise. As if claiming what's his. I notice his hand in one of the photos. He's wearing a plain band, but I know it's mine—the same one I gave to Gabe earlier in the night for safekeeping. The one I thought belonged to my mom all this time.

It's his.

I can't look at them anymore. Can't reconcile the girl with the woman who's raised me. Can't think of the severe boy as anything other than the local mystery.

I wonder if this is the extent of what Roman wanted me to find. *Behind the wall. Where a Sevilla belongs.* But it can't be. Not if he was looking for an alternative to his curse—a way to control la Cegua. My mind churns. Gerardo hid his office behind his portrait. I look toward Roman's picture tacked on the brick wall. In the center of the chaos.

Where a Sevilla belongs.

"Behind the wall," I voice out loud, heading in that direction. Jamie looks on warily as I remove the photo and see a clearly loose brick behind it.

"Whoa. They really had a flair for the dramatic."

"They had a lot of things to hide." I wedge the brick out, the shine of metal peeking through. I take out more of them, Jamie joining in. Dried cement dust rains down on us as we keep going. Pictures of my mom and the others come fluttering down. Most of the blocks require nothing more than a strong tug, but Jamie grabs a letter opener from the table for the more stubborn ones until we reveal what's inside.

An antique chest.

Together we pull out the chest, which is a lot heavier than I expected, and place it on Roman's bed.

Jamie and I look at each other and I know he's wondering the same thing. Have we opened enough? Everything we've discovered has only led to more and more danger. Yet, now that I'm this close, I get that same electric pull that I do from the forest, and I need to know.

The latch is unlocked, broken. The chest looks ancient. When I flip the lid, I rear back.

Inside, surrounded by velvet like the interior of a casket, are mustard seeds and bones.

30

THE POWER EMANATING OFF THE BONES is intoxicating.

Jamie's voice is a hammer against the silence. "Do you think those are Roman's?"

I shake my head. No. No, they're not his. Scattered all around are the same tiny mustard seeds found everywhere in this town. The same ones that were in the letters Soledad found long ago. An attempt to subdue.

"What was he doing?"

"Trying to trap her," Jamie says with sudden confidence. "It's why he went to the curandera. Witches of Villa del Sur are buried in their local laguna with mustard seeds. It's supposed to put them to rest, so their spirits don't wander."

I gawk at him and he shrugs.

"I did some extra research."

My smile is small but filled with warmth. "Of course you did." I grab an old JanSport book bag from over Roman's bed, dump out the single binder, and slowly fill it up with Soledad's remains. The chest is too heavy to lug. "We might need these," I say.

Jamie looks a little dazed. "I'm disturbingly right there with you." And he helps fill the bag and empty out the chest. Tucked into the side of it, however, are letters. Soledad's bundled letters now ripped open. It's what Roman believed was Soledad's heart, and I wonder if she showed him the vision of her death, too, and he just didn't care.

"I saw those," I explain to Jamie. "In a vision—something Soledad wanted me to see. The letters were meant for Soledad's family but Gerardo never sent them. He was isolating her, keeping her from the people she loved. And then he killed her."

Jamie's eyes widen. "He killed her?" I nod, and he mutters, "Asshole."

Jamie reaches forward, plucking another note tucked into the morbid chest. But this paper is modern—college-ruled with the tight precise handwriting of an artist. Jamie glances at it and pales, his reluctant beat to hand it over making my heart stutter in my chest, but I take it. I can't skirt around this anymore.

The note's addressed to my mother. My eyes skim over the words.

Marina,

By the time you read this, you'll probably know, and I'm not ready . . . a kid will only hold us back . . . You know what it's been like for me. My entire life, they've told me the Sevillas die young. We're punished for something we didn't do.

She's taken too much from us, and I'm not stopping until I take something back.

I'm completing the ritual, Marina. She'll be under my control and she won't be able to refuse. I'm going to make the wish, and I can't imagine spending eternity on my own. We can both stay together, young and invulnerable.

You never have to be broke again, you'll never have to deal with your aunt, or the crap cards life has dealt you. I can give you everything. I promise, I'm doing this for us. Think about what it would mean to bring another Sevilla into the world with the way things are now. It'd be a waste of life. It'd be pointless.

I love you.

Yours always,
Roman

I don't realize I'm crying until a big drop falls onto the paper, smearing the words—*Pointless.* It's the second time I've cried in the span of a few hours, and I thought I'd forgotten how. I'd forgotten the pain that comes with it.

"Ceci," Jamie says softly over my shoulder.

"I'm the kid," I say, the realization creeping back up my neck, closing in tight like a fist. A realization that's been building under my skin like a disease. Adel had called me the parasite. My mom had been in the well, had made a wish, had known Roman intimately. This time there's no outrunning the truth, no denying the words when they're printed here in black and white.

I'm their kid. The one he never wanted.

"I CAN'T STAY IN HERE. I can't. I'm sorry." I dash from the room. *His* room. For all I know, the place where I was conceived. God, I'm going to be sick.

"Ceci, wait—" Jamie can't keep up, he picks up the book bag of bones. "It's dangerous!" I'm flying up the hidden stairs, gasping as I push Gerardo's portrait outward and stumble into the hall.

The entire manor seems to be shaking with the thunderstorm raging outside. I go downstairs to the house phone in the parlor and try my mom's cell again, angrily punching in her number, but the call doesn't go through, because nothing in this godforsaken town is normal. The line is still dead, but she needs to explain. She needs to be here now and tell me why. *Why.*

How?

He disappeared five years before I was born. *How?*

Jamie's trying to calm me. But I need to move. Figure out where to go next. How to escape. The kitchen's back door toward the forest, the front door toward the road? Do I look for la Cegua or my mother? There's a tempest inside my heart I can't ease. There's a rage screaming through my body louder than the cracks of lightning outside. I sink to the floor because I don't know where to go. I don't even know who wants me.

Roman is my father. My mother made a wish. It all went so very wrong. It's the only thing I'm sure of. But my dad is supposed to be this loser who travels the world, sending me stupid blank postcards. I suck in a breath. Travels the world. Gabe.

"Ceci, *please*, come here." Jamie's hands are on me, squeezing my body to his as if he could absorb the pain, trying to fix the broken geyser that's finally erupted. That I'm not sure will ever be tempered.

"I can't—he didn't want me. Why didn't he want me?"

Jamie's expression is shattered. He collapses beside me. He can't fix this. He can't fix *me*.

"He's dead and trapped, and my mother's a liar. Neither of them have ever wanted me. I've been a mistake. A wish gone wrong." I'm sobbing. The tears won't stop now that they've broken free.

Jamie's murmuring something in my hair but I can't hear him. The high-pitched keen of everything I've kept inside is screaming like a kettle.

"You're not a mistake. Ceci, listen. *Listen*, please."

Jamie's face swims in my vision as I bring my eyes up to meet his.

He looks through me as if seeing the fractured pieces of my thoughts filtering across my face. And he waits. Waits until he's sure I'm aware of him again.

"You're not a mistake," he repeats.

There's a sting I can't swallow. "You saw the letter. You saw."

He shakes his head. His smile so heartbreakingly tender. "The only thing I see is you. Here. Alive and beautiful—courageous. It doesn't matter *how* you got here. That's between them, between two kids, because that's what they were. You're here now—and I'm so glad about it. I am so glad you're here."

A sob bubbles out of me. I press my face to his sturdy chest, his hand on my back smoothing out the knots under my skin.

"I'm sorry," he says, voice rumbling against my cheek. "I'm sorry you've been kept in the dark for so long. I'm sorry they were so absorbed that they couldn't see you. But I do. I see you, and I want you, and I'd *choose* you. So many people would."

And it's as if his words are the final chisel. The final stroke to complete not a beautiful picture, but a real one. How often had I wanted to hear someone say those words to me? To mean it. How often did I want someone to reach in and pull me out of the depths?

It took this place, the cavern, Jamie. And it took the truth.

Jamie pulls back, running his thumb under my eyes to wipe away my tears. His eyes are glass yellow, like a rainy meadow. Like a haven in a dark forest.

"We'll get your answers, okay? But whatever they reveal, remember *you* choose. You can decide who and what is worth having in your life. Everything else can go to hell."

I nod, my face in his hands. My throat so tight, I can't say the words raging in my heart.

Like before, impulse takes over instead. I lean forward, press my lips to his, feel his mouth soften under mine. It doesn't take long for his fingers to twine around my hair, and we're lost in each other again. Lost then found. Searching then reaching. Tethered.

Even when our mouths clash in desperate movements, as if he can absorb every bit of sorrow, he's gentle. He's loving. It's a kiss unlike any I've had.

I'd live forever in this moment if given the chance.

We break, our foreheads touching, our breaths warm on our faces. His fingers lace through mine. *Home.*

Then the front door crashes open, and my mom steps through, soaked from the storm, just as a streak of lightning spears through the sky outside. Fear darkens her face because right behind her is Adel.

31

"MOM," I SAY, everything fleeing from my thoughts the moment I take in the gun at her back.

"Cecilia." Her eyes are pained.

Jamie lunges for the fire poker but a shot goes off and I scream. I think maybe it hit him because he stops moving but then a rain of plaster trickles down from the ceiling.

Adel *tsk*s, blood running down her face. "That's right. Girl with the gun makes the decisions." She casts Jamie a disapproving once-over. "This is a mid-Florida hunting county, you jerk. Did you think I would only carry one gun?"

She sounds so young. So high school, but this is someone who's been stuck in a hole for over twenty years. The edge of unkempt violence leaves an unsettling residue in her voice. The storm continues to rage outside, rain dripping from both her and my mom to soak the rug beneath.

Adel nudges my mom forward with the gun. "Look who I found outside," she deadpans, moving the sopping red hair from her face. "Heard a sinkhole gobbled up the exit to State Road 40. Looks like la Cegua doesn't want anyone skipping town."

Mom pushes away from her. “I came back because I remembered everything.”

Adel scoffs. “Oh, good, so you recall betraying us now?”

Betraying?

Mom’s mouth tenses imperceptibly. She arches a brow, donning her epic bitch face. Another mask. “You wanted him for yourself, didn’t you? I thought you’d be happy resting in eternal bliss together.”

Adel laughs. “Same old, same old. And here I thought I was the only one who didn’t mature.”

I try inching away while she’s distracted. Jamie notices what I’m doing, catches my fleeting gaze toward the ancient rifle hanging in the library. He’s a lot closer than I am but . . .

“*You* can stop sneaking your way over here.” Adel looks at Jamie then, who stops doing exactly that. She sighs, impatiently. “Come here,” she tells him, as if he were a child to scold. Jamie hesitates at first, but she brings the gun up to press to the back of my mom’s head and I can’t help but whimper.

“All right, all right.” He holds his hands up, and I want to scream at him to run. The second he’s close enough, Adel whips the gun across his temple.

I scream, rush for him as Jamie crumples to the ground.

“There,” she says. “Now we’re even.”

The gun swings to me, and my mom lets out a cry of protest.

“Please,” I say, holding my hands up, “just let me check and see if he’s okay.”

Adel glances down at Jamie. She nudges his shoulder with her boot. And I see it, the hitch of breath. “He’s fine. And we have a date with a cavern.” She nods to the book bag he dropped. Crouches down and unzips it. She meets my eyes. “Oh, you clever, clever girl. This changes everything. Maybe we really can get what we all want. After I bring Roman back.”

Mom and I gasp at the same time.

I think of the other part of the ritual she'll need. La Cegua's heart. "It won't work," I say.

Adel hoists the bag's strap over her shoulder. She reaches for her waistband and pulls out the doll. She smiles.

"I think we'll be okay."

Oh god. She gestures for us to walk outside ahead of her, leaving Jamie behind.

I cast him one lingering look before shuffling forward. The rain pelts us immediately.

"Adel," Mom cries. Our feet squelching over the muddy garden path. "Why don't you just leave town? Start over."

Adel practically growls. "You don't think I tried that? That's the first thing I did. I couldn't get past the damn bridge." She edges us between the hedges. The slope toward the forest and down to the circular garden door. But what if it doesn't appear?

"Don't do this," Mom says. "It didn't end well for you the first time. What makes you think it'll work now?"

I look back. A shadow shifts in Adel's eyes. Part of her fears the consequences. She knows this isn't benevolent magic, and she's asking to toy with a vengeful supernatural spirit all over again.

She looks at me and smiles. "Because this one's special. Wouldn't you say? Either way, things can't get any worse."

We make it past the magnolia trees and even before Adel pushes me to move aside the vines, I know it's there. I can feel the pulse beneath my skin.

Adel inspects the garden door for a long while. Judging by the surprise and relief in her expression, she's used to seeing something else. As if it never materialized for her before.

Adel kicks open the rotting door to the forest path, pushing us both ahead of her. Another streak of lightening cracks through the sky.

I'm drowning under the downpour of rain as we push our way forward. Suffocating under my circling thoughts. Jamie's crumpled figure fogging every corner of my blurred vision.

My mom moves as if to hold my hand, but Adel immediately tells her to knock it off, and despite the threat of the moment, I don't think I'm ready for that either. We tumble through the thick mud. The layer of water making every step down the path grueling.

Adel walks behind us, having an equally hard time traversing the path. But I still feel detached from it all. Like those sleepwalking dreams where it's not even me roaming the forest. My mind is what's struggling.

"I'll get us out of this," Mom says quietly. "You must be so confused."

"I'm not," I say, voice probably loud enough to be overheard.

Mom stops. "You're not?"

Adel waves the gun in the air. "Hello? No stopping."

But realization fills Mom's expression. "She found you."

La Cegua is who she means. La Cegua, who's been waiting. For me—the last Sevilla.

Adel stomps closer to us. "Hello—"

"Wait!" Mom whirls on her. "Goddammit, wait."

"I found her," I say, arms crossing, rainwater falling into my eyes. "I went to the cavern. I made wishes I'm not proud of and I found out too late that there are deadly consequences because my *mother* who went through the exact same thing years ago that cost three boys their lives didn't bother warning me and telling me the truth before she dumped us here. Why did we even come back, Mom? If you planned on keeping me in the dark forever, why bring me here and risk me finding out everything? There's a yearbook with your picture in it!"

A ripple of defensiveness shutters through her. "I didn't remember!" Mom struggles with the ring on her finger, twisting and turning it until finally she gets the thing off and tosses it to me.

"Gabe kept trying to remind me, but it wasn't until the ring—until I was leaving town with it on that it all came back."

I look down at it. Roman's ring. The one I'd been wearing all this time.

"You weren't supposed to find anything," Mom says. "I told her to keep you out of it. Like the rest of this town, you're not supposed to see the truth! It's part of our last bargain—*my wish*." Her nose wrinkles with the bitter words. "And I don't know, Cecilia. I guess—I guess part of me always knew I'd have to come back here eventually. This place is a curse. But I won't let her hurt you. No matter what."

I want to say that Soledad wouldn't hurt me, but I don't know anymore.

Adel lets out a harsh laugh. "Tell her the rest, Marina. Tell her what happened to her dad. How you couldn't save him."

Mom bares her teeth at her. "You don't know what the hell you're talking about."

Adel wipes the water from her face. "Oh, I don't? *I* was there. Since the moment that witch tugged on his generational curse, I've been there, even before you." She turns to me. "Roman found the cavern first, like every Sevilla before him, and as soon as he did, he showed us. It didn't take long before we figured out what the cavern could do. The magic it held and the promises it offered. He'd given us all a gift. Everything was going fine at first: our wishes were coming true; we were all getting what we wanted. Then Dominik's little brother went missing, and Dominik couldn't take the guilt."

A roll of thunder clashes and we all flinch.

"It wasn't a gift," Mom scoffs. "Roman was using us. We were his little guinea pigs to see how bad things could get before he made his wish. He became obsessed with figuring out how to have everything he wanted without the consequences. How to break his curse. First he thought he could bind la Cegua. He'd convinced us all it was possible. Said we could wish for immortality. He could give us everything and more."

"And that's what you wanted?" I ask. "To be alive forever?"

Adel laughs bitterly, answering even though the question's not directed at her. "Who wouldn't want to be young and hot forever?"

My mom gives her a look of utter disgust. "And how's that working out for you?"

Adel taps the gun to her chin as if she's thinking. "I'll let you ask me by the end of the night. *If* you're still around."

Mom rolls her eyes. "Roman painted this picture about true love being the only thing to break generations of wrongdoing. And I believed it. He told me that all I had to do was wish for us to be together, immortal. To wish for him to be spared from the curse."

"But you didn't love him enough," Adel snaps.

Roman had wished, without the others knowing, to have the knowledge on how to break the curse. *Die. Or have someone you love and truly loves you back to plead for you. Even if it costs them.*

He didn't care what it would cost her. So it was him that didn't love *her* enough.

"I went down to that cavern," Mom says. "Even though after Dominik died, I'd told myself I'd never step foot in there again. But Roman dragged me." Her face darkens. She points at Adel. "*She* was there, too, always clinging to him like a tick. He told me everything would go back to the way it was once I did this." Mom's face is stricken, and it hurts. It hurts to see her like this. To ever think of her being pushed down by anyone.

"In the cavern, she waited for us—la Cegua—in all her horrifying beauty. She took off her veil. And she was animal and death." The night sky fills with the buzz of insects. Electricity erupts across my skin and even though we haven't gone farther, I know the cavern is coming to us.

"I was about to make the wish. La Cegua knew before I even opened my mouth. She clocked Roman's hands on the back of my neck and showed me . . . the cavern transformed, and I saw myself holding you. Just me and you, kid. I held your tiny hand as you squeezed, as you opened your gorgeous eyes—and I *knew* that you were mine, and his, and that I carried you already. And I couldn't lose you. How could I want to live forever if it meant you would stop existing?"

Pain wells up from every recessed corner of my body until I'm drowning in it.

"The Cegua was tricking you." Adel's pale face flushes with fury. "Roman could've figured out how to make everything right; you just didn't give him the chance. Because you've always been selfish and you never loved him."

"*I* never loved him?" Mom stabs a finger to her chest. "Roman saw the same thing I did. He knew I was pregnant. Knew what it would cost me to make that wish and he didn't care!"

A kid will only hold us back.

"If Gabe hadn't shown up at the cavern when he did, if he hadn't knocked him out, I could've lost *everything*." Gun be damned, Mom takes a step closer to Adel, grips her arm. "You saw him, Adel. He wasn't right anymore. He was messing with power way too big for him. Binding her bones with his blood. You saw his *face* . . ." Adel takes on a tinge of yellow as if remembering. "He looked like a monster. And what did you do? Pleaded for his life because he told you to, because he'd kept you as his last resort and he didn't care what happened to you either."

"Fuck you," Adel says between her teeth, pulling away. "At least I tried to save him while you and your little friend only looked out for yourselves. I told the Cegua how much I loved him, had always loved him, how we deserved to be together, and I was punished for it—not by him, the so-called monster, but by that spirit bitch."

Adel stares Mom down ferociously. "And you know why I wished for all of us to live forever, Marina?" Her laugh is bitter as acid. "Because I wanted you to stick around and witness what you'd lost, but I couldn't even have that, because she let you go."

My throat goes tight. Adel had said she'd been punished for finishing what my mom couldn't. She'd been released the moment we got into town, but Roman was not. Roman was still stuck there.

Adel dashes to my side, pressing the gun's lip to my temple, bruising the skin. My mom sucks in a breath but doesn't dare move. "So tell us, Marina. I'm sure Cecilia would also love to know how you got free from la Cegua. Why did she let you go?"

Another fracture of pain fissures across Mom's expression. When it seems she won't say anything, Adel digs the gun deeper into my skin and something in her expression must make my mom spill.

"Stop," she chokes out. The storm builds around us, her words loud to be heard over the rain. "I didn't just walk away from the cavern that day. For *five years* I didn't age, and no one remembered me except Gabriel." Shock strikes me like I'm a tuning fork. *Five years.* "I knew you'd stopped growing too," she says to me. "I could feel you inside me—I wasn't showing. You barely had a heartbeat. But every test would still come back positive, and I just *knew*. It was supposed to be my twenty-second birthday and I looked the same. The cavern never made itself known to me again. That kind of loneliness . . . it gets to you." Mom swallows hard. "I was carrying another human *inside me* and neither of us would ever grow beyond what we were. It was all some sick joke—the bullshit promises Roman made, the decisions he took from all of us. I hated him for it. I was so, so angry. I needed it to be over and I couldn't live like that anymore."

A terrible ache grips my chest. "What'd you do?"

Her face goes empty. The swirling pain I know that's raging inside her is suddenly masked. Something we're both experts at hiding when we want to. "I tried to end it. There was this invisible perimeter around the entire town that prevented me from leaving. It was like hitting a thick wall. I got in my car, took the back road, and floored it."

"I take it it didn't kill you," Adel says at my back.

The buzz of electricity is even louder in my ears. Louder than the storm.

Mom shakes her head. "No. The car stalled right where the boundary was instead of smashing straight through like I figured it would. Like I'd hoped. It was a dark time for me—" She has to stop for a moment. "I'd brought a backup in case that didn't work. I won't go into the details but before I could do anything, I saw her. La Cegua was watching me from the trees like I was some freak show made for her entertainment. I got out of my car, screaming—a total mess." Her laugh is disparaging. "I don't know what I thought that would accomplish. But I followed her into the forest. Threw Roman's ring at her, told her I didn't want any of this. I still don't understand how you ended up with it."

I don't understand either. I found it one day in her purse. When I'd been looking through it for money. She never seemed to care that I'd started wearing it. It's because she didn't remember it at all.

"I didn't care if la Cegua got mad—she couldn't do anything worse. I yelled and yelled. Begged for one last wish—a bargain. Told her you had as much of my blood as you did his. I'd learned a little about her by that point. Knew what she'd been through. I wanted her to see that none of this was my choice, just like her fate wasn't hers." Mom's eyes fill with tears again and meet mine. "I wanted so desperately to see you grow up. I wanted to grow old with you—I wished it with all my heart. To forget everything and move on. I grabbed her feral hand and placed it on my stomach, and I couldn't see her face but something changed then. The air grew lighter, softer. She left her hand there for a while, almost as if she could see you inside me."

A connection built before I was even born.

Mom shrugs as if she could hardly still believe it. "She let me go. And maybe being a horrible mother was my consequence, because it's impossible to get everything you want in life." Her eyes close briefly. "But that's not the truth. I just never knew how to be a mom to you, and maybe I can blame that on how I grew up, but those would all be excuses. I've been selfish and afraid that if I tried and failed, it meant I was never supposed to be a mom to begin with. That maybe I was supposed to rot in this town with the others, become a forgotten relic at the bottom of a lake. Maybe I was never worthy of you." My chest threatens to tear with every word. "I owe you so much, Cecilia. And I'm sorry. I am so sorry, milagrito."

Her little miracle. Now I understand why she calls me milagrito.

Finally hearing her say everything I've ever wanted to hear from her shouldn't cause this much pain. It doesn't fill me as it should. An apology can't undo everything.

And whether it was brought on by her words or not, the well materializes before us, the ground shaking under our feet.

32

"GUESS THAT'S OUR CUE," Adel says the moment the quake stops. "Come on in, ladies, story time's over." She flicks the gun between us and the cave's lip. "It's time to put the witch to rest."

Lightning crashes nearby as if in challenge, illuminating the sky as we make our way down.

Adel pushes me forward first and we climb down the many steps. The air is mud-filled and old, but no longer comforting. The cavern releases another quaking shutter as we work our way down, and we stop, all of us tensing. Even a ripple of fear seems to work its way through Adel's otherwise cool facade.

But the shaking stops.

The cavern opens up before us, like a dream made reality. The ghostly echoes press in like a thick weight, and the soft drips of water trickle from the cavern's exposed cavities. I expect to see her, the way I have in visions, alive and real. Waiting. But only the stone version of her greets us.

With all this rain, the runoff has filled the spring considerably, creating an overpowering smell of damp air.

I'm careful treading onto the slippery bank.

"Here we are." Adel cracks her neck. "Home sweet home."

I can't help but wince. There was a time when this place did receive me like a home. But now I understand it was like a scent to lure prey.

"Roman, you gorgeous idiot," Adel mutters to the cavern, and I feel my stomach drop. I see the cavern walls ripple with shadow. Because he's been here. This whole time. Every time I've been here, he's seen me. "Left a bit of your legacy to run around and prolong this." Her voice darkens. "You should've told me."

An ache deep in my stomach.

"I don't understand," I say, watching my step. "Why bring us here with you? What do you need from us?"

"From her?" She gestures at Mom. "Absolutely nothing." And she shoots her. Right in the stomach.

"No!" My scream is earth-shattering. The entire cavern flickers with colors at the sound. My mom falls against a boulder, red spreading across her shirt. She looks more surprised than in pain. She falls to her knees, and I scramble toward her before her head can hit stone.

"Mom! Oh my god, Mom!" My hands are a shaking mess. I move her shirt up and see the wound is pulsing blood. Too much blood. It pools on the floor beneath her, falling in rivulets toward the spring.

"No!" I scream. I look to la Cegua's statue. "Help her, *please*. Save her. I wish for you to save her!"

The cavern walls don't shimmer. The statue doesn't move. My mom is still bleeding out.

I bare my teeth at Adel. "*Why?*"

Adel shrugs, but she's staring at my mom like she can hardly believe what she's done either.

"Motivation," she says. "She'll survive, once you bind the witch and make her."

My mom's chin is quivering. Her entire body is shaking but she's still alive. She grabs my hand. "I'll be okay," she says.

"Mom." My vision blurs with tears.

She pulls me closer. "You need to leave," she whispers. "Escape. The binding doesn't work, I've seen it. You'll get yourself killed. *Leave*, milagrito."

"Clock is ticking," Adel says.

I back away, shake my head. There's no way I can leave her here. No, I have to try to make this work.

I clench my fists. "What do you need me to do?"

"Bleed," says Adel, opening the bag of bones and tossing in the doll. The cavern gives another violent shake.

You need to bind the bones and her heart with mustard seeds and the blood of her enemy. I am her enemy. Because I'm the last Sevilla, the impossible choice that I thought was Roman's is now mine to make. Has always been. I was always meant to come back here and face it. La Cegua forever the marionette master.

Adel doesn't waste time. From her jacket's pocket, she produces a thin fillet knife in a leather sheath. A fisherman's tool to gut.

"We can break a million curses," Adel says. "But the only way to get rid of her for good is to strip her of power. An hechizo to bind a witch's corrupted spirit. Put her to rest, so to speak."

Control, greed, power. It's all they ever wanted from her, even in the afterlife. They're lying to themselves if they think this will bring Soledad peace.

Then, Adel's approaching me with the knife.

"Relax," she says. "It's like a paper cut." She tucks the gun into the waistband of her pants, wrenches my wrist toward her, and makes a deep slash on the palm of my hand. The skin splits, curls back. Hot blood pours out, excruciating pain vibrates along my arm, until I can feel it everywhere, until my vision goes cloudy.

Blood pours over the bones, over the doll's stitched dress, and a hiss of steam rises from the bag before Adel tosses everything into the water. At first, all is quiet. Then tendrils of veiny shadows geyser from where the bag sinks and spread across the spring, covering the statue's feet and tightening around her like rope.

La Cegua's statue groans, cracks as she moves, fighting the bindings.

"Isn't she terrifying?" Adel hums.

Large rocks tumble down from the ceiling, one heading right for Adel's head.

She yelps. Drops the bloody knife into the spring before diving out of the way. My mom is still slumped behind me, hand to her wound. Her gaze is glued to la Cegua.

The statue is transforming, becoming more corporeal. La Cegua is stretching the stone body as if testing its limits. Fury radiates from her. Thousands of worms and millipedes, ants and other dark-dwelling insects skitter out from the perforated ceiling.

Her veiled face meets mine. I can almost imagine her bone mask hiding beneath and glaring back at me. But she's not the only one upset. I want to scream at her.

Of all the memories she showed me, she could've told me who I was. What I meant to her—that our affinity to each other was only because of a centuries-long vengeful crusade. And not because the loneliness in her resonated in my hollow heart. Because I've felt for her. I really have.

La Cegua stops midmotion. Her stone head inclining. The dark shadowy bindings at her feet are slipping.

"I don't know how long the binding will hold!" Adel screams. "Make the wish!" She holds the gun up, again pointing it at my mother, whose breathing has turned too shallow. "Bring Roman back first!"

I think of all the memories I've seen of Roman. His cruelty. His obsession. But I have no choice.

"I wish for Roman Sevilla to come back!"

La Cegua stares me down. Through the veil, I can almost see a grotesque smile. The shadowy bindings around her as thin as thread. "And please . . ." I add. "Heal my mom."

The walls flicker between a kaleidoscope of colors, a nauseating whirlwind of places and dreams. Of wishes and memories. I fall to my knees, crawl toward my mother, who's already sitting up. A ghostly wind streams in from every crevice, hitting us with hurricane strength. It all feels like too much. The wind stealing my breath. The images take on sharper focus, like a holographic screen showing us la Cegua's past. Soledad. Not a vengeful creature or spirit, but a young woman.

Murdered.

Just like in the vision she had shown me, I watch the scene play out. A crackle of lightning through the perforated ceiling. Gerardo staring down from the ledge, breathing hard, bloody. He's staring down, down . . . and when I follow his gaze, to the rocky platform in the spring's center, the statue isn't there. Instead it's her. Her body strewn on the slab like an offering. Her mantilla, her dress bloody and tangled, covering her face. Covering the bruises of her neck where Gerardo strangled her to death.

The cavern flickers between morning and night, the dress flattening on a decomposing corpse as the days go by. The water silent and still like glass around her. Spreading throughout the cavern, tendrils of spilled incandescent magic like glittering oil fall from Soledad's body and seep into the rock, seep into the water. They reach and reach toward the ceiling but never high enough to escape. Never high enough to return home. Eventually the cavern is made of her, of her magic and blood and vengeance. All of it her tomb.

It all suddenly stops. The images, the wind. The hollow sounds of ghostly wails. It all goes utterly, disturbingly still. My mother's already sitting up.

At the water's edge, where I'd bled just moments ago, stands Roman Sevilla. In the flesh. Darkened veins of power branching under his skin.

33

MY MOTHER'S CRY STRIKES a blaze of fear through me. It's devastation and anger. Brutal, brutal grief wrapped into one sound. She struggles to her feet, the oozing wound at her waist gone.

"Marina." His voice is cold. So cold.

Roman takes a few steps toward us, the ground trembling beneath like the beginnings of another quake. The cavern is slowly crumbling, starting with la Cegua's statue. Her stone hand is turning to dust, finger by finger as Roman becomes more and more solid.

The image of her dead body strewn on the rock is gone.

Mom comes to my side. Her hand clasps mine. I keep her at my back as if I can shield her from this pain.

Roman cocks his head. Blinks animal-like as if putting us all into focus. His eyes, which had seemed endlessly black, settle to the rich brown I always find when I look in the mirror. A color so familiar it opens a wound in my chest.

His expression softens.

Adel comes forward, too, shaking off water from her gun. "Hello, Roman," she says. "Wait until you see everything we've missed."

Roman's attention, however, is solely on me. He's an artist, too, I remember. He studies my features like he plans on carving them into his memory, etching the shadows of my face.

"You're mine," he croaks—his voice layers thick, silenced for twenty-three years.

I straighten, though every part of me wants to crumble. Because there's no denying it, not with him standing in front of me. He's my father. This boy's DNA is half mine.

But I shake my head. "I'm not *yours*."

You didn't even want me. It's left unsaid, but he still flinches as if he heard. As if it was aimed at him with deadly precision.

Mom's shaking hand covers her mouth. She's always looked young to me, but it's staggering to see how time has gone by for only one of them. It's a difference she must take in too. Her hand lowers to her side in resolve, in control.

"Roman, you know this isn't right," she says, and his gaze shifts to her, hardening slightly. "You won't come back the same."

"The same as what?" he asks, voice layered and old. "The boy you loved?"

Her eyes close briefly. "Human. You're as touched by twisted power as she is."

Half of la Cegua's stone body has deteriorated. A cascade of tiny rocks showering into the water.

Roman grows in height, in the thickness of his shoulders, as age etches across his face.

He steps out onto the dry bank with us, the pool's water receding. A little cry draws my gaze to where Adel perches on a rock. She's staring at her hands as they elongate and grow freckles of age. And I wonder if all the wishes are being undone with la Cegua's power bound.

"Humanity is overrated." Roman flashes a crooked smile. A boyish expression on a maturing face. It's all wrong. "I've been trying to tell you, Marina, we can be anything we want. I'm not even upset that you left me here. I understand why you did it. I can see her now—" He gives another longing glance in my direction that thrashes my heart in my chest. "But I want you to see the full possibilities. You believed in me once."

"I've grown a lot since then." Mom's shoulder presses against mine. La Cegua's stone head rolls and shatters against her dais. "And I—I didn't *want* to keep you here. I just couldn't . . ."

Roman's brow quirks. "Wish to save me because you didn't really love me?"

"That's enough," I say. "You can't talk to her like that."

Roman steps back, bows his head. "I'm sorry. You're right."

I look back at la Cegua. The sight of her pitches a stone at my heart. "What's going to happen to her?"

Roman looks back, too, his jaw hardening with deep-rooted hatred. "She's faking it."

The cavern quakes are getting stronger. Flickering images like damaged film on the cavern walls—Soledad. Her face thrown back in a laugh. Her hidden smile.

"What?"

"She's toying with us," he says. "I'm still connected to this place. To her. I feel her power. She can't be bound because she doesn't have a heart. I learned that the hard way."

"Then why?" I say. "Why did you want me to find her bones?"

"I wanted you to find my room. Everything I'd uncovered was there. You had to have seen it . . ."

"Your wall of experiments. I saw it." And I'd done my own search, without his help, without using my friends. My mom's warmth presses against me. Or someone I claimed to love.

It's not regret that crosses his features, but something else.

"Then you know the only way to get rid of her is for a Sevilla to give up what they most desire." Or die, he doesn't add. He looks pained. But I don't know him. I don't know what's sincere or not. The darkened veins under his skin aren't comforting either. *A monster.* "I'm sorry that falls on you, Cecilia. It was cruel to bring another into this." He glances at my mother. "It's not that I didn't want you . . ." He tries to reach for me.

I back away. "What does that mean, though?" I demand. "What am I supposed to give up?"

"Family." Adel's words cut through. She's squirming in her skin, looking trapped between aging and youth. Like a glitchy filter. "That's what you want most, isn't it?"

My mom's hand squeezes mine. Family . . .

Noticing my reaction, Roman pins his feral glare on Adel. "No one knows what they really want," he snaps. "Desires change all the time. Why don't you leave this to us? You did your part; you can go now. You're free."

"But"—there's already hurt in her eyes—"what about . . . us?"

An invisible string tugs on his lips. The expression says it all, and the heartbreak on Adel's face is gutting. Despite the kind of person she is, I *feel* that look.

Adel stands there. Staring at him. Her eyes clouding, losing purpose. Desolation painted in raw brushstrokes along her jaw. She doesn't move as the cavern releases another shudder. Doesn't seem to notice the rock column trembling precariously behind her.

"Adel!" I scream, but she does nothing. Doesn't even turn around to face her death as the column falls. As it crushes her body, pinning her to the cavern floor.

Blood slopes into the spring.

"Oh my god. Oh my god." I smother my scream against my hands.

My mom hugs me to her chest. "Roman, stop this! You're putting my daughter in danger."

"Our daughter!" His anger bubbles to the surface. Not a moment spared for the girl who gave up everything for him. "Don't you realize she was already in danger?" he growls. "Didn't you think her days were numbered too? She can have a chance at life if she just gives up one thing!"

But he doesn't offer to give up what *he* wants. Power.

I'm trying not to look at where Adel lies.

"I can reason with her," I say, my voice shaking. "I'll call to Soledad." There's nothing left of her statue now, but that was never her. She is more. So much more, and if I could just . . .

"There is no reasoning with that creature!"

I flinch at the pain in Roman's voice. "She killed my father, and his, and all the ones that came before, and she took my life too. She would do the same to you. Cut your life down for something you had no part in. She's done it to us for generations." To us. To the Sevillas. "She was playing you. Nothing she shows you can be trusted."

I swallow down the hurt. I'm not sure why I feel hurt. Why I'm so bothered by the thought that la Cegua's quiet presence or her sorrowful pain could be lies.

Roman steps closer to me, extending a careful arm as if I were a cornered animal. I get the feeling he wants to wrap me in his arms. Make me feel safe. And I'm tempted to give in. In seconds, he's been made to look the age he would've been had he grown up in my life. Had he seen me through school, through heartbreaks, through every moment when I desperately wanted him there.

Wanted my parents.

"It's an illusion." Mom looks between us, tears in her eyes. "Whatever he's showing you, Cecilia. It's not real. Only one of you can leave this cavern unscathed, and he knows it."

Black, inky hair falls across Roman's face, and he pushes it back impatiently. "You don't know what you're talking about. Once the Cegua is dead, I can make everything right." He looks down at his hands, stained in power, as another violent shake rumbles under our feet.

We need to leave. The cavern won't hold up much longer.

Roman doesn't say a word, but there's a shift in the air.

My eyes raise. Gabe is at the top of the crumbling steps holding the shotgun from the library.

Jamie is right beside him. Half his face is covered in blood, and still, still he's so strikingly beautiful. He's okay.

And now he's here, putting himself in danger all over again.

"Jamie—"

I move toward him, but I'm wrenched back.

Roman clamps onto my upper arm, whirling me to him. My mom falls backward as if pushed by an invisible hand. And I think he really is connected to la Cegua's power.

I'm fading into the black, fathomless gaze of my father. I hear my mom scream something distantly. A shot goes off.

But it's all many, many miles away, because I'm here.

I'm safe in his arms.

His hands are calloused but warm. Loving but hard.

My father shows me the life we can have. The life we *should've* had. The electric buzz I get near the well becomes something physical, worms its way under my skin and into my veins.

A power. An invincible gift.

Stolen. Possessed. The words are low, so diminished I almost don't hear them but they're there, in the quiet pockets of energy flowing into me. Connecting me to this man I don't even know.

The grip on me tightens.

I see myself in the car, in the back seat. My parents are in the front, laughing. Singing along to this horrible song. My mom turns around to nudge me, encouraging me to join them, but I just roll my eyes. I've never felt this safe.

We stop in front of a large building. Find parking on a busy street with other parents dropping off their kids, unloading mattresses and dressers, brand-new laptop cases while they hold back tears. Their babies are leaving, entering the next phase of their lives, but the parents are always there to catch them if they fall. I hug my mom. My dad. I lock them in an embrace so tight I might decide to go back home.

Controlled. Caged. Lied to.

My veins swell with power. I'm nauseated with the bitter taste of something foreign rummaging in my body, finding me wrong.

Killed. Stolen. Forgotten.

More memories, wishes, filter through my head in light-breaking speed. But I'm starting to see someone else in those thoughts too. A woman is always there, standing back in her white veil. Watching as the world moves on without her. But I see her.

I see her.

Her head lifts in my direction. I watch slowly as she lifts her mantilla and shows me her true face. And in it, I see horror, I see beauty, but most of all, I see truth.

34

I PULL AWAY FROM ROMAN. My nail rakes across his cheek. Whatever my mother sees in my face makes her go white with terror. The cavern has almost completely collapsed around us. We'll be crushed under its weight.

I can tell I'm not right. Roman, as he stares back with a wicked look passing for loving, is not right. But it is tempting. Everything he showed me could be true. Everything I've ever wanted could be mine if I take it. But none of it would be real.

The things you want most have to be earned.

I look at Jamie. His expression is worried, but there's something else there too. Something fortifying and knowing, as if he has no doubts in me. It gives me the strength to do what I do next.

Because I know how to bind her, but even more, I know how to free her.

La Cegua is before me, everyone shouting as if from a distance. It's only me and her for this moment. Her true face should horrify me, but it doesn't. I grab hold of her hand with my bloodied one and fear crosses her expression.

"I wish you would remember what it is to love, and be loved in return. For everything to go back to how it's meant to."

Her heart. It's there, withered and forgotten, but there nonetheless.

"No!" Roman's scream pierces the encased silence. Parts of him are already going dull. Translucent. "Don't do this. You're my blood," he begs. "You're a Sevilla!"

"I'm sorry," I say, and I mean it. "I'm sorry I'll never get the father I deserved."

As Roman disappears, anguish on his face, I feel the bank crumble under me. Sink into the crystal clear spring where her bones now rest. I don't let go of her. I pull her with me, because she's here, in my heart, in the power streaming through my body, and I will take her home.

I SURFACE FROM LA LAGUNA as if from a long, long dream. I don't care that my feet are bare on the rocks, that my ragged dress drags against the muddy shore. Because there they wait. My family stands between the two large boulders that mark a trail. A trail to our pueblo.

The woman I never thought I'd see again rushes forward. Fire-clayed skin and hair of spun white. A sound pulls out of me—a name, prayer, and cry all at once. I fall upon my mother's arms with the full weight of pain I've carried for centuries. "Mamá. Mamá, forgive me. I wish I'd never left. I wish I'd stayed with you."

"Sh," my mother coos, trailing her strong hands over my hair and I am filled with light. "You have always been with us, corazón. Always."

My sisters come forward next, wrap me in their loving arms and soothe a loneliness I felt bone deep. My grandmother pulls my face to kiss my head, to remind me of what it's like to be surrounded by love.

The women of my family each bring me flowers and adorn my hair. Clean my skin with water from la laguna. Bring me tea and fill my pockets with the black seed of mustard.

All the while, they tell me, I am home. I am home.

I WAKE TO FIND a dark sky freckled with stars. The blush of a new morning spreading slowly across. There's a promise in there somewhere. A vow of new days ahead.

My mom's face fills my vision next. Sooty tears track down her cheeks. The relief I see when she looks in my eyes is like a balm. An assurance that I'm me. Untouched by magic.

Mom pulls me up, and though every part of me aches, I can't protest. I wrap my arms around her too. Feeling her shoulders shake, her breathing ragged against my neck. We're in the meadow, where the cavern's mouth—the wishing well—used to be. The coral stone collapsed inward, swallowed by the last sinkhole I hope this town will see for a long while.

But it's gone. There's no electric pull. No hollow sound of forgotten places. La Cegua is home. And Roman . . .

An ache forms in my throat.

I know my life is better without him. But it doesn't change the yearning. The secret wish that was buried along with him.

Over Mom's shoulder, Jamie and Gabe are there, bruises spreading across their faces and arms. Despite how it obviously hurts Jamie to smile, a beam spreads across his mouth that fills every crevice of my once hollow heart with light.

The three of them wrap me in their arms. "Let's get you home," Gabe says, picking me up like a child waking from a nightmare.

Exhaustion presses at the edges of my thoughts, but I want to tell him. "I'm already here. I'm already home."

35

Weeks later

THERE'S PAINT UNDER MY NAILS. On my jeans. It feels like forever since I've fallen into a project like this. In love. Consumed.

Filled to the brim.

My back is curved, hovering over the canvas. Daylight filters into my room, onto the sewing machine Gabe helped me restore last week. I add the final details, going over her brow, the gentle curve of her bow-shaped lip.

The face could belong to any of the women in my life. But I paint her not as la Cegua, but as Soledad. A girl that could represent any young woman forced to lose herself in the shadow of some ambitious man. I don't want her to ever be overlooked and forgotten. I paint her with a sharp upturned chin—head bowed for no one. Atop a horse, in a field of primrose and wild mustard, and no mud. Just wind.

There's a knock on my open door before Gabe pokes his head in. "You ready, kid? She's waiting for you." He looks at the painting. "She seems happy."

I tilt my head, studying it. Her mouth is unsmiling, but her braided hair is a crown on her head, her hand gentle on the horse's neck. She is glowing, safe.

Outside, I find my mom in the garden. We look the same—her covered in dirt, me covered in paint. Giving life to untended things.

She wipes the beads of sweat along her brow, pushes back the dark wisps of silky hair. She packs in the mustard plant amidst her roses. It's traveled with us to every house, and now it can finally take root.

When her eyes meet mine, her smile is hesitant. Pained.

She told me last night, she thinks we didn't get enough time. And maybe we haven't. Maybe we could've wished for more of it, more chances to fix the broken pieces between us.

At the dining table with Gabe last night, we'd gone through all the postcards he'd sent throughout the years, and he told me stories from each place. Mom listened quietly, sipping her tea but I know it hurt. Slowly we're unraveling the lies, the half-truths, the secrets she's had to tell me throughout the years. It hasn't been easy.

I hike my bag higher over my shoulder, and she walks forward, looking almost shy.

"How are you feeling?"

I shrug. "Excited. A little nervous."

"It's a long drive," she says.

"She's going to do great." Gabe grabs the massive portfolio bag from my hand, kissing the top of my head. I'm still getting used to the random acts of affection, but that's just the way Gabe is, and I don't really mind it.

"We'll see you in about a month for the break," he says.

Even at this time of day with the sun winding its way down, the manor seems to glitter with a brighter light. Every crystal window sparkling like the top of a cavern lake. I'm going to miss this place while I'm gone. I'm going to miss these people.

And my *room*. Jamie can sell living out of a camper for three months and bathing in public restrooms all he wants, but I know it's going to be brutal. Brutal and wonderful. A few months of freedom right before I start the art program in Vermont for the fall. Right before Jamie moves to his mom's new house only an hour away from campus.

The acceptance letter that came weeks ago is now framed in the library room where the rifle used to be. Another Sevilla relic for the house. But one to be proud of this time. Because I am proud. After emailing Dorset, thanking them for the opportunity but deciding they weren't the right fit, I followed Myra and Di's advice. I submitted my Nightmare series to a few different places. The dark charcoal paintings that felt too raw. That showed the harsh, ugly fragments of me I thought no one would ever want to see. Turns out, some did.

"All right, no more moping." Mom pats the bottom of her eyes so her mascara won't run. "This isn't goodbye, it's see you later. And it's a celebration!" She turns up the volume on her little Bluetooth radio playing one of her favorite songs. She's wearing her ultimate 1950s gardening housewife getup, because she wouldn't be Marina without being a little extra.

She starts singing louder, noticing the mild embarrassment on my face.

Gabe pinches the bridge of his nose. And Mom sidles closer to him, picking up his dirt-smudged hands and moving them as high in the air as she possibly can in her five-foot stature.

Every word in the song is punctuated by a little hop.

Gabe sends me a pleading look but I know he's secretly loving it. When he glances back down at my mom, the smile he gives her . . . well, it could really make a girl think everything will be okay.

I hear the side gate latch, and again, I sense him before I see him. Not like I did with la Cegua, but like a softness in the wind, the feeling of hovering over the edge of falling.

Jamie comes bounding into view from the side of the house, a huge grin on his face when he sees them dancing.

I quirk a brow. "*Don't* even think about it."

"I got you to dance once; I could do it again," he threatens, coming up to me, grabbing my hand, and placing a soft, lovely kiss on my knuckles. His mood-ring eyes are warm and brown and full of something too big to name yet. But maybe one day.

"You guys are too cute," Mom says, having stopped singing to gush at us.

"The cutest," Gabe adds with more than a fair share of teasing. He's spent way too much time around us.

"Shut up," I say.

In front of the house, Gabe and Jamie load up the trunk of my car and make sure the hitch to the camper is sturdy. They're both in their classic hands-on-hip, dad-inspection mode.

Again, I catch my mom giving Gabe the once-over as he crouches, for no reason, by one of my perfectly inflated tires.

"You know," I start. "Gabe's a *really* nice guy. I know that's not your usual type, but—"

"Shut up," she says, laughing.

I look at her. Really look at her, and I'm so glad she's giving someone a real chance. Someone who deserves it. Because she deserves it too.

Her hand cups my face, smelling like all my favorite lotions and that soft rose oil she loves. "Don't go soft on me now, milagrito." But her eyes are so tender.

"Me?" I say. "Never."

Her expression sobers. This is where we'd usually walk away, pretend there was never a flash of vulnerability. But we stay rooted, and instead of stopping herself from saying more, she hugs me.

"I love you. You know that, right?"

I swallow down what I'd usually say, and instead I hug her back. Hold her tight.

"I know, Mom. I love you too."

She grips my hand as she walks me to the car. We all take turns hugging goodbye and I'm surprised to find myself so teary-eyed, so choked with emotion. But I'm so very glad I feel it all.

The moment he's in the passenger seat, Jamie pulls out a binder. *A binder.* Granted most of the papers inside are crumpled and spilling out, but still.

He looks at the first checklist in his itinerary. "Okay. So we've got an hour to pick up Di and give her a ride to the airport. Do we have Myra's gift for her to take—" He looks at the back seat, to the black-wrapped present. "Perfect. After that we have about twenty minutes for a food and bathroom break before hitting I-95."

He's so proud when he shows me what he has planned for the rest of the day, and I know his newfound organization feels heavenly for his brain. But I can't help teasing him a little.

I turn the El Camino's ignition, roaring it to life, and slide him a smirk. "God, every day I learn something new about you—like you're a total control freak on the road. You must be going through one of those infamous ten-year mind shifts. Pretty soon you won't even like me."

"Impossible," he says. The wind from the open window whips back his hair.

I feel my face go hot, and he leans over to kiss my cheek, something reassuring and quick, knowing there are so many more moments ahead.

"Is there enough time for kissing on this itinerary of yours?"

He flips to the last page, and I laugh because he's made a list of travel rules.

He reads aloud. "The first says: kiss all the time."

"You're ridiculous."

"The second: always agree to disagree."

"A good rule," I say.

"And the third: tell her you more than *like-like* her."

I look up at him. The truth laid bare on his face. My entire body goes warm and effervescent.

"You know, I had a feeling," I say.

"Well, you have great instincts."

And because I made a promise to myself that I wouldn't leave things unsaid between us, I say, "I more than *like-like* you too."

Jamie puts his hand palm up on the seat between us, an invitation to interlace my fingers with his, which I accept. His face is all sweet, lovely edges. A wish come true.

"I know," he says. "I had a feeling."

And because it's the first rule, we kiss.

At the gate, we wave goodbye to Gabe and my mom, and I turn onto the main road feeling the warm breeze of an incoming season. The same warmth spreads through my chest.

Sometimes on the long stretch of the road, I think I see her, in the woods. Silent and watchful. But I know it's not her.

La Cegua, Soledad, is gone.

Never again the vessel to someone else's dreams.

ACKNOWLEDGMENTS

THERE'S A FREEDOM THAT COMES with finishing another book. A relief to get the world and characters out of my head and onto the page. As a writer, I can only hope my words transport and free the reader to explore in shoes other than their own. It was such a joy to escape into the world of vengeful spirits and small haunted towns. I've noticed that each book has been its own unique experience, and this one poured out of me. I appreciate how rare that is, since drafting a new story can often feel like pulling teeth. So I'm eternally grateful this book child decided to behave.

The unruliness lives strictly within its pages and characters.

I have many, many wonderful human beings to thank, both for keeping me alive and nourished while the story poured out, and others for making sure the contents produced a shape worthy of the stunning cover. Speaking of covers, I absolutely have to praise the incredible talent of Zando's design team, cover designer Jenna Stempel-Lobell, and artist Cesar St. Martin.

A billion stars and wishes to my most deserving champion, Danielle Burby, who has been a life-changing force of goodness and my very own wish-granting spirit in the form of a literary agent. Thank you for all that you do and all that's in store.

And if magic itself had a name, it would be Tiffany Liao. You have shown me an editor's warrior spirit, fighting for every aspect of a book's success. I can't tell you how grateful I am for your guidance, insightfulness, and general editorial genius. I look forward to many more celebratory drinks in teacups with you!

Sometimes you just find the person who gets the story you're trying to tell but knows exactly what's needed to make it so much better. I was lucky enough to work with two such special someones—Tiff and TJ Ohler. TJ, thank you for answering endless questions and countless emails, and for supportive, invaluable notes that truly elevated a story still working to take shape. You are a brilliant editor and I can't thank you enough!

An enormous outpouring of gratitude to the entire team at Zando for your unwavering support and all the magic strings you pull in the background to make everything possible. Thank you for taking a chance on me and my stories. Thank you, Molly Stern (CEO), Shayna Holmes (Managing Editor), Kayla White (Managing Editorial Associate), Andrew Rein (Head of Sales), and Ashley Alberico (Director of Sales). Huge thanks to the marketing team: Nathalie Ramirez, Anna Hall, and Natalie Ullman, and the publicity team: Chloe Texier-Rose, Julia McGarry, and Emily Morris. Much gratitude to Rachel Kowal (copy editor)!

I must say, the fear of leaving someone out does not get any easier, but please know that I see the efforts, support, passion, and creativity of all the book bloggers, readers, booksellers, and authors that have taken the time to boost my work. None of this, and I mean none of it, would be possible without you. A special thanks to Karin Yung, Jessie @ExclusivePalmBeachLiving, Javi @rosegoldenby, Lo @thereisalwaysatbr, Stephen @gallifreygamgee (thank you for always checking in), Desirai @librilabra, Emma

@es.reading.corner, Nikki @take_me_awayyy, @magickpumpkin, Marisol @marisolreadsbooks, Mari Rona @mari_rona_reads, @breezys.books, Carla @carla_is_reading, Stacia @stacialovestoread, Feather @firestorm_of_books, and so many more! Audrey Estok @audreyestok and Ju @joleanart, thank you for the gorgeous character art commissions!

My local booksellers, y'all are champions and worth your weight in gold! Thank you, Spellbound Bookstore, Writer's Block Bookstore, White Rose Bookstore, the Barnes & Noble in Altamonte Mall, and Book Haven Books.

Tara Lundmark, mi amiga, thank you from the bottom of my heart for your friendship throughout the years and for your willingness to read the earliest drafts of my books each time. I value your opinion so much, and I look forward to gracing my shelves with your books. Verena and Kelly, thank you both for your notes and encouragement through my early drafts, I appreciate you so, and my shelves will always have a special place for your books as well! Kara, I love checking in with you as we gush about our recent reads and catch up on life. Here's to many, many more years of friendship.

After debuting, I've been lucky enough to encounter such incredible people with such enormous talent. To the authors I've met along the way, you're all an inspiration. Ginny Myers Sain, I can't wait to do more events with you and finally have that margarita night. Terry J. Benton-Walker, I love to watch your career soar! You're so deserving, friend. Nina Moreno, my mentor and friend for life, thank you for all your encouragement. When are we going to Epcot together? Mexico, first, of course. Shelly Page, Jackie Morera, Alex Brown, Sher Lee, Angela Montoya, Amparo Ortiz, Lauren Yero, Jessica Parra—you're all such brilliant stars. So lucky to know you and consider you friends. Ginny, thanks so much for introducing me to your talented group of friends, I will be joining those Zooms soon! My Mad Woman Literary friends, I'll see you all in the retreat! Isabel Sterling, you fit into so many groups in my life—fellow Mad Women, Do The Words Slack group pal, and overall wonderful friend. Thank you for always being such a positive force. Speaking of the Do The Words gang, will forever love you, Erica Davis, for being my knight-in-shining-awkward at the social event and for every moment after! Love your friendship. Huge thanks to the entire Do The Words clan for keeping me sane and listening to my spirals.

Gratitude cannot encompass the entirety of what I feel toward the people that kept me emotionally nourished and semi-sane. Yeny, I'm pretty sure in another life, you were a sister, or we are somehow cosmically tied. Thank you for the friendship that filled something I didn't even realize was empty. My life is so much fuller with you in it. Our buddy reads, our endless conversations in every platform imaginable, the holiday shopping, the trauma dumping in the midst of kid-chaos, the unwinding phone calls in school pickup lines—I wouldn't dream of trading any of it.

Friends and family, Luisy, Claribel, Suzi, Sami, Yessica, Cynthia—I can't tell you how much your support has meant. I see you out there reposting, boosting, and caring so much when you all have such full lives to live. It's a testament to those enormous, beautiful hearts of yours.

Lisy, I love you so much. I love how we show up for each other, and how we express our admiration and appreciation for the things we've accomplished. I couldn't have wished for a better sister. And I love my bookish tattoos!!

Mami, te amo to the moon and back. Thank you for always believing in me. I see all that you do, and I'm so thankful.

And finally, the monumental task of displaying the vast amount of gratitude for my husband and my kids. Angel and Emmalyn, you two are my heart and soul. All that time I spend on my laptop, this is what I'm doing. Making worlds, but you two are still the best things I've ever made.

Leonardo, you are the true magic that fills my life. My best friend, my haven. The person who's always given me the courage to chase after my dreams. With you beside me, the dream is already here, baby.

ALSO BY

Vanessa Montalban

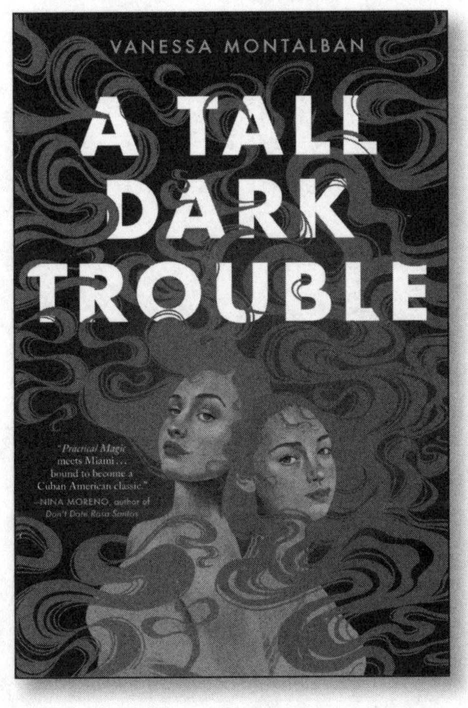